THE
GENTLEMAN
FROM JAPAN

Also by James Church

THE
GENTLEMAN
FROM JAPAN

JAMES CHURCH

MINOTAUR BOOKS

A THOMAS DUNNE BOOK

NEW YORK

A THOMAS DUNNE BOOK FOR MINOTAUR BOOKS.
An imprint of St. Martin's Press.

THE GENTLEMAN FROM JAPAN. Copyright © 2016 by James Church. All rights reserved. Printed in the United States of America. For information, address St. Martin's Press, 175 Fifth Avenue, New York, N.Y. 10010.

www.thomasdunnebooks.com
www.minotaurbooks.com

Library of Congress Cataloging-in-Publication Data

Names: Church, James, 1947– author.
Title: The gentleman from Japan : an Inspector O novel / James Church.
Description: First edition. | New York : Minotaur Books, 2016. | Series: Inspector O novels ; 5 | "A Thomas Dunne book."
Identifiers: LCCN 2016024876| ISBN 9780312614317 (hardcover) | ISBN 9781250023018 (ebook)
Subjects: LCSH: Korea (North)—Officials and employees—Fiction. | Terrorism—Prevention—Fiction. | Conspiracies—Fiction. | Political fiction. | BISAC: FICTION / Thrillers. | FICTION / Mystery & Detective / Hard-Boiled. | GSAFD: Suspense fiction. | Mystery fiction.
Classification: LCC PS3603.H88 G46 2016 | DDC 813/.6—dc23
LC record available at https://lccn.loc.gov/2016024876

Our books may be purchased in bulk for promotional, educational, or business use. Please contact your local bookseller or the Macmillan Corporate and Premium Sales Department at 1-800-221-7945, extension 5442, or by e-mail at MacmillanSpecialMarkets@macmillan.com.

First Edition: December 2016

10 9 8 7 6 5 4 3 2 1

This book is dedicated to all who spend their lives pushing the rock uphill, only to find it sent crashing down again by fools and knaves; by those who "know better" and those who know nothing; by morally and ethically bankrupt guardians of the law; by greed, corruption, and malfeasance; and by the evil in all its forms that sleeps in every heart.

Preface

This is a complicated tale. What follows is pretty much exactly what I can recall as Inspector O told it to me from start to finish. More than once I tried to interrupt him for a clarification about a squiggly relationship or a jump in the proceedings. My queries were brushed off with a curt "Pay attention!" And so that is the best I can offer to those who read beyond this note. Pay attention; it all comes clear in the end.

TOKYO—In a brazen gun attack that shocked a country tough on firearms, the head of a nationwide dumpling restaurant chain was shot dead in front of his company's headquarters on Thursday. . . . Mr. Ohigashi [the deceased] ran a fast-food chain called Gyoza no Ohsho, or King of Dumplings, started in 1967 by his brother-in-law. The chain has about 660 restaurants across Japan. Mr. Ohigashi took the helm of the company in 2000 and is credited with using aggressive cost-cutting to turn around restaurants struggling to make a profit in Japan's deflationary economy.

—*The New York Times,* December 20, 2013

PART I

Chapter One

By the time the sun had set on Thursday, there were seven corpses in four of the city's ragged collection of restaurants, cafés, tea shops, "bakeries," and illegal lunch stands. Four eateries, seven bodies. It goes without saying that couldn't be good for business. The mayor would be calling, probably after one of his big dinner parties. The police had quietly sent me the guest list. They weren't supposed to, but they knew I was interested in seeing who kept company with the mayor. None of the names on the list rang bells.

The sketchy details on the events at the four restaurants were laid out in the field reports appearing on my desk late that evening. As a matter of standard procedure, we didn't deal with local murders: wife conks husband on head; drunk knifes companion over who gets the next turn at the bottle; burglar panics on being discovered and strangles renter. As the local office of the Ministry of State Security, we routinely got copies of the police reports. On rare occasions one of these incidents had some link to our concerns. Mostly, the reports were filed without a second glance.

These particular reports did not give me a warm feeling. Initial observations by the local police were often a problem. This time, to make things worse, in the upper right-hand corner of a couple of the reports there were notations indicating that they had been copied—unedited—to the Ministry of State Security in Beijing. Nothing is supposed to go to Beijing right away. Raw reports, especially, should never go to my headquarters in Beijing. The higher-ups don't know how to read them. Whatever the original problem, it is always compounded by distant superiors who think they understand local events on the basis of barely accurate, and even more likely completely mistaken, first reports. I made a mental note to complain to the local police chief.

There were four field reports, one for each incident. I read them quickly, and then again more carefully to make sure I hadn't missed anything remotely important:

—Working-class neighborhood near edge of town, three elderly males at adjoining tables slumped over bowls of noodles—two daily specials and one of the new Vietnamese-style considered trendy. No one else on premises when patrol showed up. Owner of the noodle shop (identified as "Uighur with a limp and wisp of a mustache" by cashier who appeared out of nowhere a few minutes later) has disappeared.
     FIELD COMMENT: No further information.

—One otherwise (apparently) healthy middle-aged male—well dressed, no tattoos or scars—leaning back in red leather banquette of upscale restaurant in Yanji's finest hotel, never having gotten past appetizer from the looks of it. Maybe autopsy? Chef in custody, but not talking.
     FIELD COMMENT: Still working him over.

—Couple of hookers taking a break before work found dead as doornails behind back alley dim sum joint. Best guess judging from scene: sharing steamed buns and red tea. Shop claims it doesn't make dim sum on site. Buys off truck every other day. Manager insists "they don't have phone number" of supplier and (surprise! surprise!) none of staff can remember anything, even color of truck.
     FIELD COMMENT: Asking around.

—One tourist, blond, female, discovered on washroom floor of new Mongolian tearoom across from train station. When turned over, funny look on face. Passport nowhere to be found. No Yanji hotel has record of anyone with her description checking in. Smaller inns still being canvassed.

FIELD COMMENT: This may take a while.

I looked at my watch. The mayor would be calling soon, but even before that, the first message from Beijing would arrive, something along the lines of "From time to time someone dies in a restaurant, but seven in one night?"

I contemplated eating at home for a few months. The idea survived a nanosecond until it ran into the realization that this would mean spending evenings with Uncle O.

2

"Major Bing!" After a halfhearted salute, my new deputy, tall and gaunt, dropped a fresh sheaf of papers on my desk. "The mayor says he wants all leave canceled. Do I type up a memo to that effect? Or do I use my discretion?"

The man had arrived by train Tuesday afternoon straight from his previous assignment in the city of Tianjin, which sits close enough to Beijing so that anyone posted there feels superior to all of us in the northeast sector. They feel that way even though Tianjin is widely considered in the Ministry a poor sister, badly run. A few of the more suspicious also think it is a city marked for doom—one year a huge earthquake, another year an unbelievably destructive explosion.

Still fresh from Tianjin and with an air of superiority trailing him as if he were Ying Zheng in the flesh, the new man had spent his entire first day wandering through the office asking a lot of questions. Whether he should use his discretion was the caboose on most of them. His height, which went beyond what most people would consider reasonable, only drew attention to his shoes, which were brown, thick soled, and badly scuffed.

"This isn't our affair," I said, contemplating the shoes. They had started life as patrol boots, but it looked as if halfway through they changed their minds and made a stab at being fashionable. If Ministry of State Security officers in Tianjin dressed like this, no wonder—disasters aside—it was a city near the bottom of most people's list for transfer assignments. Only my sector and the two others near mine in the northeast ranked lower in the Ministry's beauty contest. Almost no one wanted to be assigned way up here. The general impression was that this was a place filled with country bumpkins with nothing to do during the long winters but drink.

"Let the local police here in the wilds of Yanji do some work once in a while." I looked up from the shoes. "Besides, it's almost midnight. We only type memos in the morning." I paused before giving him a tight smile. "It's a Manchu tradition."

The man was too tall for sarcasm to go over his head, but there was no sign anything had registered.

"When I was in Tianjin," he said solemnly, "the mayor had a lot of clout. He could have canceled leave anytime he'd wanted. He never did, of course, but he could have." A pompous fog enveloped this pronouncement. While it dissipated, I sat back and pondered. If the mayor of Tianjin had so much clout, why didn't he order people to polish their shoes? I wasn't a martinet, but I insisted my officers show a little pride in how they looked. It was not just fussiness. Suspects react badly when interrogated by trouser legs that drag on the floor, or get slapped around by frayed shirt collars.

I pushed my mind back to the problem at hand. "That may be, ah . . ." For some reason I couldn't place the new man's name. "But our mayor can't cancel leave, not for anyone in this office, anyway."

I did not normally lecture new arrivals on their second day. It was always better to let them get comfortable for a week or two. In this case, however, it seemed crucial to set a few guidelines before the scuffed shoes went over a cliff, dragging along a few of the impressionable members of my staff.

"You might as well file this away for future reference: We don't take orders from the locals. That includes the mayor." I said this evenly enough, as if I wasn't constantly locked in combat with the mayor, who was crooked, and lecherous, and beyond my reach because he was so well connected in ways that, even after trying for several years, I couldn't trace.

I indicated to the new man that he should stand against the wall rather than take a seat. It wouldn't be smart to let him feel too cozy in my office. If we were in for an ugly period of house-to-house fighting—and I already knew that was where things were headed— I wanted him off balance every time he walked through the door.

"You may have to adjust a little to the way things work here on the ragged edge of civilization, Tang."

His name had popped back into my head. It was Tang Xin-ho, or at least that was what had been stamped on the front of his personnel file, which I'd received and skimmed without much interest weeks ago. The file itself was an odd color, not the normal light green, and it was stuffed with commendations. That had instantly sent up warning flares. It meant every office he'd ever worked in couldn't wait to get rid of him. The first page in the file made clear that he was a direct assignment to me from the Ministry personnel office. That was stapled to a second page with red stripes along the top meant to carry the unmistakable if unspoken message that it didn't matter what I thought of him or his file—he was mine, and there was nothing I could do about it.

Tang's shoulders stiffened at my warning. He flushed to an ugly shade of red but quickly regained his composure. I could tell that he had almost clicked to attention but then, in a fit of anger or stubbornness, decided instead to test me.

Just try it, I thought. Nothing he could do would match what I faced every day at home. I sat back, making sure to look relaxed but mentally girding for a long campaign. I'd break his bureaucratic neck in the end, but it had to be done slowly, imperceptibly, by degrees, until one day he'd walk out of my office with his head at an odd angle, not quite realizing what had happened.

"Normally," I said quietly, forcing him to lean toward me, "we don't even get the full police reports on this sort of thing. Bicycle thefts, bad checks, and murder—none of them our business. We keep our eyes focused on the border, record what comes over, and spend the rest of our time tracking all of the foreign ducks and geese that make their way up here under one sort of cover or another in order to watch each other watch the border. A lot of them spend their time in the South Korean coffee shops that keep popping up, or hanging around the North Korean restaurant here. The food there is all right, and you're allowed to accept one meal a week. Understood?"

This was met with sullen silence.

"If North Korean soldiers cross the river and kill a few of our people during a robbery, we listen, we observe, we gather information, we look for patterns, and then we put the whole thing in a file and forget about it. Understood?"

Silence, even more sullen than before. I let that hang around the room for a few seconds before continuing. "But according to this note"—I picked up a piece of paper and let it float back down to my desk—"the chief of detectives seems to think in this case there is something odd going on."

"And you don't?" Tang raised an eyebrow. Apparently, that was how they communicated doubt in Tianjin.

"As I said, we have plenty to do"—my voice dropped to a near whisper—"without worrying about food poisoning."

I leafed through the papers he'd delivered, letting him stand there like a slightly bent potted tree. The new reports contained more preliminary speculation on several key issues for which the local coroner still had no good answers. First and most obvious among the questions was what had caused seven people to abandon all signs of life more or less at the same time, assuming the coroner's thermometer could be trusted. Someone had written "ptomaine?" in the margin of one of the pages.

"I admit," I said at last, "the hookers have me a little worried."

"I was thinking of the dim sum." Tang looked thoughtful.

"How do you know it wasn't the red tea?"

"There's that, too."

3

No sooner had Tang edged out of my office than the special phone in the top drawer of my desk buzzed. Only a few people had the number, and no one except me had physical access to the phone. The drawer was secured with a special lock, and I was the only one who was supposed to know how to get it open.

I let the phone buzz twice as I searched for the key, then opened the drawer and lifted the receiver. When it was first installed, I had tried to make the phone actually ring instead of buzz, because the buzz was annoying, as if an insect were trapped in the drawer. Beijing sent instructions that I was not to fiddle with the phone. It buzzed, I was informed, because that was what the regulation said it was supposed to do. Calls on that phone were strictly official; they might as well have been from poisonous bugs.

The voice on the other end was a bug, a mosquito at midnight.

"Qin here."

More bad news. It was the mayor, and the lack of even a minimally polite greeting was meant to suggest that I should leap to my feet and salute.

"Qin?" I pretended to be searching my memory.

"Listen closely, Bing. I've just been in touch with Beijing, and your superiors at the Ministry agree that for the next month, maybe more, your resources are to be fully at my disposal." He paused. "Cancel all leave."

I closed my eyes. "What is this about, Qin?"

"You know what it's about, Bing. It's about a lot of bodies showing up where they don't belong."

"What about your police, Qin? Am I misinformed, or isn't this what they get paid for, investigating mysterious events? Everyone knows this dysfunctional city has more than its share of them." I sensed the mosquito revving up again, so I kept talking. "The issue here, as far as I can tell, is unexplained deaths, several more than normal, one supposes, but numbers by themselves do not make them my concern. My concern is with matters of state security—spies, terrorists, smuggling across that damned river. You know, the sort of things that are probably minor in your constellation of corruption. Feel free to send over the results of the police investigation about the murders, if that's what they were, when you have something. I have work to do. *Ciao,* as they say in Milan." I paused for two beats. "That's Italy."

"I know where the fuck Milan is, Bing. We have a new Italian restaurant in town, or haven't you noticed? No, forget it, you're not slipping away so easily. What we have here is not just the normal triad stiffs laid out in a pizza parlor."

The sound of papers being shuffled came across the line. I knew he was trying to figure out where the bodies had actually been found, and whether he was in danger of losing the new restaurant, which he thought added class to the city. No doubt it added to his personal revenue as well. The mayor skimmed from the tax receipts, I was sure of that, but being sure and finding evidence was not the same thing.

The mosquito came back on the line. "Murder? What we have here is terrorism. I don't doubt it's your cousins from across the river. Maybe even friends of your uncle. If you can't stop these people, Bing, we'll build a wall. That's what I just told them in Beijing, build a fucking wall and be done with it!"

The mayor pointed to my Korean blood at every opportunity. This was, he whispered into a thousand ears, a source of dangerous pollution. It was true, he would say, his city was filled with Koreans whose families had been here for decades, centuries in many cases. "I'm friends with them all"—he would always say that as if wounded by the thought he might not be their friend and benefactor. They belong here, he would exclaim, which was another way of saying he could squeeze money from them and they would not complain. The point, he would say gravely, was that he knew to the marrow of his pure Chinese bones that it was a travesty, in fact a mortal danger, that someone charged with security in this sensitive part of the country was not pure-blooded.

And now he thought he had finally found a perfect way to get rid of me.

"Do I make myself clear, Bing? Terrorism! Not just your murderous thugs from across the river, but terrorism!" The word shot across the phone line like a piglet running from a carving knife. "And this terrorism is a big fat concern of the state, as you so rightly point out. Not only that, it's going to ruin the livelihood of the citizens of my city, citizens that the authorities in Beijing want to protect and see prosper. With terrorism here, tourists won't come. Businesses will go elsewhere. We're supposed to get a new dumpling restaurant later this year. I signed the papers the other day. It's Japanese. Big name, big revenues. Nothing like those trash heaps we have now. It will drive that North Korean eatery with its flashy girls out of the city."

The mayor waited, apparently sure he had gained the upper hand. In fact, I was mildly surprised by his terrorism gambit, but even more by his complaints about the North Koreans. Once in a while he beat that drum, but had to be careful because he pocketed plenty from Chinese businessmen sending too much of one thing or another across the river, and doubled that from North Koreans who needed favors on this side of the border. If he was complaining so loudly, it must be because he'd heard from his network in Beijing that it was time to put the squeeze on again. At this point, unless someone else was writing his script, I figured his next move would be to accuse me of incompetence.

"A concern of the state," he repeated, with minimal reverence. "Regrettably, in this backward corner of the country, that means you. Or has a miracle happened without my lifting a finger and you've finally been replaced as head of the State Security detail in my city? Let me point out that neither the state nor my city is secure if people drop dead all of a sudden, especially tourists. It's your job to protect us. The police obviously aren't doing it, but they're not your affair. I'll attend to them, and that monkey's ass of a police chief, later. What I'm most concerned about is you, Major, you and your incompetence."

Whenever Qin used my rank, it was always with a sneer, as if he had friends who could demote me as soon as he wanted it done. In turn, I made a point of never calling him "mayor," not to his face anyway. I knew that rankled him. For years, every conversation I'd had with the man had been a form of guerrilla warfare. I should have been used to it by now, but his constant references to "my city" always got under my skin. He talked as if he owned the place, which to a large extent was true. What was worse, he liked to parade that in front of me, secure in the knowledge that I still hadn't figured out how the mayor of a flea-bitten town got away with bribery, mendacity, moral turpitude, malfeasance, and—very often—murder, sometimes all on the same day.

If I could step on this insect I would. At the moment, all I could do was argue a technicality. "You said State Security 'detail,' Qin. Let me remind you, this isn't a 'detail.' It's an 'office.' In fact, it's a 'special office.' That's why it says on our letterhead 'Yanji Special Office.' You know what that means? It means we keep files on everyone."

I paused to let that sink in, though I knew I'd laid it out for him several times before. Once, when we met in my office and I was for some reason feeling expansive, I had even let him see the two thick file folders we had on him. I had pretended to be surprised when he walked in and had made a show of moving the files off my desk, but not before I had seen him smirk when he read his name on the cover sheet. I still don't know what I thought that would accomplish. It hadn't been much.

"And another thing," I said, "according to this stack of reports in front of me, we're only talking about one tourist, nothing plural. Just to be clear, in case the main point hasn't come through"—I was picking up a head of steam—"even if I had a direct order to listen to you from the minister of security himself, I wouldn't do it. Not in a thousand years, not even if Qin Shi Huangdi rose from the grave and delivered it in person. If he does come back, maybe you should ask him for his plans for a wall, though it wasn't a great success if I recall."

There was a brief pause. I would have bet a week's salary the mayor was smoothing his hair, something he did in moments of stress.

"I'll have you sacked," he said finally.

"Good. Perfect." Not for the first time it struck me that the mayor thought he was born too late, that he should have been a prince in the kingdom of Qin, standing near the emperor, taxing the hell out of the peasants. "Sacked—nothing would please me more. It would mean finally getting out of this town. While we're waiting for you to send the request for my transfer, I'll wager a year's salary that there is not a shred of paper on my desk giving you any special powers over me. Notice I said paper. If it's not in writing, it doesn't exist. People say all sorts of things over the phone, and sometimes the connection is not so good, so you can never be sure. Beijing is a big city, by the way. I don't know who would possibly have fed you such a line. Face it, Qin, you are mayor of a boring town at the faraway edge of the empire. My resources are and will never be at the disposal of any minor local official, and that includes you. Especially you. On top of which, terrorists don't mess with noodles. I think I can guarantee that. On the outside chance we pick up rumors suggesting a change in their tactics, noodle bombs or whatever, I'll be in touch."

It was a long speech, longer than I normally make, and I'm not sure the mayor heard the whole thing, because the line had clicked halfway through. No matter, it was on the record somewhere.

As soon as I hung up, the phone buzzed again. "Major, it's Po. Can we talk? If you haven't eaten yet, maybe I can buy you a late dinner."

Po Dawei was the chief of the Yanji City police. He'd been

promoted two years ago after the last chief ended up in a ditch with an odd, totally fatal, and yet-to-be-explained wound on his neck. The other candidates for the job all declined, so it fell to Po, who was only a lieutenant at the time, and not actually in line for advancement. He was bright in a plodding sort of way, but too honest ever to get such a promotion. To everyone's surprise, he got it anyway. The two of us kept our meetings few and far between. We were on cordial terms mostly because we stayed away from each other—that and the fact that he didn't get along with the mayor. Po wasn't much to look at, medium height, medium build, medium gait, even-tempered almost to the point you wanted to punch him just to see him react. The most distinguishing thing about him was his strange laugh, like a small dog being strangled.

"Before we get started, Po, your people sent a couple of the reports directly to Beijing. How many times have I told you not to do that?"

"They were stressed, Major. A lot of bodies all at once will do that."

"Second," I said, "if this is about terrorism, don't waste your breath. I don't want to hear it."

"I guess you've already talked to Qin. Listen, he's breaking my back on this, worse than ever. Can you help me out, loan me someone part-time maybe, just for a day or two so we can go through the motions of coordinating? Just the motions, you know what I mean. I'd owe you a favor."

"Sorry, can't help, Po, my basket of favors is empty. I'm short-handed, and believe it or not, my office has work to do. The border isn't going to take a rest while I look for a food nut with a grudge."

Po laughed. It sounded worse over the phone than it did in person. "Is that what you've concluded? A food nut? I don't think so. Maybe I'm only a local cop, but I know what I know, and I don't think so. I also don't think it's ptomaine, whatever our crazy coroner says. I'll grant you, I'm not sure if it's terrorism, but it sure is as close to a massacre as anyone has ever seen around here. Seven bodies, maybe eight, all in one night. It's going to get press attention—tongues are already wagging out there, and neither of us is going to be happy at the end of the day if foreign reporters from Beijing come up here nosing around."

"You're the chief of police," I said. "Do whatever you want. If you ask my advice, shut down every restaurant in the city for a few days. If there's no food, they'll have to go home."

There was silence on the line, so I figured he was thinking it over. Finally he cleared his throat, something he always did before announcing a decision. "I can't touch the hotel, the mayor wouldn't like it, but I guess we can shut down all the noodle shops for a few days until we're sure we know what happened."

"Excellent. And while you're at it, double your flying squads. Have them break a few dishes and turn over some tables when they barge in. It doesn't hurt to have people sore at you. Not really angry, just irritated."

"You telling me my job, Major?"

"See? You're irritated."

"I'm always irritated. Every morning I wake up and the first thought, always the first thought, is that some time during the day I'll have to deal with the mayor."

"Listen, if your boys find dual-use items under the sink in any of the kitchens, let me know and I'll send a special team over, but I'll bet you it's just dirty cutlery that caused those deaths. I can't say sanitation is a strong point in this city."

"I take it," the chief said, "this means you don't want dinner."

"You mentioned other bodies?" An eighth corpse was not what I needed.

"That's right. I can tell you more when I see you."

"Noodles are out. So is Italian."

"Let's meet in Fuzhou Alley in about fifteen minutes. There's a little place right on the corner you may not have tried. It hasn't been around long. The food isn't great, so not a lot of people go in. That means it's quiet. It stays open late. All night, actually."

"I don't care how many go in," I said, "as long as the same number come out. Upright."

"So far, you're in luck."

4

There was a full moon over Yanji that night, but it had skipped over Fuzhou Alley. A rat rummaged around in a trash can nearby. Otherwise the place was dead quiet. After a minute or two, the hairs on the back of my neck prickled. I sensed a soft footstep behind me.

"Nice to see you, Major. I hope I'm not late."

I turned around to face the chief of police. "Even if you were late, Po, how would I know? I can't see my arm, much less my watch. Isn't it against the law for a street to be this dark?"

"We like it this way. Breeds crime." He laughed. The rats screamed and scurried away at the sound.

The chief led the way to the restaurant. The floor was littered with discarded food and paper. It had the charm of a tomb that a lower class of robbers had looted. Vermin of all types would consider it homey. I hesitated before following Po in. My office was supposed to know all the dingy, dirty eateries in the city, but this one had fallen through the cracks. I'd never heard of it. I made a mental note to open a file and get an investigation under way, starting with simple things like who owned this hole, and what did they have against brooms?

We found our way to a table, not difficult because there were only six of them, all empty. As soon as we sat down, the place started getting on my nerves. For some reason, it reminded me of the old-fashioned morgues out in the countryside, the ones with small restaurants out front. They were strictly illegal, not to mention unhealthy, but so are a lot of things.

"I said the food was bad, but that might be unfair, Major." The chief looked around for someone to take our order. "My only advice is, avoid the soup."

"OK, no soup."

"Sometimes the fish dumplings are good."

I wasn't in the mood for dumplings. "They come off a truck?"

"No, we make them here," a young woman said, emerging from

the gloom. She gave me the once-over. "But we're out of dough, so you'll have to sit here until tomorrow afternoon when we get some more. Or, if you want something sooner, I have fish head soup."

Po held up his hand. "We'll skip the soup."

The woman laughed, not what you'd call musical, but not in the same league as Po.

"Who owns this place?" I asked. "It's filthy."

"You a sanitation expert?" She swept some dried noodles from the next table onto the floor. "I don't own it. I'm the manager. In other words, I manage things. I'm in charge of operations." She looked around and muttered something under her breath. "I also serve the food and entertain the cook when we don't have any customers. You want to eat, or do you want to chat? We have bills to pay, you know."

"Sure," said Po evenly, "we want something to eat. Just not soup. How about pork? And rice." He looked at me.

"Fish," she said. It wasn't a question.

I shrugged. "OK, and make sure it's a nice fish, the whole thing, not just the head. You got something fresh? Bring it out here first. I want to see its eyes."

"You want one with blue eyes or brown?" She tossed her head. "From what I hear, you got problems, and not with fish."

"Is that so?" Po asked gently. I knew the chief's eyelids drooped when he was getting cozy with someone he thought might have information. They were drooping. "I got problems?" His voice had turned silky, an even more advanced sign that he was closing in for the kill. "Listen, darling, my problems are your problems. But you already know that. You want to tell us what you've heard about blue eyes?"

"Nothing, I was just making conversation, that's all." The woman shrugged. "Let me go find the cook and then wake up the fish. I'll make soothing noises so it won't suspect anything. Maybe hum a tune. You want him smiling or just with a fish expression on his face?"

The woman disappeared again. Po frowned and jotted down a

note on a tiny paper napkin. "She's from out of town, Harbin we think. Came here about six months ago. We're still looking for her file. Harbin says it was transmitted, but it never got here."

"You believe them?"

"The Harbin police are earnest."

"But . . ."

"But not always very efficient. Anyway, we have been watching the lady, testing to see if we can use her. A dark place like this will sooner or later turn into a meeting place for troublemakers."

"And?"

"She's very combative, never gives an inch. The consensus is that she is probably too hard to control. The fish is usually OK, though. It's from the river."

"Not much you can do wrong with river fish." I didn't want to get off into a long conversation about food preparation, and police sources were none of my business. "Over the phone you mentioned another body."

"I did, but we're not sure yet if it's connected with the others. Actually, we're not sure how many bodies it might be. That's why I needed to talk to you."

"I told you, I don't want to hear you say the word 'terrorism.'"

"All right, I won't. How about the word 'bomb'?"

I sat back. "That's the second word I don't want to hear. Go ahead."

"This other body, or bodies . . . There wasn't much, not that we could find on first look, anyway. It was already past sunset, and there was no sense taking our big light trucks out there when it's dark. Runs the hell out of the generators. We found the place about fifteen kilometers north of town. Some farmers in the area called and said they heard an explosion. Four or five calls, all at once. The dispatcher says the calls came in just about the time we got the first reports about the bodies in the restaurants, maybe a couple of minutes later. Incidentally, those calls about the restaurant bodies also came in all at once. Might be coincidence. Might not."

"Not much there, you said. Enough to identify?"

"Hard to say. We'll go looking for more bits and pieces as soon as the sun is up. I've told the local patrol to put tape around the scene, but that won't keep anyone out, so we might lose a little evidence overnight."

"A little?"

The chief shrugged. "Maybe most of it. Want to come along to see what's left?"

No, I did not want to come along to see what was left. Until they were sure it was a bomb, it was police business, and I wasn't about to get pulled into it. "Apart from the timing of the calls, what makes you think this has anything to do with the bodies in the restaurants? The initial field reports were not very useful as far as I'm concerned."

"They were early, Major." He wasn't taking offense. "You can't expect miracles from the street cops up here. They don't get paid much, not after all the deductions."

I'd heard that excuse before. These "deductions" were vaguely worded. I was sure they went via a circuitous route into the mayor's pocket, and I figured the chief thought so, too, though we'd never discussed it. "You're breaking my heart, Po. Any results from the interrogation of the chef in the hotel? Any more information on the tourist?" It wasn't my business, but I didn't want any unpleasant surprises.

"The chef says he didn't even know anyone was in the restaurant. He was preparing a sauce, he says."

"A sauce. Anyone check to see what kind of sauce? What about the serving staff? Were they preparing sauces, too?"

Po turned toward the kitchen just as the woman walked out holding a medium-sized fish that was moving its tail and looking around the room.

"It jumped into my arms," she said. "I didn't whistle or snap my fingers or nothing. When your time is up, it's up, I guess." The fish goggled at us. It didn't look all that healthy to me.

"Throw it back," I said. "It might be someone's mama. We'll just have pork and rice if you have any. And go easy on the pork fat.

I know it was Chairman Mao's favorite dish, but tonight I'm not in the mood for a heart attack."

The woman looked at Po. "You want me to throw this fish back? And order pork in a fish restaurant?"

Po shrugged. "You and the cook make yourself a meal of it if you're hungry, but it's on your tab. The major and I are granting it a limited pardon."

We finished dinner without much conversation. When we were done and outside again in the dark, my mobile phone rang.

"Yes." No phone number showed up, but I knew who it was even before I heard the voice. "Yes, uncle, I'm working late. There were noodles and vegetables on the counter if you had wanted something. No, you won't starve. Eat some crackers, then. I'll call when I'm on my way."

Po shook his head. "You should get a housekeeper or something to look after the old man. Make it easy on yourself."

"We had a housekeeper. In fact, we already had three this year. They can't stand it. They say my uncle is from another planet, and no amount of money will induce them to stay."

"But he's still with it, right?" Po tapped his finger on his temple. "All there, from what I hear."

"And what exactly do you hear?"

"Just this and that, Major. Nothing special. Yanji is still like a small town, and we keep our ears open."

"That's good, Po. If your ears hear any more explosions going off, let me know. Otherwise, no reason to keep me up to date on your investigation, unless you run across signs of a noodle bomb. Thanks for dinner."

"What about some cooperation? You have a new deputy, don't you? He'll be useless for a few weeks. Why not send him over to me for a couple of days? I'd be grateful."

As far as I could tell, the new deputy would be useless to me for more than a few weeks, but I didn't want the locals poaching on my staff. It set a bad precedent. Anyway, Tang might pick up a few bad local habits, and that would only make things worse. He already seemed to have brought along baggage from his previous assignment that I was going to have to pitch overboard.

"Sorry, Po, nothing I can do for you right now. You handle the mayor; he's the stone in your shoe. I have problems of my own. We'll be in touch again next week, sooner if something big comes up. I'll keep my eyes open, though I doubt if there is anything in this business that falls under my jurisdiction."

"What about the tourist? Foreigners are in your jurisdiction, aren't they?"

"I'm specifically enjoined by Beijing from dealing with anything that has blue eyes. Headquarters has its reasons, I suppose. Good night."

I decided to swing back to the office, but the long way, not through Fuzhou Alley. A good walk would give me time to think, and with luck, Uncle O would be asleep by the time I finally got home. He'd sleep most of the morning, then about noon drift into his workshop to plan bookshelves for the rest of the day. He planned more than he built, but he had built plenty in the three years he'd lived in my back room. I told him to stop until we found a way to deal with the ones already stacked up around the house. Besides which, we could barely afford the lumber. On this, as on almost everything else, he ignored me.

Back at the office, I went into the file room to see if there was anything on the owner of the dirty restaurant. There was nothing on the owner, but at the very back of one of the cabinets was something better—an old-style piece of folded cardboard containing a single yellowed paper with entries on both sides, typed on an old typewriter. According to the paper, the place had been a large and prosperous silk shop during the Japanese occupation. Soviet Red Army troops had looted it when they came through in 1945. It was looted again and partially burned down when the Kuomintang troops hurriedly left town in 1948. The PLA took possession of what was left of the building and turned it into a local police headquarters. During the war in Korea a small wing to the main building and an underground storehouse were added, turning it into an intelligence base, which doubled as a medical supply station when the fighting got heavy. It remained in the army's hands until the Cultural Revolution, when gangs of Red Guards, who terrorized the Korean autonomous region and ran roughshod through Yanji, took it as their base of operations and an interrogation center that was broken up into a series of small underground torture cells. When things returned to normal in the mid-1970s, there was another fire, this time burning the back half of the building to the ground. The last entry on the paper noted that in 1979 the place became a restaurant whose full ownership, very curiously, could never be determined. The only operating certificate dated back to 1985, which meant it had expired several times over. I was tempted to close the place down on security grounds, but decided to leave well enough alone for the moment.

The second file I wanted to see was on the noodle shop where the three old men had been found dead. Whether they had actually died there, I didn't know. I also didn't know exactly what I was looking for in the file. Mostly, I wanted to make doubly sure that seven local deaths, more if Po was right, weren't going to cause me trouble I didn't need. The noodle shop's file was fuller than the first one because for some time we'd had a low-level watch on the Uighur who supposedly ran the place. Uighurs were rare up here in the northeast. They were from the western fringe of the empire, not Han people, largely Muslim, and considered more and more by Beijing to be troublemakers. Uighurs thought China was occupying their land, oppressing them. I didn't have to make a judgment on that, so I didn't. All I knew was we were supposed to keep an eye on them if they showed up in our area, so that's what we did. Alert bulletins from Headquarters arrived at least once a month to remind us in case we forgot.

In the file there were several elliptical reports about characters we didn't like moving in and out of the restaurant, taking an overly long time with their noodles, leaving newspapers they hadn't read on the tables when they walked out without paying their bills. It was one of only three noodle shops in Yanji that an ex-triad chief who called himself Mike hadn't put the arm on. The two other shops which he hadn't touched were both run by the Russian mafia. We knew Mike was afraid of the Russians. We also knew he was looking for new opportunities. Noodle shops were small potatoes.

We'd sent the file on the Uighur's place to Beijing for review along with a request for a technical team to be sent up to wire the place. The file and the request sat there for nearly half a year, and then three months ago the file had come back with a note: "No interest." That surprised me. It also annoyed me enough that I hadn't lifted the watch. How the Uighur left town without my knowing it was something I needed to find out, assuming he had actually left town. I didn't have to close the place. Three dead customers would probably be enough to queer the business for a while.

The file on the upscale hotel where the chef had been making a sauce while his sole customer keeled over was missing. There was no recent signature on the checkout sheet. The last record was from three years ago, signed out to my former deputy. "Former" because he had been shot in the head by a local gangster working for someone—another of our local thugs—my uncle had soon afterward tossed into the hold of a coal freighter. My uncle hadn't actually done the tossing himself, but he was the proximate cause. Both of the thugs—the gangster and his boss—had been in Mike's employ; they were supposed to pass along to him whatever money they got from whatever rackets they ran, minus what they thought they could keep without his finding out. What Mike did with his money I didn't know. He didn't throw it around. He only had a shabby apartment in Yanji, which was his base for shaking down noodle shops throughout the northeast.

The only thing I like less than the triads, even ex-triads, is missing files. I made a mental note to ask the file clerk if she had any idea what was going on in her file room.

That was enough for one night. I was going out the front door when the duty officer glanced my way.

"Anything up, Major? You're here late, or early depending on how you look at it. The sun will be up before you know it."

"Late," I said. "I'm here late. Have you looked at the duty log recently? We're hemorrhaging diners."

"Yeah, I heard about it when I ate before I came in."

"Oh? Where was that?"

"My usual place, an Indian restaurant. It's called the Bay Leaf, very artsy interior."

"And the food?"

"Some people call it 'curry from hell.' It's OK if you need to sweat."

"What was the rumor?"

"Someone is poisoning restaurants to get them to pay protection money."

"Nice theory." I stepped over to the duty desk. "Too simple. By the way, there's a file missing."

"Uh-oh." The duty officer knew what I thought about the sanctity of the file room. "Want me to do anything? Look around for it?"

"Just keep your bottom glued to that chair until your relief arrives. And answer the phone, will you? If it's the mayor, don't tell him I'm at home."

"No, sir. You want me to call you?"

"You know that the only time you're supposed to call me at home is if the entire North Korean Politburo paddles across the river in a rubber boat and asks for asylum."

He grinned. "And if you don't answer?"

"Leave a message. No, wait; cancel that. No message." I didn't want my uncle waking me with a sly look on his face as he said he had something I might find interesting.

I took a roundabout route home, past the new department stores with the names of swank European designers plastered across the front, and stopped off in a bar I visited sometimes. I liked the place. It stayed open until dawn, and no one ever bothered to look up when I walked in. A long drink later, I felt prepared to face Uncle O.

Chapter Two

It was already getting light when I opened the front door to my house. I smelled burnt vegetables, so I knew my uncle had been in the kitchen. That meant he was up early. Sometimes he got dressed around sunrise to go for a walk. He maintained that the air at dawn was healthy. The police had warned me that he was walking aimlessly and that I should keep my eye on him, but I knew my uncle didn't know the meaning of the word "aimless." The door to the courtyard was open, so it was a good bet my uncle was in his workshop, contemplating the design of another bookcase. There was no reason to check. He didn't like to be disturbed in his workshop, and I wasn't in the mood for conversation.

I had slept for a couple of hours when sounds from the alley, piglets squealing, woke me. The neighbor raised them, illegally. He and his wife were mortal enemies, but they shared the profits from the pigs.

"Good morning to you." My uncle stood in the doorway to my room. "I have something that might be of interest."

"How about later? I only got in when the sun was coming up, and I need a little more sleep. Can't we shut those pigs up?"

"I know when you got in. I heard the door open, and I heard you creeping down the hall. Floorboards creak louder when you walk on tiptoe, did you know that? You want breakfast?"

"Since when do you make breakfast?" I let his observation on creaking floorboards slide past without comment. It was meant not very subtly to suggest that I still had things to learn about operations. Ignoring his jibes was useless. My uncle always knew when one of his darts had hit home. It was all the more galling when he made a show of not pressing the point.

"Do you think," he asked, "I have lived to this old age without knowing how to make breakfast?"

I gritted my teeth. He was waving the victory flag in my face, pretending that what I had said was more important than what I had ignored.

"What do you want with your tea?" My uncle pressed his advantage. "We still have an apple."

"If you are telling me I need to go shopping, I already know that. Maybe this afternoon I can do it. Meanwhile, go ahead, eat the apple, it will do your digestion good. All I need right now is sleep. Do you mind?"

"I don't mind. I'll go out for noodles."

"No."

My uncle caught something in my tone. "Problem?"

"No problem. You should realize that noodles are not good for you all the time. Too much starch, that's all."

"This sudden concern with my health is nice, nephew. It hits me here." He touched his chest. "But I'm not going to die young, and I'm not giving up noodles."

I could tell he wasn't really concerned about noodles at the moment. "You have something else on your mind, am I right?"

"Not on my mind, no. But I still have something you might find interesting, which is where we started."

This was exactly what I did not want to hear him say, and he'd said it twice. I threw off the quilt and yawned. "What you mean is, you know something you think I don't, and you're dying to tell me. You're also going to tell me it's urgent."

"It's not urgent for me, it might be for you."

"All right, what is it?"

"Mike is back."

Sleep did a two-step out the window as I sat bolt upright. "Where did you hear that?"

"Around."

"When did you hear it?"

"Yesterday."

I lay back down again and stared at the ceiling. "Not good enough, and you know it, uncle. 'Around' and 'yesterday' score low on the answer scale. You have more. I need the details."

My uncle smiled. It was his totally impenetrable, most annoying smile. "You wish. In this case, I don't know much more. Details?" He shrugged. "That's what investigations are for."

"I'm tired, uncle. I had a bad dinner last night, and I'm in a black mood from lack of sleep. I have a new deputy who is going to give me a worse headache than I already have, and the mayor is on one of his bureaucratic jihads against my office." I rolled over and shut my eyes.

"Not to mention terrorists killing diners," my uncle added, "and the tragic loss of a blond tourist whose passport is missing and whose husband is the owner of one of the biggest manufacturing plants in the country. Makes phony designer bags, or something."

The husband was news to me. So were the bags. I sat up again. "How you do know this? And don't tell me you heard it 'somewhere,' or I'll burn every last one of your bookcases." It was an idle threat, but the thought of it made me smile.

"Which do you want to hear first, the news about Mike or this interesting food problem that is already making trouble for your friend the mayor?"

"Forget the mayor. Give me what you know about Mike. And I mean everything."

"I told you, he's back. Showed up in Changchun a week ago. Someone spotted him here on Tuesday at the train station getting into a taxi."

"And if he showed up on Tuesday, and you knew about it, why didn't I know about it before today, which is Friday, as if I needed to remind you."

"Probably for the same reason you don't know that he went across the river on Wednesday night."

This news was galling, as he knew it would be. "Now you're fantasizing. Mike wouldn't do that. He doesn't like boats. And anyway he couldn't. We'd have noticed. The river is covered."

My uncle was running his fingers along the top of the doorjamb. "Damned thing is out of alignment. Who built this place? Hold on, I'll get some tools."

"Never mind the door. We're talking about Mike. He would never go across the river."

"Tell him yourself, why don't you? He's sure to be back here, I'd guess in a week, two at the most. He might fly out of Pyongyang, but I doubt it."

When the phone rang down the hall in the room we sometimes use as an office for private cases, my uncle flashed that smile again. "Pretty early in the day for a phone call. Must be for you. A lady friend, perhaps. Want me to get it, or should they just leave a message?"

"I'm not talking to anyone. Could be it's for you. Maybe it's someone calling for a private detective, you know, a job so we can earn money to buy groceries." I paused for effect. "Or maybe it's one of your old friends."

My uncle laughed. "My old friends leave messages under trees. You never know who's listening on the phone."

"Then let it ring," I said. It did, eight times, before it went silent. I waited for my uncle to pick up the conversation, but he stood there, looking at me with a bemused smile. It was my move as far as he was concerned.

I decided to try a direct question, something that rarely worked with my uncle. "You said someone spotted Mike. Who?"

"We didn't exchange name cards."

"Fine, no name. Anyone you'd recognize if you saw him again?"

"Walked with a limp, leaned to the side a little. Short, bad teeth, faraway look in his eyes, like he was dreaming of another day."

"Why would a dreamy-eyed stranger pick you out to pass on something important like that? And where did this little chance rendezvous happen, uncle?" More questions for which I knew enough not to expect answers.

"If you're not going to make breakfast, I'm going out for noodles."

"The noodle shops are all closed, uncle. The police aren't taking any chances." I didn't know if the chief had actually issued the order yet, and even if he had, if all the shops had complied. I could think of a half dozen that wouldn't close until the police came and nailed their front doors shut. "Try something else for a change. You might like it."

"For instance?"

"I don't know. How about *youtiao*?"

"Fried dough? All that grease is bad for my heart. It's probably old motor oil, considering everything else that happens around here. What a country!" He disappeared into the hall, and a minute later, the front door clicked shut. I lay back and asked myself, as I do at least once a week, when my uncle would figure it was safe for him to cross the river back to his home in the mountains of North Korea.

2

Grabbing more sleep was not an option. My brain was jumping with possibilities. Mike did not go in for mass murder, but the coincidence of his reappearance and the demise of the seven diners, with more body parts possibly littering the countryside north of town, raised ugly possibilities. True, if my uncle was to be believed, and that usually turned out to be the smartest thing to do, Mike had gone across the river to North Korea the day before the murders. That timing helped, but not much. It's unlikely he would do a job like that himself. He had staff, "contractors" actually. Mike thought contractors reduced expenses. He was from south China, and very concerned with overhead.

Why Mike would want to mess up the noodle business, however, was a good question. It could be that the Uighur was behind on his protection payments, but three dead diners felt like overkill

for a simple bookkeeping problem. Besides, poisoning diners, assuming that was how the three old men died, sent the wrong message to the eating public. And why the man in the fancy restaurant?
Or the two hookers? Or the blonde?

On the other hand, I thought I could see the thinnest of silver
linings here. At least if Mike was behind the murders, it meant I
didn't have to worry about terrorists. Mike was old-fashioned;
he didn't like terrorists. They were too unpredictable, something Mike
detested. He was convinced that if terrorists were in the vicinity, it
rattled his clients. I know this because for a while we had a useful
tap on his phone. We heard him get furious once when he learned
that a group of jihadists were hanging around the Muslim Hotel in
Yanji, casing buildings for what we never found out.

"Tell them to get the fuck out of here," he had shouted into the
phone, "and tell them if they aren't gone in twenty-four hours,
they'll leave in boxes. This is my territory. I don't want their long
noses anywhere near here."

The group had slipped back to Beijing the next day and hadn't
returned. I'd sent a message to Headquarters, but I never learned if
Beijing rounded them up or if they had moved on to cause problems somewhere else.

For a while after that, Mike and I had an unspoken truce. He kept
things orderly on his end and avoided anything that might have to
come to Beijing's attention. I kept track of him but didn't make a
move. Then, as happens, there was a leadership shuffle in Beijing,
at which point things that Headquarters had previously considered
only local background noise became a matter of high policy. The
ministry launched a hard strike in Yanji, with Mike in the bull's-
eye. He left town barely a step ahead of the excitement, and he stayed
away, doing what I didn't know. The message traffic on his activi-
ties was reduced to one short item every few months. Old sources
that used to know his whereabouts clammed up. So when Uncle O
said Mike was back in town, I knew there would be trouble. Mike's
was still an open file in Beijing, and the Ministry would want to
close it. That meant a special squad would be sent up to my office,

a lot of nasty questions about procedures asked, well-established routines disrupted, and the one or two effective operations we'd established trashed—all because the slick boys from Beijing thought they knew better than anyone on the spot.

The biggest problem was I couldn't tell Beijing where I got my information about Mike's return. My uncle still had his sources, of course, and they were all good. But they were his sources, not mine. Soon after he had first arrived, we reached a strict understanding—we would never share sources. Information sometimes, sources never. Some of his sources came from the private detective agency he ran on the side, but those were dwindling because he didn't like taking on clients. Clients meant getting paid, and he thought working for money was corrupting. We did manage to take in some money from the bookcases he built. Locals had taken a liking to his skills in woodworking, which I had to admit were considerable when he put his mind to it. We agreed that half of what he earned he could keep for expensive lumber, which he said was absolutely necessary because he detested working with pine. The other half of the bookcase profits went toward food. The problem was, though he turned out a steady supply of bookcases, most of them were what he called "proof of concept." That meant they were odd shapes, basically unusable and largely unsalable. So a lender might say (and did whenever I looked for a loan) we had enough money, but not much of a cushion. We might have had more, but as everyone seemed to know, my ex-wife had taken everything when she ran away with a Japanese pastry chef several years ago.

Every time Uncle O did take on a case for his detective agency, I helped discreetly, hoping that he might build up a regular paying clientele. In turn, he helped me from time to time with my cases, or so he thought. Help, in his view, took the form of a running criticism of my investigative techniques.

For that reason, Uncle O's unsolicited offer of information about Mike, even the little he had shared, was a surprise. It wasn't much, but he knew it was all I needed to get started. As it happened, it was all I had. There was nothing about Mike in the message traffic recently. Anything on Mike was considered "Class A" in our sector, and reports with that stamp were always flagged for me to see right away. That meant they weren't supposed to sit around in someone else's in-box for more than a couple of hours. The local police hadn't heard anything, I was sure of that. The chief knew that if he had information on Mike and failed to mention it to me at our dinner, I'd make his life more miserable than it already was. If he had heard something—anything, no matter how small—he would have shared.

That left two places for me to check. First were taxis that had been at the train station on Tuesday. The mayor had his fingers into the taxi companies, and he would know it as soon as we started questioning drivers. He'd order them not to talk to us, and we would be seeing doors slam in our faces for weeks. We could try roughing up a few of the drivers to get the rest to talk, but the next time we needed their cooperation on something else—and there was always some reason to need assistance from the taxi drivers—they would be sullen and drag their feet. I could give the job of dealing with the taxis to my new deputy; let him run up against the mayor and see what it was like.

The other angle was more risky but might pay off faster—ask the few sources that I personally ran what they knew. It was still before noon, and most sources didn't like to meet during the day. They were all annoying characters, always in need of psychological stroking. I'd never met one who didn't have personality quirks that grated on me.

As a matter of preference, I met rarely with my agents, and in a few cases had never actually met them at all. Messages and information were passed through an elaborate ritual of feints and signals. Some of what I learned was useful; most of it was not. In this case, I knew I needed to check with one source in particular, and it had to be a face-to-face meeting. Sources can embellish, they can distort, they can even outright lie on paper. They can do all of those things in person, too, but I could cut the chances in half if I could watch their eyes. If Mike had been in town, even for a couple of days, I wanted to confirm that right away before Beijing got wind of it. Even if Mike hadn't ruined dinner for seven people—maybe eight—this particular source had probably heard something that would give me some clue as to why this plague rat was being visited on me again.

There hadn't been much from this source in the ten months or so I'd been running him, but whatever information he had passed had been good, and most important, all of it had been timely. Even the rumors the source passed on had turned out to be solid. In another situation, I might be suspicious of so much good information, but paranoia could wait. I called the duty officer and told him I wouldn't be in until around noon.

3

The morning was cool and the sky surprisingly clear, a nice day for a stroll. About a kilometer from my house was a small park. I headed straight there. Three people trailed behind. The second and third were my security detail—a young woman who was very good at what she did, and an older man who managed to be invisible. The first person in line was nobody I knew. By the time I got to the park, no one was following me, which meant the young woman and her companion had done their job.

The park was arranged in an imperfect square, with a couple of ragged benches on each side. There were nondescript, rarely trimmed bushes growing randomly behind all but one of the benches, which sat by itself under an old, bent tree that had always struck me as lonely and out of place. I wouldn't have known what the tree was, except my uncle had pointed it out one afternoon when we were on a rare outing together.

"You see that tree?" he'd said, walking up to the tree and patting the trunk.

"I do."

"You know what it is?"

"Other than wood, you mean?"

"Listen to me, nephew. It's a red pine, quite old, and, if you look closely you'll see it has a self-assured air. Don't let its leaning posture fool you. My grandfather would have walked over and spoken to it quietly for a few minutes. He thought red pines were noble in their own way, very different from normal pine trees, which he considered trash." Uncle O had given me a sideways glance. "If I were you, I wouldn't let anyone cut this tree down."

"I don't control tree cutting in this town, uncle. That's up to the mayor, or anyone who offers him the right combination of money and flesh."

He sighed. "If it's cut down, get me the lumber, then. We can use it; we're running low, and it will save me from dealing with those crooks at the lumberyard in Harbin. Do you know how much they would charge for red pine?"

"Obviously too much."

This introduction to a tree had not meant anything to me at the time, but a couple of months later, Beijing had sent a highly unusual split transmission message assigning a special source to the office, with explicit instructions that I was to handle things personally and with utmost discretion, nothing documented, nothing traceable, payments, if there were to be any, strictly unrecorded. The code name for the source was "Red Pine."

Officially, Red Pine and I were never to meet, except in a crashing emergency. Instead, according to the Headquarters instructions, we were to pass messages twice a month, every other month, on random days, at random times. There were three places in the city where we did that. One of them was the park. I thought this was bad, and potentially fatal, operational practice. If someone was watching, it wouldn't take them long to figure out where I went twice a month. Even my security detail couldn't succeed every time in walking a tail off in the wrong direction. And when whoever was interested put those places under constant watch, they'd find Red Pine. I figured it would take six months at the most before the source was compromised, or worse. We were in month five.

Whether Beijing would consider news that Mike had showed up again enough of an emergency for a direct meeting with Red Pine, I didn't care. It was enough for me. I sent the agreed-upon emergency signal for a meeting within the hour, waited around the house for thirty minutes, and then set off to see if anyone would show up.

The park was deserted when I turned the corner onto the path that led to the first bench. A minute later, I noticed someone standing some distance back, nearly hidden behind one of the bushes. Whoever it was wore a long coat and a cap. It could be anyone, maybe a pensioner looking for firewood. I sat down on the nearest bench and waited. I'd never seen a pensioner in this park before. The figure behind the bush didn't move. I glanced around to see if there was anyone else nearby, maybe someone in position on the walkway on the other side of the bushes. No one. I looked away to check the street entrance to the park, and when I turned back, beside me sat a young woman. She took off the cap and shook her black hair so it fell onto her shoulders.

"Neat trick," I said. "How did you do that, move so softly?" I had to get rid of her in a hurry or she'd ruin the rendezvous.

The woman looked at me coolly. "I can move in many ways, Major, so many that you can't even imagine."

I nearly fell off the bench. My heart stopped. My breathing ceased. My vision clouded. "Tuya." It was the only word that came to mind.

"Surprised to see me?"

Tuya was Mongolian. I'd met her in Ulan Bator two years back. She was the assistant to the chief of the Mongolian special police, a nice enough man who after a briskly efficient interrogation had ordered me out of the country on twenty-four hours' notice, but not before I'd fallen in love with Tuya. I hadn't seen her, not in the flesh anyway, since then. She was gorgeous, long-limbed, with eyes that held the flames of a thousand fires of a thousand years of nights on endless plains, and a way of serving tea that could make a man faint with delight or horror, depending on your point of view. I still felt queasy when I remembered how she could put her legs behind her neck.

"How?" I was slowly regaining my power of speech but was temporarily stuck on interrogatives. "What? When?"

"It's been a couple of years, Major. I wasn't sure you'd remember me. You almost didn't."

"Remember?" I took a deep breath. "Are you kidding? You startled me, that's all. Have I thought of anything else? I waited. I tried calling."

"So that was you?"

"I was in Urumchi for a few days on business. The place is swarming with Mongolians; I couldn't stand it anymore. I called your office from my hotel. A man answered. Maybe it was what's-his-name. The big guy."

"Bazar."

"Yeah, Bazar. The connection wasn't good. We got cut off."

"So you missed me?" It was posed as an interrogation question, no emotion in it.

Just then, I saw a car pull over to the curb in the street at the edge of the park. No one got out.

"What are you doing here?" I filed away the description of the car—black, a two-door, European, heavy-duty bumpers. "It's not a good place for you to be right now."

"I thought you called for this meeting."

This was like having a building fall on me. "You?"

She nodded.

"Hell," I said. "That's impossible."

"Look." She moved away from me to her edge of the bench. "If you don't want to tell me why you called an emergency meeting, I'm leaving. We're never supposed to meet face-to-face. Those were my orders. I assume they were yours as well."

"Wait, don't leave. When can I see you again?"

"Bad operational practice, isn't it? Two meetings so close together." She paused a moment. "Who cares? How about dinner? I heard there's a nice noodle restaurant in town."

"No restaurants."

"Where, then? Your place?"

"My place?" I had to laugh.

"Something funny?"

"No, just the image of Uncle O walking in on us. Give me an hour or so. I'll figure something out. Can I call you? I have a sterile phone."

"Right, your uncle, how could I forget? He's well?" She pulled a card from her pocket. "Call this number. Ask if the shipment of blue purses has come in yet. They'll connect you." It was straight business, not a hint of anything else.

Then she squeezed my hand and disappeared. A moment later, the black car pulled away from the curb. It needed a tune-up.

4

I sat on the bench for a couple of minutes. I wanted to see if the black car nosed back down the street. I also wanted to let my heart rate go back down before I headed home. My uncle has special radars. He would sense in a microsecond that something out of the ordinary happened at the park. By the time I opened the front door, I thought for sure my face wasn't flushed. My pulse felt normal. As soon as he saw me, Uncle O pretended not to notice, but I could tell he knew something was up.

"Enjoyed the park?" he asked casually.

"Always enjoy parks, you know that. You've put me onto trees, uncle. I owe you a debt of gratitude."

"You won't be here for dinner, I suppose."

"A lot of paperwork at the office." I patted my pockets, looking for a notebook.

"Enjoy your evening," he said. "I found a new chisel in the alley. Hardly used. I think I'll spend the evening putting it through its paces. You can't be too sure of something like this. A headstrong chisel is a menace. There must be a reason someone threw it away."

5

"Let's get to the point, shall we? We're not supposed to meet like this." Tuya was edgy, which was good. One of us had to be aware of what the training manuals call the "operational environment," and it wasn't going to be me. We were back in the same park. I figured no one would expect us to meet there again the same day; just in case, I'd made sure no one had followed me, not even my security team. It was a crazy assumption, but then, the whole thing was crazy. Anyway, it was eleven o'clock at night, and the mayor had siphoned off the money that was supposed to pay for lighting in the parks, so from a distance no one could be sure who we were, unless they had a pair of night-vision goggles. No one in Yanji, not even the mayor, not even someone in that black car, was liable to possess night-vision goggles. My office couldn't even get them, which didn't matter because I didn't need them at the moment. I was close enough to see Tuya's face in the moonlight. "We're here, in plain sight," she said. *"Evidente."* Her eyes gave nothing away. She pulled her legs onto the bench and twisted herself into a puzzle as if she were a piece of string.

"You did that the first time I saw you," I said. "You served me tea like that, tea and those little cheese stones."

She smiled up at me, though from that angle I couldn't tell what sort of smile it was. "I told you I could move in many ways. I still can. Do you think the body is supposed to be just the way you see it all the time, legs down, head up, arms hanging at your side? You define my face in relation to my shoulders, don't you, but why? Why not in relation to my thighs?"

I exhaled slowly. Well, why not? "Fascinating," I said. "Let's leave that for another time and twist ourselves in a new direction. What are you doing here? I mean, what are you doing working for us?"

She pulled herself back up to the shoulders-and-face variety and smiled again, this time with more warmth. "The truth is, I was moping after you left. Batbayaar—you remember, my boss—said it was affecting my efficiency. I asked around. When an undercover assignment opened up, I took it. There are more Mongolians traveling here and there. There's some worry about them." She shrugged. "And I needed a change."

"But you're working for us, me."

She shrugged again. "Yes and no."

"Who vetted you? Did they know you had met me before?"

She put her fingers to my lips. "I don't know what you mean." Suddenly her body stiffened, but her expression didn't change. "Off to the left, someone's watching. Kiss me. *Tosto*."

"I don't see anything." I didn't take my eyes off her face.

When she was young, Tuya had answered an ad in a Mongolian newspaper for a waitress in Rome. Once she got there, she found that the owner of the restaurant had other ideas. Some bigwigs he worked with thought she was just what they needed at their parties. She didn't agree, and left to join a small circus, where she learned acrobatics and fought off a greasy Romanian trapeze artist for a year before going home. Her Italian was rudimentary, but I knew none, so I had to guess from context. The meaning of *tosto* was not immediately apparent. I'd look it up when I had a spare moment.

"Anyway," I said, "I don't kiss my agents on the first date."

Tuya leaned over, put her arms around my neck, and pulled my face to hers.

"Neither do I. But I value my skin. Kiss me, *appassionato molto*."

"Not on your life," I said. "Maybe some other time." I pulled away and turned to see who was watching. When I turned back, she was gone. A car passed by, very slowly. The engine needed tuning.

6

By the time I got to the office the next day, it was well after lunch. The duty officer said there was nothing new as far as the restaurant corpses went, but I could see he hadn't even bothered to check the overnight log. When I got to my desk, there was a bulky, sealed envelope next to the phone. The envelope had no address on it, no indication of who it was from or to whom it was supposed to go. I picked it up carefully and brought it out to the duty officer.

"When did this come in?"

He looked at it as if it had dropped from another planet. "Honest, Major, I never saw it before, and no one has come in that door since I've been here."

"What about the door from the bank?"

Our office was in an old, wooden two-story building. It had been built in the 1930s as a headquarters for the Japanese Imperial Army's Manchurian sector. After the Japanese left, the place had fallen into disrepair, which meant the Ministry, with not much internal discussion and even less of a budget, considered it perfect for the regional office. The building was set back from the street, with a broad open area all around. That gave it an aura of unassailability. It also meant voices and other sounds from within the building were unlikely to be heard by anyone passing by. There was a decision not to build a security fence, since that would have looked like we had something to fear, whereas it was the general population that was supposed to be worried about us.

A few years ago, someone—one rumor said it was the deputy minister—sold the open land to a developer, and not long afterward we were surrounded by tall buildings. One of them, with a Bank of China on the ground floor, came right up to our front door. "No sense in wasting good space," the developer said when we protested. The Ministry sent a surveyor and a counterintelligence team up to look things over for a week, and they decided that going through the bank all the time to get to our office wasn't very good. They recommended that we use the old kitchen door as our new entrance. That meant special locks and security cameras, all of which took months to install. The buzzer from the duty desk to unlock the door didn't always work, and no one could remember the combination to the lock, which was very complex in order to defeat "the enemy," so we spent a lot of time drinking tea at a little place on Dooran Street, around the corner. There were always some hookers there, especially in the afternoon. Most of them were happy to joke about their customers, so we kept our ears open. If anyone from Beijing Headquarters showed up on a surprise inspection visit and asked what we were doing drinking tea with hookers, we could say it wasn't a complete waste of time.

In the last couple of weeks, I'd gotten the impression that something was going on. The girls were quieter, smoking more, less eager to chat. Sometimes that was because they were having problems with the mayor's demands that they work longer hours, or party with his crooked friends. This time the mood had seemed different, but no one would talk. And now there were the deaths of two of the girls—I didn't know which two, yet—outside the dumpling shop. Technically, these weren't my business, but if I could show the mayor was connected to the murders, I might finally be able to bring him down. Beijing liked us to bring in the heads of corrupt local officials. It made the minister look good.

Chapter Three

The envelope stared at me for twenty minutes or so as I thought about opening it. It ought to be scanned, I realized, but then I'd have to make a record of it. Whoever had slipped it into the office obviously didn't want that. It didn't look like a bomb, unless it was a noodle bomb. It might be poison, anthrax or something. They had problems like that in the west, Uighurs and so forth, but not here. Well, so far not here. They'd even had problems in Beijing with Uighur terrorists, and Beijing was far from their homes in Xinjiang. It wouldn't take much for them to get a little farther, up here to Yanji. The owner of the noodle shop where the corpses had been found was a Uighur with a limp, so maybe we weren't so safe up here in the northeast anymore. But why kill me? Equally, of course, why not? I represented the central authority, didn't I? No matter to some angry Uighur that I wasn't pure Han. Even if, as my uncle said, I had only a drop of Chinese blood, they'd be happy to spill even that drop. On the other hand, it could be the North Koreans. I was in charge of the office that was supposed to keep tabs on their security people, and from time to time, I made their lives difficult. Maybe they wanted to send Beijing a message. Or it could be they were still angry about what I'd done to one of their agents in Mongolia a few years back. Less likely, it could be to scare me into sending my uncle back home. The possibilities were endless. The outcomes, on the other hand, were few, none of them good.

All of a sudden, I realized I needed to look up *tosto*. If Tuya used it again, I wanted to be ready. After she had lived in Italy and learned a little of the language, Tuya had gone back home to train as a contortionist at the Ulan Bator University of Contortionism. On graduation with honors, she was recruited by the Mongolian special police. Now she was here, in Yanji, working as my agent. Or, as she put it, "yes and no." She must still be working for the Mongolians in some capacity. The Mongolians acted like they were off balance all the time. To hear them talk, the Russians and the Japanese and the South Koreans and the Chinese were all pushing them around. I didn't buy it. From what I'd seen when I was there, the Mongolians had a good security organization. People who have conquered the known world usually do, even if it was a while ago. They knew how to watch their borders by going out and watching from some distance away. Yanji was a good place to watch a lot of other people's operations and pick up early warning signs. Putting Tuya in Yanji made sense. In that case, it meant she was a double. On the other hand, given how she'd been assigned to me directly from Beijing, maybe not—unless the screening in Beijing was worse than normal.

Maybe she was not quite a double, sort of a 1.5. It was possible that Beijing was working with the Mongolians. They were developing good relations with Pyongyang, and it wouldn't be a surprise if someone in the Ministry thought that the Mongolians could give us access we didn't have but badly needed.

It would have been better if they'd let me know she was in my region, but maybe not.

Maybe, maybe, maybe. This couldn't go on. I couldn't concentrate when I was around her, and now I couldn't concentrate when I wasn't. Something had to give. I reached over and tore open the package. If it exploded, it would save me a lot of heartache.

Nothing happened. There was a light wooden box, and inside of that, another box that had a yellow rose embossed on its lid. I lifted the smaller box to examine it under the lamp on my desk and looked at the four sides. It was nicely put together. The lid fit perfectly. It didn't look as if it had been constructed in a factory. Uncle

O would know what sort of wood it was. He would probably even be able to guess something about the person who constructed the box, maybe even when it was put together and where—assuming it didn't blow up when I lifted the lid. Just as I decided to remove the lid, my special phone buzzed. I unlocked the drawer and picked up the receiver.

"Major, did you get a package?" It was the chief of police. He was talking fast.

"I did. From you? Very pretty, though I don't think it's my style."

"Don't open it. Don't rattle it. Don't do anything. I'm sending the bomb squad over."

"You have a bomb squad handy? Since when?" I moved my chair back from the desk a little. "Calm down, will you? It's just a box."

I heard a conversation offline. Someone shouted, and then the chief piped up again. "If there is anyone in your building, get them out. You, too. Leave the box and get out!"

"Walk, run, crawl?"

"I'm not kidding, Major. I'll explain later. Right now you need to evacuate your building. And I mean *now!*"

"OK, see you later."

"Let's hope so." The chief hung up.

I walked into the front office. "Time to leave," I said to the duty officer casually. He was a nervous type, a good trait sometimes but not now. When his nerves jangled, he froze up. I needed him to stay unfrozen. "Send a message to Beijing telling them we're evacuating the office." I put my hands in my pockets and looked nonchalant. "Bomb scare."

The duty officer froze. "Huh?"

"You heard me, type a close-down message and send it. Take you a couple of seconds."

"You want me to encrypt it?"

I could see his eyes were getting a very nervous glint. "Sure, why not," I said. He was going to need prodding. "Then we'll put all the pieces of you we can find in the nice box someone sent me, and we'll keep it in the file room for your replacement to bring flowers to every New Year's Day. No! Forget encrypting it. Send the message in the clear."

I followed the duty officer into the communications room.

"What do I say?" He had a funny look on his face.

"Closing," I said. "Closing, bomb scare. Will advise." I saw him shut his eyes and turn to the keyboard. He typed one key, then stopped, his hands frozen in midair. "That's good," I said gently, "you're doing real good. Go on, type another word. Then let's get the hell out of here."

Just as we got to the street, I saw a car backing away. It did a 180-degree turn, the driver gunned the engine, and the car disappeared into a side street. A moment later, two cars came screaming at us from the other direction. The first one hurtled past and turned the corner with a screech of tires. The second one braked and spun around. The chief of police jumped out and shouted an order at two policemen in the backseat. "Get out, get out now and secure that package!"

The two of them emerged from the car, but neither one took a step.

"It's OK, Po." I ignored the two police statues. "The package is in my office. It looks harmless enough."

"Says you. Let's not take any chances. My bomb squad is out back. They'll handle it. These two"—he slapped one of them on the back of the head—"will be used as dog meat."

There was a muffled explosion, the sound of glass shattering, then black smoke curling out from one of the windows on the second floor of our building.

"Odd," I said.

"Not odd," the chief said, irritated. "I warned you it was a bomb."

"Yes, you did. The thing is, it was on my desk, and my desk is on the first floor. Why did it blow out a second-floor window?"

"Physics," the chief said. "Mechanics of bomb explosions. Who the hell cares! The main thing is we need to secure the place and gather evidence before it disappears." He turned again to the statues.

"OK, the damned thing went boom. The coast is clear. Now get in there and start looking for clues."

One of the two shook his head. "It was a bomb, Chief, everything blew the hell up. We're not going to find anything."

The chief walked over and leaned so close into the man's face that his hat fell off. "Did I ask your advice? No, I didn't. Did I give you an order? Yes, I did. You want to discuss it? How about I put you in the hospital, maybe we can talk about it there."

"Po," I interrupted. "A word if you don't mind."

The chief glowered at his man for a moment longer, then turned to me. "What?"

"A word in private."

Po looked around. "You want to go somewhere else? A noodle restaurant, perhaps? I think we've closed them all down. We can talk there in private."

"No, down the block will be fine." When we were about thirty meters away, with no one in earshot, I stopped. "I saw a car leaving just as I got out onto the street."

"So?"

"It was going in reverse, very fast."

"Did you get a good look at it?"

"Yes."

"Don't tell me. You know whose it was, but I'm supposed to guess."

"It was the mayor's car. The one he uses when he thinks no one knows it's him. The right driver's-side tire doesn't match the other three."

2

"That was going to be my first guess." The police chief made a face. "Maybe the mayor was out for one of his surprise inspections."

"Yeah, surprise. His driver whipped the car around in a hurry.

Here's what I want you to do, Po. Just wait. Watch and wait. You know as well as I do that he is up to something."

"No idea what you're talking about, Major. None." The chief turned to go, then turned back. "You sure you're OK? I can plant some people in the neighborhood to keep watch. Nothing elaborate. A couple of guys dressed like street sweepers."

"Not necessary." The day the local police had to guard one of the Ministry's field offices would be a bad day in hell and an even worse day for me. "Headquarters will send a team up here to find out what is going on. They're probably already packing. They'll arrive in a few hours, and once they're here, they won't want your people hanging around." The last thing I needed was a team from Headquarters snooping in my sector because of a bomb, two bombs if you counted the one in the countryside. I had to come up with a way to wave them off.

"We don't call it hanging around." Po was annoyed with my choice of words. "We call it collecting evidence. It makes good paperwork for the files, long lists of things and people and events. Sometimes we even catch criminals with evidence. Hard to believe, Major, but it happens, even with the sad bunch working for me."

There was no sense going back and forth with him over theories of evidence, especially now. "Just say it was a gas line explosion, why don't you? Routine incident, that sort of thing, barely even rates a written report. You can fill in the evidence later."

The police chief looked doubtful. "I don't think I can sell that. There are no gas lines on your second floor."

"Maybe there are, maybe there aren't. How the hell would you know what's in a State Security building? How does anyone know what's on the second floor? No one ever goes up there." I thought about it. Not no one. "OK, don't try to sell that explanation if you don't think you can do it with a straight face. Maybe just try renting it out for a couple of days. Long enough for me to make a few enquiries."

"But if this is terrorism . . ."

"It's not. We both know it isn't terrorism, not the normal kind, anyway. If you have to, go ahead and pretend to conduct an investigation so you don't seem to rule things out too soon. But I don't have to pretend. I'm telling you it's not terrorism."

"OK, if you're so sure, then what is it? If it's not terrorism, what do we call it?" Po held up his hand. "Never mind. I'm just the police chief. I don't have to know what State Security thinks. I don't even want to know. I tell you what. I'll pull everyone off this incident for three days. That's all I can give you. I can explain three days as normal incompetence, personnel shortages, failure of communications equipment, or even the need to concentrate on those seven bodies. Then someone will talk to someone else and my phone will ring and the mayor will be on the other end telling me to have a report finished on a certain building explosion within twenty-four hours or find myself in Hubei directing traffic."

"Three days is fine, Po."

As the chief climbed back into his car, I looked around for my duty officer. He was on the corner talking to a woman. When she saw me coming over, she lowered her face and hurried away into an alley.

"You know her?" I watched the woman disappear.

"Yeah." The duty officer had no guile, which was good. "She's the manager of some sort of fish restaurant I go to when I get off late. The place is open all night. It's new. Sometimes I need a break from Indian food."

"Curry from hell."

"Yeah." He grinned.

"How's the fish at the lady's place?"

"Nothing special."

"She just happened by after the explosion?"

"Could be. I think she lives in the neighborhood."

"You think so?"

"Look, Major, I don't know exactly. She's not my type."

"That's good. You wouldn't like her type."

"Sure, if you say so."

"I say so. You know where she's from?"

"She's local as far as I can figure, though once in a while I catch an accent."

I hadn't caught an accent when I was in the restaurant, but the duty officer had a good ear for that sort of thing.

"You stay away from her place," I said, "until I tell you it's OK. There are other fish in the sea."

"If you say so. The fish are from the river, but if you say so."

"I do. And keep away from her, too."

He shrugged. "Sure, I told you, she's not my type. She's too tough for me."

"Good, then we understand each other. Let's get back to work."

The duty officer scratched his nose. "How come only the second-floor windows blew out?"

"Physics," I said. "Bodies in motion." I gave him a hard look. "Understand?"

He shrugged. "What do we tell Headquarters?"

"Nothing. We don't tell them anything. Send an all-clear as soon as you can, before they start to worry. Tell them it was a false alarm. Maybe they won't order anyone up here. I don't know about you, but I could do without those smug faces poking into our quiet existence."

"You're the boss. Should I encrypt this one?"

"Might as well. It will make things look more normal."

3

A couple of minutes after an encrypted "All normal" message was sent to Beijing, a curt reply came back. This one was sent in the clear. "Make up your mind. Bomb or no?"

The duty officer brought it in to me. "You want me to tell them again it was a false alarm?"

"Sure, put it in extra-big type this time," I said. "They must have decided against sending someone to snoop around. Hard to find people to come up here to waste time with us dull-witted peasants, I guess."

"Yeah, you said it." The duty officer hesitated. "Strange, the explosion didn't ruffle the papers on my desk. Even the area map on the wall didn't go cockeyed." He seemed sunk in thought for a moment, then emerged again. "You want me to call someone to repair the upstairs window?"

"Maybe later. You sure your commo equipment is all right? Nothing jarred out of place?"

"Sending and receiving both worked fine."

"No wires worked loose? The roof antenna didn't get pushed over? It must have been closer to the blast than the map on the duty room wall."

"There aren't any wires, and we don't use an antenna anymore." He was smart enough not to ask why I didn't know about the equipment upgrades. "Those were replaced, ah, I don't remember when. Everything is underground cables these days. They head out from here onto a trunk line somewhere. It would take a much bigger explosion than the one we had . . ."

I frowned.

". . . than the one we didn't have to damage those cables. Maybe a direct hit from a nuclear weapon."

"Fine. You wait for that. Meantime, I'll go upstairs and look around. We'll worry about the window once I see what happened."

We never used the upstairs. No one needed so much space, Beijing thought, and years ago it had sent out a facilities team that made sure the grand stairway leading to the second-floor bedrooms was closed off. I'd gone up to the second floor only once or twice when I first arrived just to be sure I knew what the whole building contained. The locals were sure it was where we tortured people, and I knew the North Koreans thought it was overflowing with intercept equipment aimed at them. They sent people to Yanji regularly to loiter in the neighborhood to try to detect what we were doing. No one believed that over the years the second floor had really been left to spiders and mice. The Japanese had departed in a hurry in 1945, and some of the rooms still had old clothing strewn across the beds. Anything of real value had vanished long ago.

Poking around, I could see right away there hadn't been much damage. The blast had been smaller than it appeared, or sounded, from street level. It blew out one window in what I always assumed had been the commanding general's salon, next to one of the larger bedrooms. The other windows, on the opposite side of the big room, were intact. The blast hadn't even disturbed the cobwebs on that wall. There had been a desk of some sort near the broken window. It lay on its side, with what looked like a few scorch marks on the top. Other than that, it didn't look damaged. I backed carefully out of the room, trying to step into the same footprints I'd left in the dust when I entered. I poked my head into a second adjoining room, smaller than the first. An old operations map sat against the far wall. Going down the stairs back to the first floor, I noticed places on the banister where the dust had been disturbed. Some of the stairs, as well, had an odd trail on them. It hadn't been noticeable on the way up, and I'd been careful not to touch the banister.

Downstairs again, I walked over to the building's old entrance, the one that led into the bank. The door was locked, but not the right way. From the outside, with a key, it automatically fully engaged. But from the inside, the latch had to be turned twice—once to throw the bolt partway into the frame, and then again to throw it in all the way. It had only been turned once.

When I got back to the duty officer's desk, he was studying a manual. He looked up when he heard me. "Do we need window repair? They're calling for rain tomorrow."

"Who's been upstairs?" I sat down on the edge of his desk.

"Upstairs? No one goes upstairs, you don't allow it." He was unsure what was going on. I never sat on the edge of his desk, and I could tell he sensed it wasn't a gesture of camaraderie.

"Someone delivered a package to my office. Someone went upstairs. Since when do people roam around this office like it was a fun fair?"

"You said yourself, maybe someone came in through the bank entrance."

"Who has the keys to that entrance?"

He gulped. "You do."

"And who else?"

"No one." He said it quickly, without having to think.

I let him hang for a moment before breaking the tension. "That's right, no one."

The duty officer closed the manual and held it up for me to see, his effort at changing the subject. "It's for my communications test next week."

"What test? I thought you already knew that stuff. That's why you're my communicator, isn't it?"

"It is, but they are always coming up with new technology. New equipment arriving next month, more secure they say. I need to know how to use it."

"You mentioned cables. You know where they are routed?"

"I don't have the clearances for that."

"Who does?"

"I don't have the clearances for that either."

"Not very convenient, is it? You don't know what I need you to know."

"It's probably in your operational safe."

This time I let the silence drag on so long that he shifted in his chair.

"You know I have an operational safe?" I went over to the duty map on the wall and moved it a little to one side.

"There's an operational safe in the file room, the file clerk says so."

"What else does she say?" I stepped back to look at the map. "Is this straight?"

The duty officer knew enough to keep quiet.

"The file clerk." I turned and walked back to the desk. "What else does she say?"

"That no one is supposed to know about it, no one ever opens it, and she needed it moved to make room for more files."

"When did she say that?"

"Yesterday, to the new deputy, the tall guy with the scuffed shoes."

"What did he do?"

"He moved the safe. Or said he would, anyway. They were standing right here, so I heard what they said."

"You wouldn't happen to know where he put it?"

The duty officer had just started to say something when the duty phone rang.

"Never mind," I said. "Answer the phone. And leave that window like it is."

Chapter Four

Dead diners aren't my responsibility and wouldn't normally even interest me. On the other hand, an explosion of any size or description in a Ministry of State Security office deserves my attention, the more so if it happens in my building, particularly in an area of the building that is supposed to be off-limits. As of now, there were too many troubling coincidences of time and place mounting up: Mike shows up on Tuesday, he disappears again on Wednesday, a lot of bodies turn up on Thursday, and on Friday there is a pinpoint explosion in the never-used upstairs of my office building. I was not looking forward to what the weekend might hold.

I knew it would be a mistake to conclude that Mike was the thread that tied all of the events together. But something told me it would also be a mistake to discard that possibility too quickly. If I had a deputy I could trust, I'd be able to lay out the trail of events with him, and together we could figure out a plan to look more closely into where the lines intersected, or didn't. I would have done that with my previous deputy without giving it a second thought, but he was dead. Now the deputy I had was too sullen and, I had the strong impression, not especially trustworthy. I didn't have anything specific against him, not yet, but I was rarely wrong in my first impressions. For starters, what the hell was he doing moving office safes without asking me?

My uncle might have good ideas if I wanted to take the time to pull out the barbed hooks that would accompany his observations. It was even possible he would have a few more scraps of real information. If he knew that Mike had been in town, maybe he was holding back on an additional detail or two. He had promised me more than once that he had cut all ties with his old colleagues in North Korea, and maybe he had. Or maybe he hadn't. He wouldn't have to try very hard to stumble over a couple of them during one of his early morning walks. And for sure, by now they had tracked him down and pretty well knew his daily schedule.

I couldn't ask the police chief for his views. Po had his own problems, and anyway he was too much under the thumb of the mayor. True, he didn't like the mayor, the mayor didn't like him, but I could only trust the chief so far. Besides, even if he had manpower to spare, none of his detectives were too sharp.

It was clear I was on my own. For now, the dead diners were a problem for the police. I didn't think they'd solve anything, but they still might turn up something in their investigation that I could use. My focus had to be on Mike, the Uighur with a limp, and the prostitutes that hung around Dooran Street. These were smart girls, and they kept their eyes and ears open. I made a list and realized there was one thing missing—the manager of the fish restaurant. It was too soon to tell, but I had a feeling she'd made a big mistake showing up outside our building right after the explosion.

2

Number one on my list was finding out more of what Mike had been doing during the time he was laying low. Who was he in contact with? What sorts of deals was he exploring, and had he put out bids for new operations? We had a few pieces of paper on him in the files, but that didn't mean there wasn't more in the margins of other reports—unseen hands, low voices in dark corners, that sort of thing. It would entail going through a lot of agent reports, something I loathed doing because most of them were nothing but low-level information lifted from newspapers or, even worse these days, the Internet. This was then sold to us as precious insights from people with supposedly excellent access. We weeded out what we could, but even when we caught someone peddling crap, we rarely took them off the payroll. Beijing didn't want a lot of former agents running around loose, so we were supposed to keep them on a long leash, like old dogs that mostly slept and dreamed of better days.

Besides a few special cases, I'd made it policy that in our office, managing agents was the deputy's responsibility. Not all of the Ministry's local offices were run that way. In some places the chiefs handled many, sometimes most, of the agents personally. I knew that a lot of people in Beijing complained about my approach of leaving agent operations to the deputy, but sitting in Yanji, I was too far away to care what Beijing thought. Besides, I'd been in the same post for seven years, and if they were disgruntled enough at Headquarters they could order a transfer. That would suit me just fine. The files on active agents were kept in a special file cabinet. Only three people were supposed to know about the operations file cabinet: me, my deputy, and the file clerk who sat in the vault. The clerk didn't have access to it, but she knew what it was for, and if anyone fiddled with it or showed too much interest, she was supposed to let me know.

The file room—years before I arrived it had been made into a secure vault with a very heavy door and a sticky lock—was formerly the billiard parlor when the Japanese army occupied the building. Through the years, no one had bothered to remove the racks for the cue sticks attached to the walls. The file clerk used them to hang the checkout logs, her hat, and her purse. She was at her tiny, cluttered desk sipping tea when I walked into the vault.

"Good morning," I said, and got right to the point. "I thought we had agreed that you would never discuss the fact that there was an operations cabinet in this vault. You, the deputy, and I were the only ones who were to know it exists."

The woman brushed some lint from her blouse.

"I understand," I continued, "that you asked the new deputy to move the cabinet. Where is it?"

The file clerk finally looked up and grunted. "Deputy?" She took a noisy sip of tea and then smacked her lips. "You mean the tall man? No one introduces anyone to me. What do I do? I sit in here all day with this. This!" She waved her hand as if she were the dowager empress dismissing a eunuch.

"Where is that file cabinet?" I stared at her. She stared back. I thought it was a good time to add fuel to the fire. "And are you aware that we are missing a file?"

"I am not a magician, Major. Nor am I a shepherd of paper sheep. I do what I can to keep this file room in order. Why don't you speak to your staff?" This was her subtle way of saying that she wasn't part of my staff, and that she answered to another authority. It wasn't true, but it might as well be, considering how she treated the file room like her private preserve. She wasn't through complaining. "Your staff doesn't pay much attention to the rules. They take the installation files without signing them out, or when they do, they ignore the return date. Rules are rules, except your staff doesn't think so."

"This file disappeared, so it seems, three years ago."

"Ha! All the more reason for you to speak to the staff. Who was it?"

I wasn't going to win this tactical skirmish, not without more effort than I could afford at the moment. I let it drop in favor of the main battle. "I need to know where the operations file cabinet is. I don't suppose you could help me on that?"

"No one knows what it is for, exactly as you insist."

"Insist? It's not an idle demand on my part. Should we take a vote on it? How many in favor of tight security? How many opposed?"

This was ignored with a wave of the hand. "They all complain that it gets in the way, I hear that constantly." She looked at me evenly, daring me to contradict her. "Actually, they are right, and I've mentioned it to you before, in writing. The cabinet is rarely used,

and yet it takes up space. And space is at a premium in this cave."
She took another sip of tea, making more noise than would seem
possible given how small the cup was. "He moved it out there." The
empress waved vaguely in the direction of the vault door. "He's a
nice man. Very tall. We had a lovely conversation."

3

Walking down the hall, I spotted the new deputy ducking out of
my office and heading in the other direction.

"Tang! Hold it right there."

The tall man turned, looked at his watch, and frowned. "I've
got a meeting in a few minutes on the outside. Can this wait?"

In some MSS offices, an "appointment on the outside" is used
to indicate a meeting with a source. But Tang didn't have any sources
in Yanji yet. He couldn't. He had just arrived. He hadn't even had
time to look through his desk drawers.

"Can it wait? I don't know, can it? You were in my office, so I
assume you wanted to see me. About what?"

He looked at his watch again. "I just stopped in to say good
morning. Let's have lunch. We can talk then."

"No, I think we can talk now. Your appointment can wait."

"In Tianjin, appointments on the outside were considered high
priority."

I tamped down what first came to my mind to say about how
they did things in Tianjin. That was for another day. I pointed the
conversation where it needed to be. "Where did you put the file
cabinet you took from the file room?"

"I brought it upstairs."

"You what?"

"Look, Major, this is an important appointment. It's left over
from Tianjin. We didn't have time to make the formal handoff, so
I need one final meeting with this source. It's vital."

What a source from Tianjin was doing in Yanji was an interesting question, but I wasn't interested in the answer at the moment. "The file cabinet," I said. "Where is it?"

"I told you, I brought it upstairs. I couldn't see any room down here; I didn't suppose you'd want it left in a hallway. So I carried it upstairs until I could find a better place for it. I'm the deputy; I'm supposed to handle these housekeeping chores without bothering you. Do you have any idea how dusty it is up there?"

My answer was cut short by the duty officer, who was racing down the hall.

"Major! Special message, A-class. There were bells when it came in."

I glared at Tang. "Go back to your office and stay there. If you even stick one of your scuffed brown shoes into the hall before I tell you to come out, you'll be on your way to an assignment in Xinjiang by tonight. You won't like it there."

4

The message was from the MSS office in Harbin. Mike had been overheard a couple of weeks ago discussing a "major shift from noodles to dumplings" with a known Russian criminal boss who visited the city once in a while. Harbin wanted to know if we had anything on either dumplings or noodles that might explain this. The real question, as far as I was concerned, was why weeks-old information on Mike was just getting to me.

Three of the dead diners had been eating noodles; the two prostitutes had been behind a dumpling shop. I ought to send this query to the chief of police, but the Harbin report indicated it was from a very sensitive technical system, meaning the chief couldn't get it. At least it added weight to my conviction that this wasn't terrorism. It was old-fashioned criminals committing old-fashioned crimes, nothing that fell into my area of responsibility.

Unless a case combining noodles, dumplings, and fish added up to more than the sum of its parts. If Mike was suddenly switching from noodles to dumplings, it might explain the dead diners at the noodle shop. You want to scare people away from noodles and get them eating dumplings? You might leave some corpses over a few bowls of pho. Nice theory, but the dead hookers behind the dim sum place didn't fit. And the explosion upstairs in my office was still a problem. That wasn't normal behavior for Mike, and Beijing wouldn't like it when it did an audit and discovered why I had ordered a new window for the building. At least the report from Harbin gave me one new thread to follow. Mike had been there before he came here. The fish lady was from Harbin. OK, I thought to myself, it was a slender thread, a gossamer thread, but as my uncle would point out, it was better than none. Maybe it wasn't noodles. Maybe it was Harbin. That my uncle went often to Harbin skipped through my mind, but I discarded the thought. There was no way he was connected to all of this. No way at all.

5

I had a few leads, but leads are overrated. Most of them turn out to be dead ends. If there was a way to discard one or two before doing a lot of digging to nowhere, it saved time. A good place to start was Dooran Street, where the prostitutes hung out. They were a funny mix. The Russian girls kept to themselves a few blocks away. They were controlled by the Russian mafia, and it was a lot of trouble to talk to them, so we mostly left them alone. Dooran Street was where the Chinese and Koreans worked. Once in a while there were some Mongolians, but they were always restless and moved on after a few months. I hadn't thought too much about them before, but now that I knew Tuya was here, I'd have to keep a closer eye on them.

During their breaks, the girls of Dooran Street sat around the tea shop, the Koreans in the back, the Chinese in the front so they could be seen from the street. A few of them fixed their makeup.

The older ones sat back in the chairs with their eyes closed, a ciga-rette dangling from their lips. Between that and the steam from the teakettles, there was always a pall of smoke hanging over the tables.

The Korean girls stayed together. They drank tea and barely looked at each other. Most of them were from the North, but there were always two or three from the South. The northern girls sus-pected the southerners of working for the Americans. I didn't think so, but it was complicated and led to arguments. I thought they were a sad lot. My uncle did, too. Sometimes he took a couple of them to dinner, and gave them a little money on the side.

The Chinese girls were different. They laughed a lot. They heard plenty from their customers, and they didn't mind passing on what they heard if it meant I wouldn't interfere with their business. I knew they had to be careful, because the mayor controlled where they could walk, how much they could charge, and how much they could keep. Once in a while he selected some of them for "conferences" in a big house up in the mountains where he entertained rich busi-nessmen and party members. There were rumors that a couple of the girls had disappeared around the same time the previous chief of police was murdered, but no one was talking; when Po Dawei, the current chief, took over, he seemed uninterested in pursuing the matter. Mostly the girls just went along with the mayor because they figured they had no choice, but two of them openly resented his heavy hand. They were always careful how they spoke, so I never pressed them. They might be flashy dressers, but they knew how to be discreet when they had to be.

Those two girls were usually free around one in the afternoon. They weren't sources in the formal sense of the word. And I wouldn't call them informants. They never got paid, and I made sure their names never got into the files. As far as anyone watching knew, we just talked and drank tea. If they casually dropped a piece of useful information once in a while, so much the better. Today, neither of them had showed by the time I got there, so I ordered a pot of tea and waited. When a half hour later they still hadn't appeared, I wan-dered over to the elderly man who was the owner.

"Mei-lin sick today?" I asked. Mei-lin had come up to me one afternoon six or seven months ago and asked if I wanted company. I was alone and nothing else was going on, so I told her to sit down if she liked. If she had been sent by someone to strike up a relationship with me, that would be clear soon enough. It turned out her father had been a military attaché in Buenos Aires. When the family came home and settled in Shenyang, she was bored. She was also smart, very smart, and observant. She didn't want a factory job, and for reasons she wouldn't discuss, she drifted into nightclubs. One thing led to another, and now she was in Yanji drinking tea with me. Over the months we met in the tea shop, she never asked me for a thing. It was all one way—she provided useful information, and all she got in return was a pot of tea. Sometimes, there were sweet bean cookies.

"I said, is Mei-lin sick today?"

The old man looked into the distance. "No."

"If she comes in, tell her I owe her a cup of your special red tea."

"I won't have to. She won't be in again."

The girls at the other tables froze. One by one they put out their cigarettes and walked back into the street. First the Chinese girls, then the Koreans. When the place was empty, the old man began to clear the tables. "Maybe you should leave, too, Major."

"Something the matter?"

"Yeah, Mei-lin is dead."

All of a sudden I knew what had happened. "Who was the other girl?" I asked. "Someone local?"

"No." He paused and looked around. "She was from out of town. Rumor is she came from Harbin. But I don't know. I don't know. I don't know anything."

"Too bad," I said. "About Mei-lin, I mean. She was smart."

"Maybe too smart." The old man sat back down on his chair near the cash register. "You want something else? Your other friend, the willowy one that wears silk pants, she left town yesterday without saying good-bye to anyone. So I guess there's no need for you to hang around here anymore. Probably better if you don't."

"We'll see about that, won't we?" I could tell the old man was rattled to his bones. He usually liked to have me wander into his place at odd hours. It kept the extortion gangs away. The regular drunks hanging around would usually crawl out when I walked in. But if it made the old man feel better, there was no harm in my staying away for a day or two. I got up to leave. "By the way, you know anything about the new fish restaurant on Fuzhou Alley? I hear the fish is good."

"I don't eat fish." He looked at me impassively. "See you around, Major."

Back out on the street, I tried to make some sense of what I'd just learned. Mei-lin was as careful as a cat where she stepped. She kept away from anyone who looked like trouble. And I knew she didn't like dim sum, she'd told me so herself. So what was she doing in that alley with a new girl from Harbin? Wrong place, wrong time—maybe. Still, it was worth pulling the Harbin thread some more. I needed to look at the file on that dim sum place. Probably nothing there, but a thread sometimes turns into spun gold, depending on when you see it.

On the way back to the office, I passed the alley where Mei-lin's body had been found. I didn't want to go into the dim sum place yet, but looking around the outside was important. It gave me a feel for the neighborhood. I don't believe in ghosts, but places talk to you sometimes. A couple of police were standing nearby, probably part of the murder investigation. I didn't have much hope they would get very far before the mayor called them off. He had a habit of pushing investigations to look like he was doing something, then pulling them back before they made any progress. Almost everything bad that happened in Yanji led either directly back to him or to someone he was taking money from. He'd threatened me directly over the phone when the restaurant deaths were first discovered, but he'd probably heard things in the next day or two that convinced him another tack was needed. Spotting his car peel away right after the explosion in my office hadn't been a mistake. He meant for me to see him, I was pretty sure of that. I wasn't so sure he was behind the explosion on our second floor, but I wasn't ruling anything out.

After looking it over, as far as I could tell, there was nothing special about the alley behind the dim sum shop. It was an alley, like a lot of others. If there was a difference, it was that the police had been through the scene already and trampled on any evidence there might have been. There were some chalk marks on one of the nearby buildings, and in a trash can behind the dim sum place I spotted a pair of rubber gloves of the sort the coroner used. There were five buildings on either side of the alley, pretty much leaning against each other for comfort in their old age. All of them were firetraps, but I wasn't the fire inspector. A couple of them had windows in the back on the highest floors, which might mean there were rooms rented. Someone might have seen or heard something, but no one was liable to volunteer, and the police were too lazy to go up the stairs to inquire.

All the buildings had back doors at ground level. A few of them also had landings on the second floor, with stairs going down to the alley. The dim sum place was one of those. The ground-level door had an iron grate that looked like it was never used. The door to the neighboring building was wide open. A man stepped out and pulled a pack of cigarettes from his pocket.

"You have a light?" I walked over to him. I don't smoke much, but sometimes a match is a good way to begin a conversation. I took a cigarette from a silver case I carry around. It was about the only thing of value my wife left behind when she and her boyfriend slipped out of town. She would have taken the house, but it wouldn't fit in her suitcase.

The man lit his own cigarette, then blew out the match and dropped it on the ground. "Sorry," he said. "Too much wind back here. Maybe you ought to buy yourself a silver lighter." He was slightly shorter than I was, and looked like he could move quickly if he wanted to.

"Maybe you could learn to be polite when someone asks a civilized question. You're not from around here, or you'd know better.

Let me guess. You're from Xinjiang and you're thinking of moving drugs across the river. Looking at your shoes and your haircut, I'd say you're from Kashgar. But you're out of your element up here. It's not as easy as you thought, so you're wondering what to do next. The people across the river didn't come through with the advance, and you're short on cash."

The man's jaw dropped open. "All that from my shoes?"

"No, I got your photo when you pulled into town, and your file followed the next day. You're sloppy, you're stupid, and you should have given me a light. I might have let you go home. Now I'm going to take you back to the office and have someone beat the crap out of you."

"What if I have some information?"

"What do I care? Your type always has information, all worthless."

"This is valuable."

"I'll decide that."

"I'm a Uighur."

"I already figured that."

"Yeah, but I know a Uighur up here who owns a restaurant. He walks with a limp. He's part of my network. Actually, he's a distant relative. I was supposed to meet up with him, but he's disappeared."

"That so?"

"Yeah, he used to run a noodle restaurant, but he didn't know anything about noodles. It was just a front."

"For what?"

"Stuff."

"So, why am I interested?"

"Maybe I could get ahold of him for you."

"Why do I want to get hold of him? I don't eat noodles."

"Not noodles, dumplings. He knows about something special due to come through here. I don't know exactly what it is."

"You said dumplings."

"A machine or something. He wanted me up here to help him arrange things. He said it was complicated and there was a big payoff if I did it right. He wouldn't go into detail over the phone."

"I guess he wouldn't. So you jumped on a plane and got up here, figuring you'd help out your relative. That is, you jumped on the plane after you set up a deal for drugs across the river. Who's your contact on this side?"

He shrugged. "I never met her."

"Her?"

"Maybe him, I don't know."

"Listen." I moved in closer so there wasn't much space between us. "I think there is a difference between hers and hims. I'll bet you know what I mean. And I don't want a run-around. Who's your contact?" I pushed him against the wall with one hand and grabbed him around the throat with the other. "Don't think I can't break your neck if that's what I decide to do. One Uighur more or less wouldn't even register in this town."

He gave way as I pushed him, and that made my nervous system scream at me that something bad was about to happen. I moved right in the same instant his right hand came up holding a knife with a killer blade. He would have gutted me like a sheep if he'd moved a faction of a second faster. Instead, he sliced the sleeve of my shirt. I slammed him against the wall so hard he dropped the knife and slumped to the ground. That's when I stepped on his hand.

"Hey!"

That's the first reaction they all have when I step on their hand.

"Hey, yourself." I stepped down harder. "This is one of my favorite shirts."

"Wait, wait!" Fear was in his eyes, so was pain, but most of all, recognition.

"You're the guy who ruined someone's hand in Mongolia; we heard about you."

"Was I? Oh, yeah. I meant to break his arm in four places, but I crushed his hand instead. You want the same?"

"No!"

I let up for a moment, then stepped down hard again. "Which will it be? You lose your knife hand forever, or you tell me something useful."

"It's a her. We never dealt directly. She's not from around here. Really, I don't know anything else."

"You have a phone number?"

"Phone?"

I put my heel on his wrist. "Not only do you lose your fingers, but your worthless hand is going to hang from the end of your arm until the day you die because your wrist will be pulverized. Don't repeat the question. The fucking number or your wrist, you choose."

"It's on my phone. I can't remember numbers so good."

I took my foot off his wrist and kicked his knife across the alley. "Get up. Get your phone out of your pocket, slowly, with the hand that still works. If you pull another knife on me, I'll kill you."

He stood up slowly, nursing his hand. "I think you broke it."

"I sincerely hope so. Give me the phone."

He retrieved it with difficulty from his pocket. "Can I go see a doctor?"

"Are you kidding me? You're coming back to the office to answer more questions."

6

When I got back to the office, the duty officer looked harried. "Glad you're here, Major."

"Now what?"

"Phone call from your uncle. I just hung up. He makes me nervous, I hope you don't mind my saying. Something about the way his mind hops around."

My uncle had told the duty officer it was imperative to speak to me. On hearing I was not available, he left a message that I should come home as soon as possible. It was urgent.

Normally I would have given myself time to look through the files for what I needed, and only then would have called home. What my uncle considered urgent never fit my definition. But there had

been enough odd events over the past few days that I was jumpy. Besides, ever since he had returned from one of his frequent trips to Harbin last week, he had been moody, even more than normal.

"On my way," I said to the duty officer. "If my uncle calls back, tell him I'll be home soon."

"What shall I do with this guy?" He pointed to the prisoner, who was leaning against the wall and moaning softly. "What happened to his hand?"

"He caught it in a door. Put him in a holding room. Better yet, call Jiao in and tell him to work this guy over." Jiao was our best interrogator. Every special office in the country wanted to grab him, but I wasn't giving him up. "Tell him we need to find out where that noodle shop owner is, the Uighur with the limp. If this guy complains, tell Jiao to hit his other hand with a hammer so he won't favor one of them. I'll be back. And do something with this phone." I tossed it to the duty officer. "Have someone see what it tells us about this guy."

7

Uncle O was waiting in the small room we use as an office for the occasional client that might come around in need of his once-in-a-while detective agency. He sat behind the desk, a bulky thing with six drawers and a place for pens along the side.

"Uncle." I looked at him carefully. "Is something wrong?"

He turned away. "No, nothing. I shouldn't have called. You're busy."

Normally I would have been suspicious at this expression of deference to my work schedule. But his voice was not right, the set of his shoulders was wrong, and the spirit, that annoying spirit, was nowhere in evidence. This made me even more uneasy than I already was. For all the fights we had, for all he was irritating, he was at least a reliable force of energy in the universe. Now it looked drained away. He seemed broken. Something strange hung in the air.

I wasn't sure how to deal with this. "Maybe a cup of tea?" I offered. "I'll go make some."

He was silent, seeming to shrink away by degrees even as he sat in front of me.

"Uncle," I said, "this is awkward. I mean, we don't say much to each other most of the time. But this . . . this is not right."

"Oh." He turned back to me finally. "Yes, it's right."

I was startled to see his eyes were red.

"Nephew, look at me." His eyes searched my face. "What am I?"

"You're . . ."

He waved his hand. "No, don't bother. You have no idea. You don't know me. Even I don't know me. At least, I didn't. But something has happened."

There was nothing for me to say; he wanted me only to listen. For once, I let him go on.

"This will sound very strange. If you want to laugh, go ahead." He gave me a defiant look that almost reassured me, but it faded quickly, and he seemed even smaller than before. "I'm sorry," he said with a finality that made me shudder.

"About what?" I said it softly, for fear anything louder would shatter him before my eyes. I'd never felt so unsure what he was up to. Sometimes he made me angry, most of the time he made me frustrated, but this was something completely different.

"All at once, out of nowhere, last night I heard voices of despair and hurt, cries of misery and pain and loneliness. I heard all of them, from everywhere, from all time. How could I have missed them before?"

"Uncle . . ."

He held up his hand again. "No, say nothing. Give me a minute to get this out. Maybe if I hear the words in my own voice, it will make some sense."

His eyes pleaded with me. I was suddenly convinced he was dying right here, in front of my eyes.

"I've been alone," he said. "Ever since my parents were killed in the war, I've been alone. My grandfather filled a space, he held me upright, he set me into the world. But he was alone, too, and that's what he taught me. How to be alone. How to keep myself apart, because that was how I could preserve some spark in this sea of insanity. My brother . . . your father . . . if only . . ."

I searched for something to say, some reassurance, but there was nothing.

"I'm not talking about falling and scraping a knee. I'm talking about what is all around, what has always been around us." He stood up and moved to the window. "You'll find it strange coming from me, but there are great tides of horror, of deepest, deepest horror, that toss us about, nephew." He moved aside the curtains and looked outside. "And we don't pay attention. Echoes of voices of despair from centuries ago, from eons ago. I heard them all, every single one of them. They rang in my ears, softly at first, and then louder and louder. Moaning, screaming, crying, the last breaths of the wounded, the tortured, the lost. How could I have missed them until now? I have been a fool. All these years, wasted, gone, torn away, and I heard none of it?" His eyes were growing dull, the lids half closed. "And now what can I do?"

"Look, uncle, maybe you're a little depressed. It happens when you get old."

"Don't, don't even think you can make a happy face and I'll snap out of this. This is not depression, nephew. This is not some black despair inside of me. Listen! Listen! I'm sane, I'm completely in control, I'm not drowning, I'm not going to kill myself. I don't have to, I'm already dead."

"You heard voices?"

He snorted. "No, not voices. There aren't voices speaking to me. I don't hear someone telling me to blow up a building or knock off a government official."

"But you said . . ."

"Will you listen to me for once! Try and listen, forget you're a fucking interrogator."

"All right." I had a sense he was coming out of it.

"Have you ever seen the sun shine?"

"Of course."

"Have you ever laughed?"

"Yes."

"Been with a woman."

"Uncle . . ."

"Answer me."

"Well, of course . . ."

"That Mongolian woman, you love her?"

My radars started turning. What did he know? Why would he bring up Tuya all of a sudden? "I thought we were talking about . . . well, what about you? Have you?"

"Have I what?"

"Ah, been with a woman?"

He almost smiled. I clutched at that for reassurance, but it slipped from my grasp.

"You want to know, nephew? You want to talk about that?"

I felt as if I were sliding into a pit. "Well . . ."

"Good, I didn't think you did. Neither do I."

A deep, almost terminal sigh came from somewhere. He put his hand to his eyes. I had the feeling I'd lost him again.

"Never mind," he said. "Let's just leave this where it is. I realized something that I never knew before. A portal opened. I may pack up and leave later today. I can't stay here."

My heart froze. "Where will you go?"

He smiled, and suddenly a shaft of sunlight came through the window behind him.

"Dramatic." He pulled the curtain shut. "Remarkably dramatic."

"Really, uncle, where will you go?"

He turned back to me with a look of resignation on his face. "I don't really know. Someplace warm and sunny."

"Hainan Island?"

He wrinkled his nose. "Portugal."

PART II

PART II

Chapter One

That Luis should be in northeast China to visit a relative of his who ran a hardware store in Harbin made no sense, but accepting his explanation was the easiest thing to do. Luis was an old friend, a half-Chinese, half-Macanese police inspector in Macau who had helped me years ago and to whom I always thought I owed a debt of gratitude.

"You owe me, you know, Inspector."

"I know, Luis. It often occurred to me to inquire how you were, but then things went a little haywire at home and I had to join my nephew up on the border in this, the Great Center of the Universe, the Celestial Kingdom, the Land of Chou, Country of the Great Wall and Little Else. It is very confining. The youngster wants to know where I am every minute, and the only place I can go by myself is here in Harbin, supposedly to buy lumber for bookcases."

"What a coincidence," Luis said. He was even thinner than when I first met him years ago on a tricky investigation that involved body parts and a red Louis Vuitton suitcase. Luis was stooped now, but he retained a quiet nobility in the way he walked. As he talked, his head moved, almost as subtle counterpoint to his voice. You might think you didn't notice it at first, but gradually you realized that talking to Luis was like talking to twins, one reinforcing the other. "I mean, a real coincidence, that you should come to Harbin for lumber, and at the same time I should come here to visit a relative who owns a hardware store. Remarkable."

He smiled heartily, which did not suit him in the least and was probably why he rarely did it. He was only doing it now, I was sure, because that was how they had rehearsed it. It was not a coincidence that he was standing outside the lumberyard as I emerged, couldn't be by any stretch of the imagination, and there was no chance that Luis thought I would buy the story. Sooner or later I'd find out what this was about. In the meantime, there was no reason not to play along. It was the least I could do for him. Besides, it might turn out to be more interesting than sitting in the workshop in my nephew's house thinking up new ways to build bookcases, an activity that helped preserve my sanity and—not to be overlooked as a benefit—also irritated my nephew. He was, as far as I knew, my only living relative, and we got on each other's nerves.

"Yes, come to think of it," I said, "I could use a new chisel, Luis. Shall we go visit your relative's store?" I already knew the answer.

Luis smiled again, though it was more for himself than something for my benefit. He recited his lines with wry humor that made clear he hadn't written them and thought the whole thing was foolish. "My uncle's store burned down in 1937, Inspector. Imagine my surprise on learning that earlier today. It was a shock. I had been looking forward to seeing him."

"Imagine!" I said. "What a shock! Should we have tea and talk about old times?"

Luis led the way to a tea shop on a quiet street not far from the lumberyard. There were two old ladies seated at a table in the rear. Neither looked up when we entered. If they weren't working for Luis, I would have been surprised.

"Nice place," I said, looking around. "You've been here before?"

Luis stared at me. "Inspector, you are too suspicious for your own good. This is not far from my hotel. I found it yesterday while I was wandering around looking for my uncle's store."

"The one that burned down in 1937?"

"Is there another one?" Luis laughed. "My mother's family is from here, I give you my word. They went south one short step ahead of the Japanese. My uncle stayed, figuring he could make money selling hardware to the Imperial Army."

"I hope he at least collected the insurance."

Luis looked thoughtful. "No one suggested that might be a question."

2

Once the tea arrived, brought by a shuffling old man who served us without saying a word, Luis took a notebook from his jacket. "As long as we're here"—he cleared his throat—"maybe you can help me."

I sipped some tea and looked at the two ladies. They were hunched over their table and ostentatiously comparing manicures. Presumably, they already had the microphones calibrated so didn't have much else to do for the moment. "You know me, Luis, if there is some way I can be helpful, all you need do is ask. And if you need me to repeat anything"—I nodded and smiled at the old ladies—"don't hesitate to tell me."

"How would you like to come to Portugal?" Luis sat back in his chair and looked around the tearoom. "You must be tired of this by now, ready for a change of scenery, am I right? How long have you been stuck here?"

"In China? A couple of years, I suppose, three maybe. Too long, whatever it is. I've lost all sense of time. My nephew and I galloped off to Mongolia not long ago. Extremely odd place. Very few trees where we were. It gave me the shakes."

"Well, there are plenty of trees in Portugal. You like seafood, yes?"

"Up to a point. We get a lot of river fish where my nephew lives."

"Yanji is not famous for its cuisine."

"Did I mention Yanji?"

"Inspector, this is why I am glad we are meeting again. There is no one else with whom I can have quite so fine a chase through the preparatory brambles."

"Luis, I salute you. Did you write this script yourself, or are you merely interpreting it, knocking off the rough spots along the way?"

Luis looked at the old ladies. One of them shook her head slightly. "Excuse me, Inspector." He got up and walked to the rear table, and the three of them exchanged Portuguese insults. I don't know Portuguese, but I know insults when I hear them. Finally, the two women walked out, one of them trailing a wire that must have been uncomfortable if the rest of it was coiled where I assumed it was.

"Nice ladies," I said. "Too bad they had to leave so soon."

Luis put both hands on the table, a sure sign that he was nervous but getting to the point. "Inspector, this is something big. I don't know the details, but someone I trust and who holds considerable power over my employment convinced me that it was big and that we needed help. We needed the best, I was told. So I thought of you."

"Chinese flattery or Portuguese? Very musical, but to no avail; I'm not working anymore, Luis. Do you think I'd be in Harbin if I had something better to do? I make bookcases and write a little poetry when the spirit moves me. Otherwise I'm done, played out, washed up, taking up space. Besides, I can't very well do anything sitting in Yanji." I smiled at Luis to grant him the point. He nodded without comment. "My nephew watches me all the time, and when he isn't, the local police follow me around like dogs trotting after a bag of pig's entrails."

"You won't be in Yanji, don't you see? You won't be in China at all. Think of it, Inspector, someplace new, fresh vistas, no one to tell you what to do or how to do it. Just like things used to be, you'd be your own man."

"More flattery, Luis, or have you lost your mind? When was I ever my own man?"

"Come on, Inspector, I watched you in Macau, remember? You were practically a free agent. Maybe back in Pyongyang you had strings—"

"Ha!"

"OK, ropes. But when you got outside, you operated like a free spirit. Don't try to tell me otherwise."

"So what exactly do you need this free spirit to do for you?"

"I told you, I don't know exactly. All I know is that you and I are to meet somewhere."

Now it was my turn to stare at Luis. "And where is somewhere?" I just asked out of habit. I already knew because he'd already given it away, just like he was supposed to do.

At last Luis gave me a real smile as he slid an envelope across the table. "I'll be there to meet you. Pack light, we'll have to move fast."

Chapter Two

I'll leave you here, Inspector." Luis seemed ill at ease.

"Why? Something the matter? I mean, other than the fact this isn't Portugal. That's where I thought you told me we were going. Instead, we bounce through the airport in Lisbon, board another plane, and sit in Spain. Naturally, I'm curious. Actually, more than curious."

"You don't like it?" Luis was glancing around as if he expected bad news.

"Oh, no. It's fine. Where are we?"

"Barcelona."

"Ah, yes. Barcelona is a pleasant city, isn't that what people say? Nice weather. Plenty of things to see."

"Speaking of things to see, there's one of them. Don't make it obvious. Just cast a casual eye off to your right. See that van across the street?"

"Green one? With the flowers painted on the side?"

"You're being watched."

"Me? I'm being watched? How do they even know who I am?"

"Spanish security is very efficient, Inspector. Very thorough. And very tough. They are still using training manuals from the Inquisition." He stopped. "Pardon me." He bowed slightly. "A reference without meaning perhaps. The Inquisition I speak of was an unpleasant episode six hundred years ago."

"So I've heard. Word gets around, Luis." I cast another casual eye at the van. "Well, we're in Spain, so what's the problem? I thought they all napped for an hour or two after lunch. They sleep, we stroll away."

"That's what they'd like you to believe."

"You're skeptical?"

"Inspector, yes, this is Spain. The Catalans would like you to think it isn't, but it is. We've endured living next to the Spanish for a long time. If a Spaniard tells us it's sunny outside, we dress for a storm."

"And even so, you're going to leave me alone here? Luis, I thought we were friends."

"You are my dearest friend, Inspector." His brows knitted. "Not counting Lulu, of course."

"Without saying."

"I'm leaving you because what interests the green van most is that a half-Portuguese policeman from Macau—"

"They know that?"

"I told you, they are efficient. And they are curious why one such as I is walking with someone . . ."

". . . such as I. And what would that be? I'm still using the Costa Rican passport I had in Macau."

"Bad idea, I'm afraid. They will already have checked it."

"But I didn't have to show it to anyone at the airport when we landed here."

"No, you showed it at the Lisbon airport when you arrived in Europe."

"You mean there are Spanish agents working in the Portuguese immigration office?"

"I told you, Inspector, their training manuals go back to the Inquisition. They could infiltrate a plate of *bacalhau grelhado*."

"Pardon?"

"Cod, grilled with olive oil and lemon. Tiny potatoes on the side. A plate of lightly fried dumplings stuffed with fragrant morsels of pork. A glass of wine. Ahhh." He clicked his tongue against his teeth. "Would you like to try it?" He looked at his watch. "Maybe a late lunch?"

"Here, in Barcelona?"

"True, it would be a pale imitation of what you could get in Sesimbra, but worth a few euros."

"Luis, am I mistaken or is someone getting out of that van with a basket of flowers?"

"Bastards!" Luis said under his breath. "Let's move into the shade, Inspector, behind those trees. I'll sketch out for you where you should come in contact with someone who can help guide you through this operation. See? They're trying to work their way toward us." He took a handkerchief from his coat pocket and patted his neck. "They always do this to me, make me sweat. Life is much simpler in Macau. Lulu, lunch, and love." He shook his head and replaced the handkerchief. "We never should have let that bastard Rodrigo Borgia get away with his holy line."

"He drew a line?"

"A Spaniard, wormed his way into the papacy. Gave everything to Spain. Left us with Brasil."

"I thought you liked Brasil."

"I like women from Brasil, Inspector. But that's different from geography. No need to rake over papal politics right now, even those only five hundred years old. Perhaps later." He turned abruptly, very unlike Luis.

Across a narrow single lane of traffic was a long line of plane trees overarching a broad, straight walk. On either side were benches, and down the center was a watercourse broken every twenty meters or so with a small waterfall. The shade was cool, but more than that, the sound of the water splashing and gurgling as it made its way to some outlet, probably the Mediterranean about half a kilometer distant, made the whole place seem to be dozing. Luis picked out a bench and sat down.

"This is good, Inspector. It reminds me of Lisboa." He had recovered his composure.

"It reminds me of Pyongyang," I said.

Luis looked startled, and then amused. "Home is where the heart is, eh, Inspector?" An air of nonchalance passed over his features. "Tell me, Inspector, out of curiosity, how did you convince your nephew you needed to get away on such short notice?"

This was not an idle question. It was not simply "out of curiosity." It was something he needed to know.

"Someone worried about what I said, is that it, Luis? Does someone think I might have said too much, compromised your operation? Maybe that's how the Spaniards were tipped off?" I paused. "Don't worry, my friend. I made something up. It worked. My nephew doesn't suspect anything except that I'm old and maybe getting a little crazy. Just take my word."

Luis took out his handkerchief again. "Humid," he said.

"This operation of yours, Luis, give me the outlines. So far I know nothing." I nodded toward the green van. "Or are you worried about someone overhearing? What if they have long mikes or something? They might learn something about dumplings, and then where would we be?"

Luis paused a fraction of a second before whispering harshly in my ear. "Dumplings? Why? Who said anything about dumplings, Inspector?"

"You did, fragrant morsels of pork, you said."

Luis instantly relaxed. "So I did. No need to worry. The motorbikes come up the street in packs every time the traffic light changes. I only have to pace what I'm telling you to match the lights. We can fill in the rest of the time with a fairy tale. If they hear anything, it will annoy them, or amuse them, or baffle them. One never knows with Spaniards. If they were Catalans, I would be sure. They would listen to us for five minutes, then go out for lunch and a bottle of wine. These, however, are tougher boys and girls."

"Girls?"

"Oh my, yes, Inspector. Do you think the long-legged beauties walking past us in the airport in Madrid were sweet pastries, like something you pick out at Pastéis de Belém?" He clicked his tongue. "You'll make that mistake once, then never again, I guarantee."

"Not like Lulu?" Lulu was the woman of Luis's dreams. She was at least twice his size, and Luis, as far as I could tell when I saw them together, loved every millimeter. She also ran a small restaurant in Macau, where Luis got free lunches.

Luis looked away. I heard a small sigh in between the roars of motorbikes. "To work, Inspector, to work," he said finally.

"I'm listening."

"You may remember," Luis began, "the operation several years ago in Macau."

"May remember? Luis, something like that is never forgotten."

"This is different, different but similar in that it is also one of a kind. Easier, simpler in some ways, but equally foolproof."

"A great relief, though it wouldn't take much to make this one easier. That Macau operation was the most complicated . . ." I thought about it. "One of the most complicated operations I've ever seen."

"You'll have to go back to Lisboa immediately."

"Where? Why are we sitting here if the action is in Portugal? We could have stayed there. Saved a trip, and avoided the bad cheese sandwich on the plane."

"No, that wasn't possible. We had some things to clean up, there and here. I told you, when you landed in Lisboa someone—we know who—flagged your passport and passed it on to the Spaniards."

"Yes, so, why travel to Spain, then?"

"Trolling, Inspector."

I could feel my blood rising. "You mean I'm bait?"

"Not quite bait. Chum, perhaps. And over there in that van are the sharks. This is good."

"Good for whom?"

"Never mind." He patted my knee. "Barcelona is perfect for what we need, believe me. The local service hates Madrid almost as much as we do. They're watching the green truck, too. Don't look around, but they're here. We use them, they use us, and everybody's happy. In this case, they owe us a favor. They already know what they need to do. After lunch, God willing, it will be done."

2

Luis put down his fork and patted his lips with his napkin. "You enjoyed the meal, Inspector?"

"Not much bad you can do with seafood."

He looked disappointed. "That's all you can say? When have you had octopus this good? Outside of Portugal, tell me where you've had better, I'll go there right away."

"Business, Luis. Leave the octopus to one side for the moment. You said after lunch that God willing, it would be done. Well, was God willing? Was it done? And what, if you don't mind my asking, does it have to do with me? You never really had a relative in Harbin, did you?"

Luis folded the napkin and put it carefully on the table. "More wine?"

"No wine, Luis. No fruit. No dessert. I want to know what the operation is, because this is going to be a crazy operation. I could smell it a kilometer away, as soon as you gave me that phony story about your uncle in Harbin. That green truck was waiting for us, why? I don't want to sit here, pleasant as it is, by this window and watch the passing scene. I'm warning you, as an old friend, if you don't get to business in the next five seconds, I'll say *adeus* right now and go back to the airport. And if the Spanish service wants to drag me out of the ticket line and into a fifteenth-century dungeon, they can go ahead. Their training may go back five hundred years; mine goes back a couple of thousand."

"All right, Inspector." Luis looked around for the waiter. "Let's at least have a glass of port. Settles the stomach."

"Luis . . ." I moved my chair back from the table.

"Yes, yes, Inspector. I'm getting to the point." He had long, slender fingers, and they were drumming on the table. It wasn't a nervous gesture. He was annoyed, but I sensed he was also stalling for time. He wasn't focused on me. Something else wasn't where he needed it to be.

The waiter appeared and handed him a piece of paper. "Ah," Luis said, "the bill, the tally, the reckoning for this wonderful lunch." He looked relieved.

"Luis, there are no numbers on that piece of paper. Do the Catalans write out a bill in longhand?"

Luis looked at the paper once more, then tore it into small pieces, took out a match, and burned them in an ashtray before lighting up a cigarette. "Do you mind if I smoke?"

"If it helps. I have to warn you, Luis, I've gone along with this up to now because I needed to get away from China. And I'll admit it, finding out why you were sent to recruit me became something of an obsession. But right here, right now is as far as I go if you don't tell me what this about. Burning your instructions does not give me confidence."

Luis smiled to himself, a softening around the lips and around his Macanese eyes. "Now it is you who flatter me, Inspector. Do you think I know what this is about? I know this much"—he held up his little finger—"and I don't care to know any more than that. When we are done here, I'm on my way back home. Nothing else that happens is my business, and that's how I prefer to keep it."

"You go home, and I go where?"

"Listen closely, Inspector, I'm only going to say this once. There is a castle in Lisboa, high on a hill, a rather steep hill."

"What is it with you Portuguese? There was a fort in Macau, as I recall, on the top of a steep hill where you ran the last operation. I nearly killed myself getting there."

"But you didn't, that's the point. And this will be easier because you don't have to go all the way up to the castle. It's not so secure."

"Outside the gates is better this time?"

"For what you need, yes."

"No cannons? In Macau there were cannons. I had to count them. It was a painful experience, I'm telling you now, Luis. Let me hear that there are no cannons this time."

"No cannons, just benches, and easy enough to count. There are only four of them. Besides, it is a very pleasant place, tranquil, no

Chinese ladies practicing with swords. You take the tram most of the way up the hill, get off at the spot where there is a view of the river. You can linger if you like, it would be strange if you didn't. That's what tourists do. Take some pictures, listen to the guitarist who sits on the ground, leaning against the fence. Tap your feet and move your hips, get in the spirit of the place."

"I assume the guitarist works for you."

Luis took a long draw on his cigarette and shrugged.

"Fine," I said. "I linger and wiggle. But no dancing, I can't dance. Then what?"

"Then you walk up the hill."

"I knew it!"

"As I said, a little steep, but nothing a man in your shape can't handle."

"That's it?"

"Not quite. You'll get more instructions at your hotel."

"From whom?"

"It would be appealing to tell you that I'm not at liberty to say, but I can't."

"Why not?"

"I'm not at liberty to say because I don't know. This isn't how we do things in Macau, but we're here, not there, and I can only do as I'm told. I was told to tell you that you would get a message at your hotel, it would be plain to you when you got it, and you would know what to do."

"Am I allowed one clue?"

Luis shrugged. "Socks, I think," he said, and stood up..He took a final puff on his cigarette. "Time to go, Inspector. We'll stroll."

3

After landing at the airport in Lisbon, I caught a cab to my hotel, was shown my room, and then went out for a walk. If someone was going to be following me here, I wanted to get a sense of how good they were. Perhaps we could stop to have coffee once we both tired of the game.

I walked aimlessly for about twenty minutes, then turned a corner and found a tram that was about to leave on its way up a very steep hill. The city, apparently, was full of them. I jumped on. No one pushed in behind me, which meant either no one was following or they had let themselves lag too far behind. At the first stop, short of the summit, I got off and walked briskly down a narrow side street, lined on both sides by old buildings, many of them painted in bright colors. I ducked into one and waited. No one came poking along. Out on the street again, I set my sights on a blue building and slipped through the door. The proprietor, an Iranian judging from his demeanor, looked up from his newspaper. It was a leather store. He watched me closely. A woman, probably his wife, walked over.

"Nice bag." She pointed to one on the shelf in front of me. I changed my mind. They were not Iranian. Syrian maybe. "Bring it home to your family." She started to speak in Chinese, but when I didn't respond switched to English. "We get a lot of Chinese tourists," she said. "You're what? Japanese?"

I shook my head. "No family. Thanks just the same." I watched the window. No one walked by. I didn't think I'd been tailed, but there was no sense in assuming anything. If they were there, they could be waiting up the hill.

The man pretended to be gazing into space. I knew he was paying attention.

"You have a back door?" I asked.

He closed his eyes and nodded slightly.

"Is it unlocked?"

He nodded again.

"Anyone ever use it?"

He shrugged, his eyes still closed.

"Thanks," I said. "Nice bags." The wife picked up the one on the shelf and murmured something to the man. He shrugged again and went back to reading his paper.

"Well." The wife bowed slightly. "Come back when you get a family. Sayonara."

From the back door I went down a flight of steps to another street, even narrower than the first. I waited to see if anyone came out the back door after me. Nothing moved.

When I got to the bottom of the hill, I was in one of the city's main squares. The sun was setting, and a cool breeze was blowing in from the Tagus River. I found a café and sat at a table next to two young women. They looked to be tourists, well-to-do students perhaps.

One of them leaned over to me. "Do you know your way around?"

"Not as much as I should." I smiled at them. She spoke in English, an Australian from the sound of it.

"I mean, do you know where the castle is?" She held up a map and then turned it upside down. "I don't know how to read this. We're hoping to go to the castle tomorrow afternoon. Have you been there?"

"Not exactly." No one else came into the café, and from where I sat looking out the front window, no one seemed to be loitering outside. "The castle was described to me by an elderly aristocrat who claimed to be a descendant of someone who once owned property on the site. He intends to go to court, reclaim the land, and build a condominium up there with an exercise room on the roof." I smiled again.

"Oh my God!" The first one turned to her companion. "We have to get up there tomorrow morning." She turned back to me. "Thanks. Maybe we'll see you there."

"I thought you needed directions." I pointed at her map. "Never mind that. It's easy, you can't miss it. Get on the tram, I think it's the number 8 just in front of that textile store across the square." I had no idea what number tram went where, but neither of them did either. "It takes you up to the castle, or very near. Once you get off, you have to climb a hill but don't worry. There are benches along the way."

The next morning, after a roll and coffee and a quick look at a map, I was on my way to the castle. I had given the Australian girls the wrong tram number, which was good because I didn't want anyone who recognized me showing up in the middle of Luis's operation. These young ladies didn't know me, but tourists had a habit of assuming that if they've talked with you even for a moment, you're an oasis in the middle of a desert and they need to stop to chatter.

There was no guitarist at the overlook, and a fogbank had settled over the river, so no one was standing around taking in the view. A young couple was in an embrace in one of the corners and paid no attention to me.

4

When I was most of the way up the hill, I came upon the benches, four of them, about two meters apart. They were placed against what looked to be the outer wall of the castle, just as Luis had described. Two of the benches were occupied, each by an elderly man in a tracksuit. Both appeared to be slightly out of breath. Then there was an empty bench, and next to it was another, with a middle-aged man sitting close to the edge. He was not dressed in any way that would call attention to his presence, nor did his face have anything about it that would stick in the memory. It was almost as if he weren't there. At his side was a magazine; on top of that sat a bottle of water, Evian, with a yellow cap. The man glanced at me and then looked away. After a moment, he looked back in my direction. He watched me patiently, without expression. Finally, he picked up the water bottle. "You look thirsty, my friend."

"We're due for rain," I replied, using the phrase Luis had dictated, and sat down beside him. It made no sense for me to sit here rather than on the empty bench. Anyone watching—and surely someone was, even from the second story of the old house across the quiet, narrow lane—would wonder why I should sit next to a stranger when there was an empty bench available. If he had been a pretty girl, it might have been different, but he wasn't.

The man waved the water bottle at the empty bench next to us. "You're right. It's just been painted and it's still wet. See the sign?"

When I looked closer I noticed there was a small piece of cardboard taped onto the seat. The hand-lettered sign said PINTURA FRESCA.

"That looks like Spanish," I said.

The man grinned. "Exactly who we don't want sitting there."

"OK," I said. Whoever they were, this group of bench sitters seemed to know what they were doing, up to this point anyway. I figured the old men on the other two benches were not there by accident. "I'm listening."

The man sighed and picked up the magazine. "You're late, so we'll skip the preliminaries. This is what you need to know. Our information is that a restaurant supply business in Yanji is attempting to buy a machine."

"You must be joking." I stood up and turned to go back down the hill. I didn't really want to see the castle.

"You're not interested? You want your nephew to find more dead bodies, perhaps?"

This caught my attention, as he knew it would. I sat down again. "What do you know about what goes on in Yanji? And what do you care?"

"More than you might imagine, Senhor Inspector. What if I told you that the supplier of dim sum, the one your nephew has been trying to find, is up to his neck in other things?"

"Like what?" I hadn't gone into any of this with Luis, so I was momentarily at a disadvantage. Not knowing where they got their information meant I didn't know how much they were bluffing. "Poisoned dim sum?"

"Close." He turned the pages of the magazine slowly.

I stood up again and counted benches. This one was the first in line starting from the bottom, so there was no mistake. Luis had been very specific on the operational details, though he had left out the empty bench. He'd given me the code phrase and told me about the bottle. Evian, he said, didn't have yellow caps. The one thing he hadn't done was to prepare me for the substance of the conversation. As he'd said, he didn't know himself. And by now, he was on a plane back to Macau for long, languid weeks of lunch with Lulu.

"The rain in Spain?" I said softly and examined the old stone wall behind the bench.

"In Granada a week ago." The man sounded annoyed to be forced to reply to the second of the two identification phrases Luis had given me after we'd already blasted past the first.

I sat down again. "And I suppose the real problem is counterfeit red bean buns? Packaged as Japanese but actually sent to, where . . . let me think. Singapore!"

"This is not a joke, Inspector. Someone in Tokyo has supposedly ordered five dumpling machines from a Spanish confectionary machine-parts supplier. Or that's what the invoices say. We know there's only one, and it's actually going to Yanji, or at least that's the transshipment point. It's probably being shipped in sections."

"What a breakthrough! Dumpling diversion on a grand scale! Or don't you think this is a dumpling machine? What's the matter, you don't trust invoices?"

"No, as a matter of fact, we don't."

"We?"

"The people who are paid to worry about such things. I personally am only enjoying the morning." He smiled and looked up at the second floor of the building opposite us. The exterior plaster was cracked and crumbling, exposing the old brick underneath. Vines had grown up almost to the roof on one side. The pale green curtains in one of the windows moved slightly.

"And you want me to do what about these dumplings, exactly?" I was stalling, and none too cleverly. "Anyone bothered to clear it with my Ministry, by the way?"

"You're here, aren't you? Do you think Luis appeared on your doorstep with plane tickets to Lisboa by accident? Plane tickets which, incidentally, you accepted. It's a little late to play games with us. Anyway, you don't have a Ministry anymore to hide behind, or have you forgotten? As a matter of fact, your Ministry of People's Security would like to get its hands on you, or hadn't you heard?"

The retreat behind the barricade of "I can't do anything until my Ministry says so" had been automatic and might even have worked with someone who knew less about me. This man had tossed it aside, like an angry bear flinging a rabbit over its head. Sometimes the angry bear act is just that, an act. But sometimes it reflects a sense of authority. I adjusted my initial impression. The man might be more central to this operation than he let on. He was not just a bit player delivering a message. Luis's role in all of this was still a mystery I wanted solved, but couldn't solve at the moment.

What remained was the obvious question, so obvious there was no need asking—why would anyone go to such elaborate lengths to recruit me over concerns about dumpling machines? No one was going to tell me at this point, certainly not sitting on a bench near the castle gate, but it wasn't a question that could lie around for very long. A few seconds later, I came up with one more question that I needed answered, maybe even more urgently than the first: What did this all have to do with the restaurant deaths in Yanji?

"Dumpling machines," I said. "Maybe that's not it at all. Maybe the real concern is that dumplings from Japan are radioactive. Their vegetables are, their fish are, why not their dumplings?"

"Let's not sit here all morning, Inspector."

"You realize I could tell you that I don't want to play. What would you say to that?"

He shrugged. "You know what they say, you can't go home again." He paused. "You really don't have a choice. You shouldn't have gotten on the airplane if that's the case. You shouldn't have sat down on this bench if you didn't want to play. It would have been easy for you to walk right past me. No one would have stopped you. You could have turned around and gone back to your hotel, packed your bags, and left for the airport. The clerk would have handed you the return ticket. In fact, this morning while eating your roll you could have decided not to come up here at all. But you did.

You did everything without being under any duress. It was all your own doing. Now you're in, one way or another. No exit."

"You are not Portuguese." It dawned on me why this man had registered in such a strange way on my mental map. He was operating in foreign territory. His gestures, his posture, his accent—they all fit someone who wasn't on his home turf. "So, who are you? I like to know who I'm dealing with, when and if I decide to deal with them."

"Inspector, this meeting was supposed to run two hundred and seventy seconds according to the scenario. We practiced it five times. I knew it might run over because I'd heard you could be difficult, so I got permission to give it an extra thirty seconds. You're almost out of time." He yawned and looked at his watch, which I could see had a stopwatch on its face.

"There's a minute left. When I get up and leave, the door closes. And you'll be on the wrong side of it. So will your nephew." He leaned back and looked up at the sky through the trees that filtered the sunlight. "Your choice."

"My choice," I repeated, rather pleased that he hadn't answered my question, which told me I had probably been right. He was working for someone other than the Portuguese government. "In that case, only one question. Why me?" I left aside the second question—Why did they keep bringing up my nephew? Were they trying to get to him through me? Was he involved in something that had attracted attention halfway around the globe?

The man stood up and stretched. As he did, one of the old men two benches away put on a fisherman's cap and strolled up the lane toward the castle. He no longer looked like he was out of breath, or even that he was old. At that moment, a workman emerged from the house opposite us, crossed to the empty bench, ripped off the Wet Paint sign, and sat down. He pulled a small, sharp, ugly knife from his belt, took an apple from his pocket, and began to peel it. Just downhill from the row of benches, at the entrance to the ruins of a church, a short man in overalls appeared with a large black dog, which pulled at its leash and whined.

That left one exit not covered, a narrow street straight ahead that seemed to lead down the hill. The man beside me put his hand on my shoulder.

"Not a good route, Inspector. It leads nowhere. Dead end." He looked at his watch again. "Fifteen seconds."

"What good am I to you if I accept under duress? You can't trust someone like that."

"Yes or no. Ten seconds."

"All right, but I'm warning you from the start, even if I play along you might not be happy with how I do. And what should I know about socks?"

The man walked away without saying anything more, leaving his magazine on the bench. I sat down and flipped through the pages. There was nothing. They were all blank.

As I walked down the hill, the black dog sniffed my shoes and then looked up at me with greedy yellow eyes. "Nice dog," I said stiffly and continued on my way.

5

Back at my hotel, the clerk waved as I entered and pointed me to the concierge desk. I do not normally take direction from hotel clerks, but in this case I was tired and, after the morning's events near the castle, not in a mood to risk another confrontation, which I felt sure I would lose. I sat down and waited. The lobby was pleasant, filled with brightly colored, oddly shaped furniture. The bar along the back wall was deserted. What I needed was a drink, I thought to myself. Vodka, if they had such a thing here. Russian vodka if it was available, otherwise Finnish, Mongolian, or Polish, exactly in that order. As I considered whether I would want a single or double, the concierge, who had glided out of the shadows, cleared his throat and shuffled some papers.

"May I help you?" His voice was pleasant, almost musical. It probably had been a requirement for getting the job.

"That I don't know." I set aside the question of vodka for the moment. "The desk clerk suggested I see you. About what, I thought you would have some clue."

"And you are . . . ah, here it is. Room 336. Your name is . . . ?"

"Alejandro."

He frowned. "That's a first name."

"You think I don't know that? My father thought if I had to fill out forms my whole life, it would be easier if my last name was also a first name." The concierge could clearly see what my passport said. Maybe he was just trying to test me, or get under my skin.

"You are from Costa Rica? You don't look Costa Rican."

"That's because I am Dominican. When they hear that, many people say I don't look Dominican either, and they are all wrong. Do you doubt my patrimony?"

"No, no, of course not. I'm just interested, being in the travel business."

"Because if you doubt my patrimony . . ." I rose from the chair and looked menacingly at him.

"Really, nothing of the sort. Please, make yourself comfortable. Can I get you a drink . . . ah . . . senhor?"

"Call me Alejandro, as I pointed out already. And you are?"

"Senhor Alejandro." He extended his hand. "I am delighted to meet you. I apologize for not recognizing you immediately. Allow me to introduce myself. I am Bernardo Prehola Sineola des Cartes Vin. Not so simple, I fear." He smiled and showed his teeth. They were picture perfect—doubtless another requirement for the job. "I think you may know my uncle, Luis?" This was not really a question, but he posed it as one.

I was not so easily taken in as this fellow might have thought. Why would I believe Luis was his uncle just on his say-so? Why would I believe anything he told me, including his name? The meeting on the benches had put me in an unusually suspicious frame of mind. "Luis?" I pondered. "Do I know a Luis?" I knitted my brow. "Plays the guitar?" I ventured hopefully.

Bernardo Prehola Sineola des Cartes Vin looked over at the front desk clerk and then sighed deeply. "Inspector." He was speaking softly. "In your room, under the laundry bag in the bottom drawer of the chest, you will find a note. It makes no sense to anyone here."

"You've read it?" Somehow it didn't surprise me that he knew who I was. Luis had picked the hotel, so I supposed his people had someone in place to keep an eye on me.

"Read it? Of course!" This was said with some surprise, as if my even asking the question revealed some deep flaw in my understanding of the universe. "Would we leave notes for guests when we didn't know what they said? In this case, we know what it says, but we don't know what it means. Don't worry, it is clearly not our business to know, but I wanted to be sure you retrieved it before the maid came through to freshen your room."

"She hasn't been there yet? And what would the maid be doing going through the drawers?"

"It's complicated, I'm afraid. Just understand you have one of the cheaper rooms . . ."

"And?"

"And the Spanish couple in the next room asked that their room be cleaned first."

"Spanish couple?"

Bernardo blushed slightly. "They registered as Mr. and Mrs., but the staff have been comparing notes and are doubtful." He reached in his drawer and discreetly took out an envelope. "I believe this is yours," he said quietly. "It fell out of your luggage when you arrived." He shrugged. "Things happen."

6

The door to my room was ajar. Since I hadn't left it that way, it meant the maid was probably there already. I stepped quickly inside to catch her unawares. Right away I heard what sounded like voices coming from the bathroom, and then a pretty laugh as what sounded like the taps to the tub were turned on. The bed was not made; bedding and dainty underclothes were strewn across the floor. I looked in the closet, and my eyes focused on a red dress just as a short scream came from the bathroom. My first thought was to complain to the concierge, followed immediately by a second, better thought—wrong room. I backed out quickly into the hallway. The number on the door was 335, but in an effort to be artistic, someone had made 5s look like 6s. Then it occurred to me. Was this the "Spanish couple," the one the concierge had not so slyly suggested was up to no good? Before I could answer, a maid appeared from out of a doorway across the hall, carrying towels.

"I'm cleaning your room." She pointed to the small sign hanging from the doorknob. "You can't come in until I finish. It's hotel policy. Especially since you're a single male." She gave me an acid look. "We've had incidents."

The maid was middle-aged, very plain-looking, though her eyes held more intelligence than she seemed to want to convey. She spoke English with a refined accent, as if she had learned it at a good school.

"Listen," I said. "I'm an old male. I couldn't even begin to cause an incident. In any case, I don't want to make any trouble." I pointed at my room. "There is a pair of socks I need to get from the drawer. It won't take me a few seconds, then I'll be out of your way."

"There is nothing in the drawers. I looked carefully when I was cleaning. We have to go through the drawers to make sure the previous guest didn't leave anything."

"But I am the previous guest. I checked in yesterday. And I know I put socks in the drawer. Also a clean shirt and a change of underwear."

Her mouth looked doubtful, but her eyes drilled into me. "Are you accusing me of stealing your underwear?"

This was not a conversation I wanted to have standing in the hall with someone I had a feeling was charged with doing more than cleaning rooms. Perhaps Luis's people had floor watchers, the same as we had. It made sense. Most hotels were crawling with guests who were not who they said they were.

"How about I call the front desk and ask if the maids are supposed to rummage around in the drawers of the guests? Or would you like to put everything back where it was?"

"No, go ahead and call." She stood her ground. "I'm not worried." She pulled a piece of paper from the pocket in her apron. "Is this what you want?"

"I don't know. If it's what I think it is, everyone but me seems to have read it already. Should I?"

"It's a series of numbers. Lottery numbers. Phone numbers, maybe. We haven't had a chance to check. Could be suspicious. How do we know it's not? We're supposed to watch for unusual things these days. Terrorists."

"We?" I filed the question away, though the answer seemed clear enough. "I see, very good, you haven't had a chance to check. Well, by all means, shall we try these numbers and find out where they lead?"

The maid shook her head. "I'm going to replace your towels. You are going to stand in the hall." She paused. "Understood?"

I gave no hint either way.

"If you put one foot inside the room while I'm there, I'll have you arrested. And don't think the hotel won't back me up." She waved the paper in front of me. "This is evidence of criminal activity. Terrorism, maybe."

"I thought you said it was lottery numbers."

"It is whatever the police want it to be, and they will want it to be what they are told to want."

Another question for my mental file: Who was going to tell the police what to think? Surely not this woman, she was too far down the chain. There wasn't a midlevel in any organization I knew that would replace towels. I decided it was time to go on the offensive. "Are you going to let me see the paper, or not?"

Again she stood her ground. "It is against hotel policy for guests and cleaning staff to exchange anything other than linen, towels, and pleasantries. It says so in the regulations posted on your door. You should read them."

"I should. I will. Meanwhile, how about you give me the towels, and we bid each other farewell. Something pleasant, perhaps. I don't know Portuguese. Maybe you could help me with such a phrase."

A few minutes later, I was in my room looking at a series of numbers on the piece of paper the maid had finally handed over in return for several large euro bills. Fortunately, a wad of those had been in the envelope the clerk at the front desk had handed me, along with a note in Luis's handwriting. *For matches,* it said.

The paper from the maid had been folded many times, and creases made some of the numerals hard to read, but it looked like 341932 51332405516. It was a phone number, so lightly coded it would have made me laugh if I weren't so annoyed. This was what Luis said I should expect? The only thing to do with a phone number is dial it. I pulled the international dialing instructions from the desk drawer, found what I wanted, then dialed the number. There was a faint click, and then a voice on the other end, a woman, answered in Spanish. Based on what I'd heard the hotel clerk say, I figured it was hello.

"Sorry," I said in English. "My Spanish is rusty. Do you have an English speaker?"

A male voice came on the line. "Hello. May I help you?"

"I'm calling about some machinery that's been ordered." I didn't know exactly—not even really approximately—where this was supposed to lead. But based on my conversation with the man on the bench, I knew the general subject. It wasn't normal to know so little about an operation, but so far in this one, nothing was normal. Probably they didn't trust me. At this point, I wouldn't trust me either. All they knew was whatever Luis had told them and whatever was in a probably thin file with a few vague reports. It wasn't much, and it made me a risk, but one they had to take since, as far as I could tell, they needed someone in a hurry. They also probably didn't want me to sound rehearsed, since that would risk putting the other party on guard. Better if I was making things up as the conversation moved along—just like a normal conversation. I was used to this; it was not so different from working in Pyongyang. Walk in darkness, operate in darkness, stay alive in the darkness. If higher-ups didn't want to supply a flashlight, that was just the way it was.

"Order number?"

"It's in my luggage at the airport. I thought I put it in my briefcase, but apparently it was in a suit jacket." I paused, figuring there was no turning back. "You know how it is, traveling."

"Actually, I don't. Most customers keep track of these things rather well."

"You are looking to lose a big order of *màquines dumpling*?"

There was a slight intake of breath over the phone. "That's Portuguese. I assume you mean dumpling machines." He paused. "There's no trouble, I hope."

"That's what we'll have to see, isn't it. The order was to be filled a week ago. It did not arrive." Here I was hang-gliding, relying on invisible currents to keep me aloft. "There is considerable concern something happened to it. That's why I was sent over here. Straightening out these things on the Internet or over the phone is a nightmare. Face-to-face, that's what we believe in."

"Perfectly right. May I have a name? I can pull a file." No hint of suspicion in the voice, though a trace of annoyance.

"No, I do not want you to pull a file. I don't want anyone to do anything until I get there. I don't want anything prettied up. My company wants to know what happened and whether we can trust you in the future." If hot air was going to keep me aloft, I might as well make the best of it.

"But—"

"Never mind. I can't make it today; we are looking at alternative suppliers. Tomorrow will be good. About two P.M.?"

"Of course, señor, ah, whom shall I tell our salespeople is coming?"

"I don't want to meet salespeople. I want to meet your vice president in charge of international operations."

"But he'll be—"

"He'll be at the front door to greet me. Two o'clock tomorrow. *Adios.*"

Given that I had no idea whom I was talking to or what I was supposed to say—other than that the morning's conversation on the bench had been about a machine, something to do with dumplings—I thought I deserved high marks for improvisation. The number I had called was in Barcelona; I figured that out from the 3493 sequence of the numbers the maid had handed over. Maybe that was why Luis had hurried me to Barcelona—so I could see the city, but even more important, so somebody would see me there. That's what the green van must have been all about. Didn't Luis tell me I was chum? As for the note, the maid must have found it in the drawer before I got there. Whether she'd been sent to get it, or she just happened on it looking for loose change, there was no way to know. If she was working for someone trying to spoil the operation of the man on the bench, she wasn't very good. She was tough enough, but a little too flustered. And in the end, she could be bought. East or west, in darkness or bright light, one thing always worked—cash.

Chapter Three

Maybe I fell asleep, maybe not. Anyway, twenty minutes later there was a soft knock on my door. When I got up to answer it, there was an envelope on the floor. Someone had slid it partway under the door. It was a plain envelope, no name on it, sealed with a wide strip of tape that had dashed lines like those painted down the middle of a road. After wrestling with the tape, which was not regular sealing tape, for a couple of minutes, I tore the bottom of the envelope open and extracted an airline ticket. It was for a flight leaving at eight fifty in the morning the next day, and arriving in Barcelona at eleven forty-five. That would barely give me time to get wherever it was I was supposed to be to meet the vice president to discuss whatever it was I was supposed to discuss. Maybe there would be another envelope in the meanwhile, or the maid would be back to rearrange my socks. A note attached to the ticket gave me some reassurance. *The cash from Bernardo was your advance. Must have receipts for all expenditures.* If I'd had any doubts that this was a government operation, they were gone.

That night I went out to dine at the cheapest place I could find, figuring it would have the best food. Luis had told me the grilled octopus with some little potatoes would be good, that and a glass of wine. I found what I wanted at the top of a flight of stairs on a hillside overlooking a plaza. The place was crowded, with only two tables left. I indicated the one with the view of the lights below, but the waiter shook his head impatiently and steered me to the other empty one, sitting off by itself facing a stone wall covered with a series of faded advertisements for what looked to be guitar perfor- mances. Before I could ask for a menu, he raced away. A few min- utes later, he was back in bad humor. He took my order with barely concealed annoyance and rushed off to serve another table with six workmen and nine bottles of beer. When he returned with my oc- topus, he put the dishes down with a clatter and said, "Wrong ticket. Leave at seven fifty-five." He poured some wine into my glass from a carafe. "It's on the house," he said, and hurried away. A mo- ment later he swooped back with a basket of bread. "Dumplings," he said, and used his head to indicate the table behind me, the one with the view of the lights. Sitting alone was one of the old men who had looked out of breath this morning. I half expected the Australian girls to show up and sit down at his table, but no one disturbed him. When I left, he was drinking his way through a bottle of wine and doing a good job of pretending he did not know I was there.

Back at my hotel, I found my underwear folded on the bed, and no extraneous paper in the drawers. I went down to the desk to ask if I would be able to find a taxi to the airport at five in the morning.

"Most assuredly. Are you checking out early? Your reservation was for three nights."

"Emergency. Death in the family."

"How sad." The clerk pulled a long face. He looked at his watch and then at his computer. "In that case, we'll only charge one extra night. Though if you'd like, we could keep your room and save you the trouble of checking back in the day after tomorrow."

"What makes you think I'll be back the day after tomorrow?"

"Only a suggestion, sir. The Spanish couple in the next room is leaving tomorrow morning as well, but plans to be back the night after that. I thought maybe you would do the same."

I leaned slightly across the counter and looked deep into his eyes. "I am going to a funeral. I am in mourning. I will not be back."

"A taxi will be waiting in the morning. The airport, you said?"

"At five A.M."

"Very good." He glanced behind me toward the front door. "Ah, the busload of travel agents has arrived." His face took on a welcome mask, a leopard grinning at a tethered goat, and he stepped around the counter. "Welcome! *Bienvenido! Konnichi-wa!* This way with the luggage."

2

The next morning the taxi was waiting. The driver was not interested in talking, nor was I. Traffic was light, the morning was foggy, and I needed the chance to review the situation one more time. I had stopped in an Internet café just before dinner the night before and, using the phone number on the paper the maid had given me, had found where I was to go after I landed in Barcelona. It was about twenty-five kilometers north of the airport. A cab ride would not be cheap. Renting a car probably made more sense, though that meant standing in line and dealing with another clerk. I decided on a cab.

When we arrived at the airport, I paid the driver, retrieved my bag from the trunk, and immediately ran into Luis inside the terminal.

"Good morning," he said morosely.

"Good morning, yourself," I said. "I thought you had abandoned me. You are supposed to be back home."

That seemed to strike a nerve, but a morose one, so he only looked all the more unhappy. "I'm sorry, Inspector. It was not my idea to run away. It was certainly not my idea to stay. There are people above me." He looked skyward. "I'm only a pebble on the beach."

I patted him on the shoulder. "Don't worry, Luis, I'm not angry. In fact, I'm glad to see you. Can we get a cup of coffee? I have some time before my plane. Will you be able to get through the security checkpoint without a ticket?"

"I may only be part Portuguese, Inspector"—he bowed slightly—"but I still know my way around. In fact, I'll get you into one of the lounges. It will be more comfortable, and we can talk without all of the announcements crashing over us. I'll meet you on the other side."

At the ticket counter, the woman informed me that I could not have a seat assigned just yet. They would do that at the gate.

"I have a reservation, do I not? Then why not a seat?" I knew I sounded officious, but I did not care. I did not like the way this smelled.

"The flight is overbooked," she said. She was more officious than I was, and it set me off one more notch.

"Perhaps so," I said, "but I did not overbook it. It says right here, I have a seat." I waved the reservation at her.

The woman closed her eyes for a moment. I could tell she was pulling from somewhere an extra drop of civility. "Yes," she said finally, "I can see well enough you have something that makes you think you have an ironclad reservation, but I can also see it says right here"—she pointed at the computer screen in front of her—"that you don't. You bought the cheapest ticket, and the cheapest tickets get bumped in an oversold situation. Just go to the gate, and perhaps it will work itself out." She handed me the ticket. "You board at seven thirty, if you do board. Fair warning, if you are not there promptly when boarding begins, it will not go well. Have a nice flight." From her tone, it was clear she did not have her heart in these well-wishes.

At the security checkpoint, one of the guards patted me down and then asked if I had any carry-on luggage.

"I do," I said. "I just put it through your scanner."

"No, the woman at the scanning machine has signaled that you have no luggage. Why not? That's odd. It's a red flag. According to your ticket, you don't have a seat and you didn't check a bag. You don't have carry-on either?"

"Well, what if I don't?"

"You just said you did, senhor. Now you ask what if you don't. Perhaps you should step over to see the supervisor."

My eyes swept the room searching for Luis. He was nowhere around. The security guard had his hand on my arm. "Shall we go?" He tightened his grip. "There are other people in line behind you."

"I'm not leaving without my carry-on luggage."

"You said you had none. And what if you did? You couldn't put it under the seat in front of you because you don't have a seat. Please don't cause a scene, senhor. I'm sure something can be worked out with my supervisor."

Just beyond the supervisor's desk, Luis appeared suddenly, like a spider dropped from the ceiling. He was leaning casually against a pillar, staring off in the distance as if in Macau and planning something with Lulu. I wasn't even sure he was paying attention.

"I'm doing this under protest," I said to the guard. "If there is anything missing from my carry-on bag when I retrieve it, there will be hell to pay."

The guard said nothing but propelled me to the supervisor's desk.

"Problem?" The supervisor, a big man with a thick neck and matching shoulders, eyed me coolly. "Let me see your passport, if you would be so kind."

"I would not be so kind," I said. "What are you doing misplacing my bag and then pulling me out of line?"

I saw Luis shake his head. He put his hands together as in prayer and closed his eyes. I took a deep breath. "All right, here is my passport. I insist we clear this up quickly. If I'm not at my plane in"—I looked at my wrist and realized my watch was still at the security checkpoint—"twenty minutes or so, I won't get a seat. If I don't get a seat, I will miss an important meeting."

The supervisor was studying my passport. "You are from Costa Rica?" His eyes narrowed as he flipped through the pages. It was a pretty good passport, but I had not looked at it in several years and recalled uneasily that it had not been perfect. Anyone who examined it closely enough might find something not quite right, an exit stamp that didn't belong, a page that was too full. "It says here you landed in Denmark a couple of years ago. You had business? What did you see? What did you eat? Where did you stay?" He was punching buttons on his cell phone and did not look pleased.

At that moment, Luis strolled over. He said something like "Ho!" The supervisor turned and broke into a huge grin. While they embraced like long-lost brothers, Luis peered over the man's shoulder and indicated I should get my bag and disappear. My bag was sitting on the edge of the conveyer belt; my watch was in a basket beside it. I grabbed both, slipped behind the supervisor still embracing Luis, and walked quickly toward the boarding gates. The bag was heavier than I remembered. Worse, I didn't have my passport. If Luis didn't retrieve it for me, I'd have to use the spare in my luggage, which wouldn't be easy to get past immigration when I finally left Europe because it lacked the stamp I needed to show when I had entered. Details. Always details.

My gate was the last one, on the far end of the terminal. Luis was there, sitting near the check-in counter, looking off into space with a worried frown on his face.

"*Ola,* Luis," I said, and sat down beside him. "How did you get here ahead of me?"

"*Ola,* yourself." He continued to stare off into the distance. "This is my territory, Inspector. Don't concern yourself about how I move."

"What about the lounge?"

"Forget about the lounge, it's overheated. What we have now is a real worry. 'Houston,' as they say, 'we have a problem.'"

"Before we start trading movie lines, Luis, do you have my passport? That bastard supervisor took it and didn't give it back. Do you know him?"

"You saw the movie?"

"Luis, my passport! That bastard still has it."

"That man and I went to the same upper school. He was my junior, and I used to get cigarettes and other things for him, so he feels obliged."

"He grew up in Macau?"

"It happens, Inspector. Don't sound so surprised." Luis reached into his pocket and produced my passport. "Here, surely you didn't think I'd leave it behind. It isn't a very good one, you know. The dates for the entry and exit stamps for Indonesia are backward. Don't you check these things when your Ministry hands it to you? I never accept a passport until I've been through it page by page."

"Idiots," I muttered as I flipped to the page with the Indonesia stamp. "It's old. Nothing I can do about it. What's the other problem?"

"Thank you?"

"Thank you, Luis. If I'd been thinking straight, I would have realized you wouldn't leave it. Now, what is the other problem?"

"Your flight is oversold."

"I already know that. They told me at the check-in counter I'd have to wait until everyone boarded. Can't you pull strings? This is the ticket I was given. Don't your people check before they make a reservation? Why did they have to buy the cheapest one?"

"Reservations are not my affair. Strings at security checkpoints and on passports, yes, I know which and how hard to pull, but on seats? No. I'm as helpless as a squid in a pan of olive oil."

"If I'm late, I don't get to Barcelona in time to make my appointment. Then what? We have your squid for lunch and call the whole thing off?"

Luis cleared his throat. "I'm aware of the timing problem, Inspector."

"Good, do you know who I'm supposed to meet in Barcelona?"

Luis looked around. There was an old woman dozing on the end of the row of seats where we sat.

"Let's get some water," he said. "Anyway, I need to stretch my legs." He stood and made an exaggerated effort to touch his toes. "Sitting makes me stiff. Old age, I guess." He smiled sweetly at the old woman, who was now alert and digging through the canvas bag on her lap.

Even before I could gather my things, Luis was moving away to a refreshment kiosk halfway down the corridor. I caught up with him as he was paying for a bottle of water. He took the change and handed the bottle to me. "Don't look now," he said, "but the old woman is taking your picture with her cell phone. She's Spanish. Her name is Dora. The Spaniards use her at the airport every other month. Sometimes she sits around in her old lady act. Other times she has on a short skirt and swivels her hips. She wears lots of makeup and a blond wig. We leave her alone pretty much, as long as she doesn't get in our way."

"Don't they realize she's known?"

"Sure, but that's fine with them. They think we figure if we watch her, we'll miss their really important agents, so we'll loosen up on her and look for someone else, at which point, she'll be better placed to do what she needs to do."

"Which is?"

Luis shrugged. "Today she's watching for you. That means they'll be expecting you at the Barcelona airport. I'm not sure that's such a bad idea, but you might as well be prepared for a reception."

"Maybe it will be just as well if I get bumped. In fact, maybe I should just bag this whole thing and go home."

Luis nodded at my carry-on bag. "Have you looked inside?"

"Why?"

"Inspector, we went to a lot of trouble at that checkpoint, and you didn't even look inside? This will be a disappointment to the head of the foreign operations department, who on my say-so has invested a lot of effort in getting you here. Please, take the bottle of water, walk over to the seating area by the window, and look in your bag."

As soon as I unzipped the bag, I realized it wasn't mine. It had a concealed pocket inside, though not all that well concealed if I could find it in a matter of seconds. In the pocket was a miniature tape recorder that wasn't mine. It was molded in the shape of a mechanical pencil. There was also a heavy guidebook of Barcelona, which was not mine, and an orange, which judging from the very faint evidence of cutting at the very top contained something other than vitamin C. Probably a transmitter, though maybe it was an explosive. Or maybe a camera. Did the Spaniards not want this orange to arrive in their country, or did they want to make sure it was delivered, on time, to a preselected target? I decided Luis was either going to come clean with me in the next few minutes, or I would hand the orange to Dora and catch the next flight back to China.

"This isn't my bag, Luis."

"It's close enough, Inspector. Maybe even better than the one you took from that store."

"The Syrian man works for you?"

"Not in so many words. How did you know he was Syrian?"

"I have a good sense of nationalities, Luis. It's a survival instinct. And you're misinformed. I didn't take a bag from that store. Is he charging you for it?"

Luis closed his eyes and frowned.

"I hate to make trouble, Luis, but I want my bag back. And without all your added stuff."

"You might find this one useful." Luis had stopped frowning but still had his eyes closed.

"I don't like oranges. Too much acid."

Luis made a clicking sound with his tongue, took a breath, and opened his eyes. "Listen closely, Inspector. Before you go to your appointment, you move the pencil out of the extra pocket and the orange into it. That activates the lens. You just squeeze the handle of the bag. There's no sound, but you've taken a picture."

"What if they inspect the bag at the factory?"

"My God, Inspector, of course they will."

"It's my neck."

"It's foolproof."

"Nothing is foolproof."

"You want out? Just say so." Luis's voice had a hard edge, nothing like I had ever heard from him.

"No. I'm with you, Luis. Though I don't know why. I really don't."

"Good. One more thing. If anyone asks, you are Japanese."

"Why?"

"Never mind. It will be explained later. You should be able to carry it off with no problem."

"What about my passport? It's not Japanese."

"Well, it's not Korean either, is it? You won't have any trouble. Have some fun with it if you want."

In a sudden turn of fate, there was room in the first-class section of the plane, and the woman from the ticket counter, who was now collecting tickets at the gate, gave me a smug smile. "As you see, it works out, and there is never any sense in getting red in the face, is there? I trust the flight will be smooth."

Luis shook my hand gravely and gave me a small salute. "Safe flight, my friend. As my mother used to say, call when you find work."

Chapter Four

After the plane landed in Barcelona, I hurried down the stairs to the taxi queue in front of the terminal. I kept my eyes open, but there was no one from the Inquisition waiting for me. The line for the taxis was short. In no more than two minutes I was in a cab, a burgundy Mercedes that was begging to be washed. The driver looked at me in his rearview mirror. "You are Japanese?" He spoke slowly in Spanish. When I didn't reply, he repeated the question in English.

"Some might say so," I said. "Here's the address. Can we get there a little before two o'clock?"

The driver looked at the address and then at his watch. "Señor, even if I had to change two tires and replace the transmission, we'd be there before two. You are buying machinery? That's a big factory where you're going. My uncle used to work there. I did, too, for a couple of years."

As we pulled out of the airport onto the highway, I was looking out the window at the scenery and not paying attention to the driver. I'd been to Europe several times on Ministry business, but never this far west. There was something invigorating about the place. I watched a few plane trees go by on the side of the road, very nonchalant in the way they stood, nothing formal or self-conscious as sometimes happens on airport highways. Then I remembered it is never wise to ignore a taxi driver. Funny things happen to meters.

"That towel on your meter," I said, looking into the front seat. "Trying to keep the sun off it?"

The driver shook his head. "Oy, señor, I'm sorry. It is a present for my grandmother. I meant to wrap it."

"Well, it won't jump off the meter by itself. Maybe it would be happier on the front seat. Perhaps you should wash it before you give it to your grandmother."

The driver smiled into the mirror. "You are something," he said. "I think we will be friends someday."

"The towel," I said.

"Of course, as you wish." He removed the towel. The meter was at zero. "I never record trips to the factory," he said, and watched me in the mirror.

"You bring a lot of people up there?"

"Recently, a lot of Japanese," he said. "When I worked there, it was mostly Europeans who came onto the production line. But after a couple of years, I left when it got strange."

I leaned back against the seat and pretended to be uninterested. "Strange is a funny word, I always say. It sort of depends on who is using it. You worked there long?"

"As I told you barely a minute ago, a couple of years." I saw him purse his lips. "If you'd rather sleep, I can just listen to the radio."

"No, sorry, I'm a little distracted, arriving in a foreign country, and my being an Asian."

Now it was my turn to watch him in the mirror. His eyes narrowed. "So you are Japanese."

"I'm afraid so," I said. "Apparently that displeases you." I bowed my head. "The offense is mine." I hoped this would not go on much longer. Pretending to be Japanese was not something I could do for more than a few minutes without hurting myself. On one trip, in Romania, I'd assumed Japanese identity for two days. I told the Ministry that if they ever made me do that again, I'd drink poison.

"No, I'm not displeased," the taxi driver said. "It's a big world. Not everyone can be from Catalonia."

"If you don't mind my asking, what was strange at the factory? My people are looking into this company, and if there is something strange about it, well, you know, that could be bad for business." I reached for my wallet. "Of course, we are always prepared to compensate for information."

"I'll tell you what was strange. You decide what it's worth. If it's worth nothing, that's fine."

"Go on, I'm listening."

"The company used to operate like a family business. The factory's been there a long time, more than two hundred years. Workers were treated well, they knew their jobs, and the owner looked out for them. When the workers took over for a few years during the civil war, the owner stayed and worked with them. Even during the worst days, even after Franco marched in and slaughtered people, the factory was considered a place of sanctuary."

"Your family?"

"We lost many, but it's done, it's past. The city has built over the bad memories, most of them anyway. My uncle worked in the factory for almost forty years. He got me a job there, and I thought I'd be set for life."

"And then?"

"And then it all changed. Things started happening. Machines broke down where they had never broken down before. The computers were unreliable, and fed the wrong information into the precision equipment. Shipments were delayed or misrouted, so we had days when there was practically no work."

"You mind if I take a few notes?" I was searching for a scrap of paper in my pocket.

He shook his head. "Just listen, OK? Paper floats away sometimes."

A careful man, I thought. "All right, then what?"

"What I told you is not strange enough?"

"Sure, it's plenty strange. But I have a feeling there's more."

"Yes, señor, there's more. After a couple of months of breakdowns and disruptions, the different shops in the factory were walled off. We weren't supposed to talk to each other, and we weren't supposed to notice when visitors came through."

"Japanese?"

"Some. They always went to the special section of the plant, to see the dumpling machines."

"Dumplings?"

"I told you it was strange. It was. We didn't know what they did in the special section. The technicians and machinists there were specially recruited from overseas and kept segregated. They were well paid, better than the rest of us."

"And then?"

"The disruptions got worse. My uncle almost lost his arm when one of the machine tools went haywire. They told him it was his fault, but my uncle didn't make mistakes. He was a craftsman. Someone had either tampered with the machine, or the computer program had been corrupted in dangerous ways, to cause injury. That was enough for me. I quit."

"They said good-bye and gave you a pat on the back?"

"They gave me some money, enough for this cab, and told me to keep my mouth shut."

"Did you?"

He looked in the mirror. "You and I never had this conversation."

"Why tell this to me? For all you know, I'm part of your problem."

"We'll find out, won't we?" He eased the cab onto an off-ramp that put us on a narrow secondary road that wound through hills and farmland. "The factory is around the next hill. You still want to go there?"

"I don't know why I shouldn't. I'm not going to try to run a machine. Besides, I have an appointment to keep. Can you hang around to take me back to the airport?"

"How will I know when you're ready to leave?"

"A puff of white smoke, isn't that the signal?"

He laughed. "Here's my card. It has my phone number on it.

Call and I'll be at the front gate in less than three minutes. You can pay me for the round trip when we get back to the airport. You have a cell phone, don't you?"

2

The guard at the front gate looked at my passport, took my picture with a small camera, and then had a short conversation on the phone. He hung up, frowned, and pointed to the metal detector. "Bag on belt," he said. "You got change, keys, anything? In the basket."

He watched closely as I walked through the detector. Then he looked at the X-ray picture of my bag. "What's in there?"

"What do you think," I said. "Look, I'm here for business. A lot of money is involved. If your company isn't interested, I'll just go home."

He scratched his neck. "I'm asking you, what's in the bag? Just checking, that's the procedure. You want to see my manual? You want to do my crummy job?" He dumped my keys on the floor. "Oops. So sorry."

"You going to pick those up? Or do I kick your sorry Slavic ass?" He wasn't a Spaniard, that was for sure. And he probably wasn't happy to be in Spain standing around all day with almost nothing to do taking orders from people who treated him with contempt and paid him less than he thought he was worth.

The guard crossed his arms. "You and who else?" We stared at each other for a few seconds before he bent down and picked up the keys. "They said I should let you in, so that's what I'll do. Me? I don't care who comes and goes. They don't pay me enough to worry. I just like some respect, you get my thought?"

I put two twenty-euro notes on the counter. "That's as much respect as anyone gets from me," I said.

Three cameras on poles tracked me as I crossed the courtyard to the main door, heavily barred. When I was a meter away, the door opened, and another guard—an ugly fellow with a sallow face—watched intently as I stepped inside. On the other side of a thick glass partition, a wiry man in a perfectly cut gray suit stood with his hands behind his back. He nodded to a third guard, who hesitated. The man in the suit shouted something. The sound was muffled by the thick glass, but from the guard's expression, I was sure it was not meant to be pleasant. The guard gestured toward his own badge, clipped to his shirt pocket. The man in the suit shouted again and raised a fist above his head. The guard shrugged and opened the door for me.

"Welcome, señor." The man in the gray suit extended his hand. "You are exactly on time." His smile was poisonous.

"And why not?" I shook his hand limply. It was better if his first impression was that I was a sack of flour. "You are the vice president in charge of foreign operations? I need to see the dumpling machines."

"Actually, the man you are looking for is out of the country at the moment. I am the vice chairman in charge of facilities and production. I'm fully empowered in his absence to deal with guests. Anything you would say to him, you can say to me." He sneered as if he had told a joke but I was not supposed to understand the punch line.

3

Wherever I was when I woke up, it was dark and cold and very quiet. My head hurt a little, but not as much as my ribs. My tongue was so swollen it almost didn't fit in my mouth. On closer inspection, I realized I was sitting on a dirt floor, with my back against a damp stone wall. I wasn't tied up or handcuffed, details obviously considered unnecessary because I had no intention of trying to stand up. A door off to my left opened, and a light shone in my face. I looked around for my bag. It was gone.

"Good, you're awake. I was almost afraid those Slavic thugs had killed you."

"Uh." My tongue wouldn't allow much more than that.

"You are probably thirsty."

"Uh."

It was the man in the gray suit. He sneered at me. "If I gave you something to drink right now, you'd drown. Your tongue will return to normal, pretty normal, anyway, in about twenty minutes. Ever had Novocain? It's like that. Don't get cute or you'll bite your tongue off and not even know it."

"Uh."

"Good, now I'll talk, you'll listen. I'd ask who you are, but you can't answer, not yet. But you might as well know, I am convinced you don't belong here, you came under false pretenses, and you'll be very lucky if one of our machines doesn't accidentally rip you to shreds because of an errant computer program that someone, perhaps a friend of yours, has for some reason altered. You know anything about that?"

"Uh-uh."

"I take it that means no. For some reason I am tempted to believe you, though I don't know why. I also don't know why you are carrying a phony passport and a tape recorder in the shape of a pencil."

I put my head back against the wall. Actually, I didn't know why I had the pencil either. I silently cursed Luis.

"It is very hard to see how you are going to get out of here alive, unless you answer all of my questions. And even then it is going to tax my ingenuity to figure out how to let you go, but I'm pretty smart and I actually do have a nice side to me." He kicked my leg. "But you won't get to see that until you cooperate. Understood?"

There was a tingling on the side of my tongue, so I figured it was only a matter of time before I'd start repeating the one answer I knew for sure, "I don't know."

"Would you like some water now? Or perhaps some orange juice?"

I indicated I would. He stepped outside, making no effort to close the door. In a moment he was back with a glass of water. "Drink it slowly," he said.

Most of it dribbled out of my mouth onto my shirt. Not only was my tongue numb, but my lips were as well. They were rubbery and cold, and completely useless. I cursed Luis, cursed his forefathers, cursed the day I met him in Macau. From outside the room I could hear shouting and the sounds of a scuffle. A short man burst through the doorway. He did not look happy.

"*Gilipollas!*" he roared. "*Pollino!*"

I braced for what I figured would be more kicks, but the new man grabbed the no longer sneering fellow in gray by the scruff of the neck and threw him against the wall. Spanish ricocheted around the room. You didn't have to know Spanish to be pretty sure it was vile. The man in the gray suit put his hands up as a supplicant and tried to scramble to his feet. The other man, smaller but with shoulders like a set of wooden blocks, threw him down again. Then he straightened his tie, composed himself, and turned to me.

"*Gomen,* or whatever," he said. "May I assist you in standing? Pay no attention to this *bobo.*" He turned and kicked the man on the ground twice. "He is an idiot, from a family of idiots. He was recommended to me by a horse's ass who I will deal with when the time comes. This one"—he kicked the man on the ground yet again—"he has shit in the milk one too many times, and I'll see to it that he regrets the day his mother, a great fat whore who sleeps with goats, conceived him."

The man on the ground whimpered and covered his face. My lips buzzed with feeling. I realized I could probably talk again but, considering the performance I'd just witnessed, decided to stick to grunts for a couple more minutes.

"The first thing we will do is to get you comfortable, new clothes, a shower, whatever you wish. You are my guest. For lunch, if you would like to gnaw on the heart of this donkey, I will gladly oblige."

The man on the floor curled up in the corner.

"Jackass! Get out, I can't stand the sight of you!" He turned and called out the door in Russian, "Come and collect this garbage."

The guard from the first entry point, the one who had dropped my keys, came into the room. He came toward me with a smile on his face, until the short man grabbed his shoulder and spun him around. "Another idiot! It has rained idiots on us. By the holy saints, have the burros taken over the world? Not him, you fool, that one, in the corner. Take him to his office and keep him there. If he tries to get out, break his neck."

The little man took a handkerchief out of his pocket and mopped his face. "You won't believe it, but this isn't how we normally conduct our business." He reached into another pocket and pulled out a tiny silver box. "Pills," he explained and put two in his mouth. "Is it any wonder I need pills? I should have retired years ago, but no. They told me I was needed, that my experience was irreplaceable. Ha! Did I believe them?"

I grunted.

"Yes, you're right. Of course I did. Fool that I am. Are you a fool, too?"

I pointed at my tongue.

"Well, we all say stupid things sometimes. I could cut out your tongue and you wouldn't have to worry anymore. Shall we try it?"

I shook my head.

"That was a joke. Don't worry. You are my guest. Here, now, stand up, and let's get you to someplace more comfortable than this."

4

After cleaning up and changing into a pair of trousers and a new shirt, both of which fit reasonably well, I was escorted to a dining room with a high ceiling and a long wooden table at which, on either side, were eight ornately carved chairs. There was a long runner down the center of the table. Squarely in the middle was an iron candleholder holding four fat candles. Three of the walls were paneled. One was mostly taken up with a gigantic fireplace. The two others were hung with massive, dark portraits of men with angry eyes and gaunt faces. The final wall, rough plaster painted the color of a diseased lemon, was decorated with crossed sabers and an ancient rifle. In front of the fireplace was a multicolored rug, but the rest of the floor was nothing but bare, wide oak planks that had been worn smooth from years of use. Seated at the far end of the table was the short man with the big shoulders. He had changed to a white linen shirt with a brown silk tie and a pair of rust-colored trousers.

"Welcome, *irrashaimase,* or whatever." He stood when I entered but otherwise made no effort to come toward me. "Please, sit here, next to me. If you are on the other end of the table, we will have to shout, which I find irritating. Are you feeling well?"

"I'm fine." My ribs ached and I had bruises on my thigh, but there was no sense detailing the damage at the moment. "Quite a room." I looked around. "Your relatives?" I pointed at one of the pictures.

The man shook his head. "No. They are friends of the family killed in the Inquisition. That was hundreds of years ago, or do you know our history?" He indicated I should sit, which I did. He pressed a bell, and a butler with big hands and a nose that looked like it had met a large truck appeared. "Get the wine, Yuri, the special bottle that's in the locked cabinet. Here is the key. And be careful."

When the butler returned with the bottle, the man sighed. "Maybe you uncork wine with your teeth in your country, Yuri. We do not. Give me back the key, then find the corkscrew. After that, leave us alone until I ring again." He looked at me. "We'll start with the soup. I assume you like soup."

"It depends," I said. "I do not like it too spicy, and never with cream. I don't suppose you have anything with seaweed?"

The man turned to the butler. "Well, you heard our guest.

See what the cook can do. And close the door as you leave, close it completely."

After the door clicked shut, we sat in silence. The elaborately carved chair was uncomfortable, probably because it was oak. The whole damned room was nothing but oak. The oak paneling on the walls was especially oppressive. It was hard to see how anyone could sit still for a whole meal in the room without breaking down and sobbing.

"This chair is oak," I said.

"Yes, sturdy as a ship."

"My grandfather would say oak was the worst thing to use if you cared about comfort, because oak only cares about itself. He would tell me that in a slightly peevish voice as if it were my fault."

"Your grandfather? An interesting man, it seems. A furniture maker?"

"He was a guerrilla fighter, but got tired of sneaking up and killing people. So he turned to carpentry."

The man absorbed this silently.

"This table." I tapped my finger on it. "Also oak."

"One massive plank." The man brightened noticeably. "Must have taken ten men to bring it in here."

"Probably so," I said. It was one massive plank, yes, but with no character. Simply a slab of wood, like a bloody steak, rounded on the edges but otherwise just as it had been when the tree had been felled and—as my grandfather would have said—lay dying on the earth, its limbs being torn away.

"I see you are admiring the table," the man said. "It is several hundred years old, and will last several hundred more no doubt. You won't find many trees like that around here anymore. What about in your country?"

"My country? We have no more trees. Every one has been cut down for chopsticks."

The man frowned and then reached for the bottle of wine. "That donkey didn't bring me a corkscrew." He went over to an oak cabinet and rummaged around in a drawer. "Success." He held up a corkscrew with an elaborate wooden handle—oak. "Let's have a drink, shall we? After that, we can have the soup, and then the main course will come—seafood. We love seafood in Barcelona. Ours is the best in the world. I think we may have something special for you as well."

After he had filled the glasses there was another long silence. Finally, I thought it was time to see what he was made of, besides Spanish curses and this bloodcurdling hospitality.

"I hope you won't think me rude, but first you have your thugs beat me up, then you give me a change of clothes and offer me fellowship around your ancient oak table beneath portraits of dear friends tortured to death long ago. All charming. What do you want?"

The man held his wineglass up to the candlelight, took a sip, and then settled back in his uncomfortable chair. "No, I think you have it backwards. The question is, what do you want? We had a deal; there is even an elaborate and carefully worded contract, but now you seem to have broken it."

I held my wineglass up to the candlelight, looking to gain a few seconds in order to pull a brilliant thought or two out of thin air. He might know about my phone call yesterday to his colleague in the gray suit, though they didn't seem to communicate all that well. It would be best if the sneering man had kept it to himself, because it had been a gigantic bluff on my part, and his boss, who had closed his eyes and was smiling faintly as he took in the bouquet of the wine, would by now have recognized that I was a fraud. On the other hand, given what little I'd learned sitting on the bench beneath the castle in Lisbon, this fellow might be talking about something that I barely understood. Either way, I was liable to hang myself no matter what I said. In that case, I might as well enjoy myself as long as I could. I took a sip.

"Your passport is Costa Rican. You aren't, of course, but I congratulate you on your imagination, and that of your organization." He raised his glass.

I nodded and raised my glass in return. It was a heavy glass, elaborate with diamond cuts and a thick square base. Nothing delicate in this country that I could see. Everything overdone. I wasn't looking forward to the soup.

"Drink up," he said, and tipped his glass back for a mouthful of the wine. I did the same, thinking to myself that he had said "organization," not factory, not enterprise, not company. Organization. Even allowing for translation from Spanish to English, it had a funny ring.

I swallowed the wine and felt my knees twitch as the jolt of alcohol dropped into my system. This was not just wine.

"We were unhappy with your predecessor. He was rather crude." He took another large swallow.

I cocked my head as if confused, which of course I was, both by the conversation and the wine. I took a dainty sip.

"You came here through Portugal." He gave me a hard look. "Why?"

This at least I could answer without getting into trouble. "I'd never been there. It seemed like an interesting place."

"Bah. The castle in that shitty little city of Lisboa is nothing. You'd have to drive to Sintra for anything worth seeing. The Portuguese love to show off Sintra. Did you go?"

"I'm a busy man, with very little time to sightsee."

"Well, there is much to see in Barcelona. Once we finish our business here, you must stay for a day and look around the city. Have you seen Gaudí? You will not believe your eyes. And besides, there is so much to enjoy at night." He leered slightly and drained his glass.

"Business first," I said. I raised my glass, silently cursed Luis, and took another sip.

The man reached over and filled my glass, after which he filled his own. "Of course, if you've been to Barcelona before . . ." The rest of the thought hung over the oak table before drifting toward the paneling in search of a window.

If he knew more than he was saying, he was certainly taking the long way around. "Surely you don't think I would just show up here out of the blue," I said. "On something as important as this, we are naturally careful. That's how the organization works." I smiled when I said the word. "I assume you are careful, too, or do I assume too much?" I glanced casually around the room. "For example, the camera over the fireplace. I assume that's why you wanted me in this seat. Would you like a profile shot? It helps in identification, I'm told."

The man looked at me carefully, his eyes narrowing. "How did you spot that camera? You must have been trained. What else have you been trained for?" He rang the bell, and when nothing happened, he rang it again, with more urgency. Again there was a wait before Yuri finally appeared.

"If that was for the soup," Yuri said, "it's not ready." The Russian smelled of alcohol, even from several meters away. He looked steady on his feet, though his eyes were not as focused as you might like for a bodyguard. "Something else you want I should do?"

"Nothing, Yuri, nothing at all. We'll have the soup as soon as it's ready. Can you bring it here without spilling on our guest?"

"Maybe," I said once Yuri had left, "we should know each other's names. It might make dinner friendlier, using names. When I say pass the rolls, I can attach your name to it. Señor such-and-such, would you be so kind as to pass me those delicious rolls? See what I mean? Or would you rather things stayed tense? I can eat dinner either way."

"Strange, you don't know my name."

"Not really. Where I work, we trust no one, we share no information, we especially do not reveal contacts. There have been too many leaks, too many people talking, too many trials, too many shipments intercepted." I was assuming what the taxi driver had told me was close to the truth.

"Why, then, would you want my name? Wouldn't it be dangerous to your organization?"

"Of course it would! That's the point." I tried to make what came out next sound self-obvious. "If I know your name, and you know mine, we have guns cocked at each other's head."

"But everyone already knows who I am, I own this company. I've lived here for decades. My neighbors respect me."

"In that case, pass the rolls."

"Wait, wait. We mustn't spoil your appetite. Let's start with the surprise."

Again he rang the bell, again nothing happened. Then the door swung open and Yuri burst through, holding two bowls of soup. "Ready," he said, and sloshed some from each bowl on the table as he set them down in front of us. "The cook says the seaweed is very nuanced. That was her word."

"Thank you, Yuri. Now, can you get the surprise? Put them on the big platter, the red and gold one, can you?" He looked more closely at Yuri. "Never mind, have the cook arrange them." He turned to me. "Please, try the soup. It is a seafood broth. Why don't you call me José for now? And I'll call you Sakamoto."

"I wish you wouldn't. I don't like Japanese names."

"Oh? And why is that?"

"Because I'm not Japanese. I'm Korean."

José's spoon dropped into his soup with a splash.

"Surprised? That was a nice tie, by the way. I hope you can get it cleaned."

José looked down at his shirtfront. "The tie was a present from an old mistress. She had good taste in most things. She was especially good with ties."

"You didn't expect me to be Korean? But why not?" I took a leap into the unknown. "That's who you're dealing with, or didn't you know that?"

José's smile was sly and gone in a flash. "We don't want to know who the end users are, that's our operating principle. We always know, of course, but we pretend that we don't, even to ourselves. We sell machinery, piece by piece. No machine has value in and of itself. No value, no soul, no heart, no moral weight. We ship all over the world. Whoever wants a machine, they must have a reason. And if they have the cash, they have a machine."

He was about to say something more when the door opened and a woman in a cook's uniform walked in, carrying a large serving plate on which, artfully arranged around a centerpiece of a miniature machine of some type, were about two dozen steamed dumplings.

Chapter Five

José beamed. "What do you think?"

"The machine? Is that the one we contracted to buy? I hope not. Can we get spare parts for something so small?"

"Good!" José slapped his hand on the oak table. "I didn't realize Koreans had a sense of humor. Please, the dumplings, try one. We have our own Spanish version, but yours are different." His face fell. "Oh, Mother of God, these are Japanese dumplings. Cook! Take these away!"

"No, no, they look fine. They actually look nearly perfect. I'm not fussy about dumplings. Names, yes. Dumplings, no."

"We thought since we were about to deliver your first dumpling machine, you would enjoy this to mark the occasion. Of course, it was supposed to be for your predecessor . . ."

"Who you did not like."

"I cannot abide a man with so many tattoos."

Things began to fall into place. My predecessor was Japanese mafia. My so-called organization was connected with the yakuza. "Yes, the organization has tried to rein that in, but it's not easy. We haven't even started trying to ease some of them out of the practice of chopping off the little finger. I am one of the first." I held both of mine up to prove I was intact. "We've moved my predecessor off to another, ah, operation. Something more suitable."

"Please enjoy the dumplings." José had reverted to full host mode. I didn't know if he had accepted my explanation or not.

"More wine? I had it fortified; it relaxes things. Then we'll get to business. And then we'll go for a tour so you can see the dumpling machine, the lovely *madre de todas las máquinas* before it is crated. This will please you?"

"So! It was not shipped yet. There has been a misunderstanding, most unfortunate. If all is in order, yes, it will please me and I'll be able to close off this chapter."

José's face fell. I had a feeling I knew why.

"If the machine works once it arrives at its intended destination, and the dumplings . . ." I paused searching for the words. ". . . are deemed satisfactory to those who know more about these things than I do, then I'm sure there will be more orders. One thing at a time, that's how we keep ourselves ahead of the crowd." I picked up a dumpling with my fork. It leaked all over my shirt and onto my trousers.

José pursed his lips. "I should have warned you. These are soup dumplings. I thought all Asians would know that."

2

Once we had finished with the dumplings—the skin was thick and unpleasant, very much like those served in the restaurant near my nephew's house—José suggested we have brandy and cigars by the fireplace. I sat in the chair that looked like it would play havoc with the camera. The microphones could be anywhere and everywhere. In some ways it was nice not knowing, like being home again. Hidden microphones never bothered me. They're much better than note takers, who tend to miss things and make you out to have said something you didn't.

José brought a bottle of brandy and two glasses from a cabinet recessed behind the oak panels. "Yuri must have smoked the cigars. If he weren't so valuable, I'd break his legs."

"He's valuable? I wouldn't have guessed it. In fact, it won't look good in my report to the organization when I describe the security setup here."

José poured the drinks. "Let's not worry about reports. Let's just enjoy this brandy and forget about business. There is more to life, you know. Business is just a necessary evil. As if there were not enough evil in the world already, eh?" He settled back in his chair and gave me a thoughtful look. "Does evil bother you?"

Suddenly the room was very still and cold. The brandy warmed me only for a moment, and then I felt an icy hand squeezing my heart. "Evil is part of the order of things," I said. "Evil is under rocks everywhere. It doesn't shock me, if that's what you're asking. I don't encourage it, but I don't hurl myself into senseless combat with it."

"Really? What would your grandfather say to that?"

I thought back to the conversations in the old man's workroom, filled with woodworking tools, and pieces of lumber leaning against the wall, each in a designated spot depending on what my grandfather knew about its history, its age, its relationship with the earth and the sky. This was very complicated, and more than once I knocked something over and put it back in the wrong spot, only to earn a scolding—often, as he got older, a bitter harangue.

"My grandfather?" I swirled the brandy in the glass. "He thought most of humanity was full of folly. After the war, when we walked past a village that had been destroyed by bombs, he'd say to me, 'No reason, none. Just felt like dumping bombs here. Remember this place. It's folly, that's what it is. Do you understand what I'm telling you?'"

"You had an answer?" José leaned forward, for some reason looking very interested in what I told my grandfather.

"None. It did no good to answer, so I would look down and shake my head." But in my memory was more than that. In my memory my grandfather grew pale, putting his face close to mine. He would say softly, like a bayonet going into someone's thigh, "You don't know, do you? You can't imagine such a thing. But I can tell you this, folly has produced more evil in the world than a thousand devils working a thousand years. Folly killed your parents; folly and grief will always be your brother and sister. And evil? Why, you don't need to look for evil, it will find you, always two steps behind folly. You watch, you'll see." And then he would walk quickly away, as if he didn't want to be near me anymore, though why I never knew. But I didn't tell this to José. It was none of his business.

José poured a bit more brandy in my glass, then an equal amount for himself. "In some ways I am like your grandfather."

I kept myself from saying what I thought at that moment, which is that this man was no more like my grandfather than a turtle is like a shaft of light through the clouds after a summer storm. But the brandy was making me bold where I knew I should be silent.

"And why is that?" I asked. "He worked with wood. And you work with machines. They are not the same at all."

"Ah, good, now we get to the essence of things. You are right, and you are wrong. Machines are not natural, that is, they are not *of* nature. They are thus unnatural in a sense. In that regard, they are, as you suggest, the opposite of wood. Yet a well-built machine is more than the sum of its parts. The screws and bolts and shaped steel, the copper pipes, the gears and pulleys and precision movements are a composition. Moreover, they give birth; their offspring contribute to civilization."

My head was buzzing slightly. "Machines are cold. They are noisy. They pollute. They do not dance in the wind. As often as not, they deliver destruction. They provide tools of folly."

"And next you will tell me they bring evil." Slowly the veneer was slipping away. His face lost the cloying smile that smothered the rest of his emotions; his voice sounded more of cold steel. "Evil, my friend, has nothing to do with machines. Nothing! If you are so concerned, tear up your contract! Go home to your trees, to your wooden dreams, to the breezes of morality that flutter the leaves of your imaginary kingdom of good."

If he had been drunk, I would have ignored the outburst, but he was stone sober and as serious as the silver pistol he had taken from somewhere and was now aiming at my face.

"I could blow your brains out with just a twitch of my finger. And maybe I should. I don't need the money your organization is paying, and I don't need the headache of every intelligence service in Europe sniffing around my factory. If I kill you and then call the police, I can tell them that you were trespassing—a Korean trespassing at a machine factory in Spain, a very special machine factory that produces very special machines, so precise, so reliable, so beautiful! They will be interested. A Korean with a Costa Rican passport! They will be fascinated! They will think we argued over the terms of our contract, but no matter how they pore over my files and invoices and accounting books, they won't find a trace of anything resembling a contract between us. They will jump at the chance to double-check all the shipments in and out of here, they will question all of the workers, they will hold the invoices up to the light and look for secret entries. All useless! But you will know nothing of this, because your brains will be splashed from here to kingdom come."

"True." This was one of those "think fast" moments when thinking is the worst thing to do. Either your instincts are up to the task, or you're dead before you can open your mouth. "But you've had visitors."

The barrel of the gun dropped slightly. I could see that José was thinking about this.

"All sorts of visitors," I pressed ahead, "and your workers, though they weren't supposed to be paying attention, watched each one. You see, we know a lot. We do not do business in the dark, my friend. After you partitioned off the factory so that the different parts wouldn't communicate without someone in the front office watching, it became more obvious that something was odd. And when the computer-driven machines started acting up, causing injuries, the workers got scared. Scared people are not the best allies."

"But no one has seen you." The barrel went back up again.

"If that's what you think, go ahead and shoot." This had to be instinct, because there is no way I would have said those words if I'd thought about it.

Sometimes even a Russian does something right. At that moment, Yuri burst through the door. "Hello!" he shouted. "Did someone call a fucking taxi?"

José stood up suddenly to see what this was. He turned, and as he did, the gun went off. The bullet went over my left shoulder judging from what it hit, which was one of the dearly departed ancient friends, shot through the aristocratic nose.

"Yuri, you are the son of a burro. Your mother . . . to hell with your mother. Get out before the next shot goes into your stupid, wooden head."

"A taxi," Yuri said. "There is a taxi waiting out in front. The driver says he was supposed to pick up a Japanese man he dropped off here hours ago."

"Tell him to go away." José was examining the portrait. "This was the great-great-great-grandfather of my mother's cousin. A bastard by all accounts. Probably a Jew."

"I can't," Yuri said sullenly.

José whirled around and moved toward the oak table. "Yes, you can. You can because if you don't you're through here. You can pack up and go back to your pathetic country."

Yuri shook his head, like a dog shaking off water. "No, I can't tell him. Because—"

"Because I'm right here." The taxi driver stepped inside. "And either I need to take this man back to the airport, or I want my fare."

José focused on the driver. "Do I know you? You look familiar. And how did you get into my house?"

"Well, I didn't climb over the fence, if that's what you're thinking. The guard at the first gate let me in, the guard at the second gate asked about my family, and here I am."

"Ah, that's it! You used to work here. Your uncle did, too, before he got sloppy."

I had my eye on José's pistol. He was holding it behind his back.

"My uncle was a craftsman, he was never sloppy. Your factory is cursed, and that's why people are leaving. Too many accidents, too many unexplained failures, too many—"

José turned to me. "Don't listen to this man."

"I owe him the round-trip fare."

Just then Yuri, who it turns out was neither drunk nor ponderous, moved like a panther. In one swift motion he leaped over the table and knocked José to the floor. There was a muffled gunshot. José gave a groan, half rose on his elbow, and then fell back. It seemed to me he was dead, something Yuri quickly confirmed on failing to find a pulse.

The taxi driver looked at José's body and shook his head. "Now what?"

Yuri didn't hesitate. "We get rid of the stiff, clean up this room, and then everyone goes about his business." He turned to me. "What is your business, by the way?"

"I'm here to check on a contract. You obviously aren't a bodyguard. What's your business?"

"I'm here to check on a contract, too. The world moves in mysterious ways, huh? You're Japanese?"

The taxi driver closed his eyes and leaned against the wall. "Does anyone mind if I'm sick?"

My mind had settled into a crouch, ready to deal with Yuri, who I had the feeling was going to be a big problem over the next several minutes. "I don't have a lot of use for dumplings, if that's what you're getting at."

"I don't care fuck about dumplings." Yuri rolled the body in the rug in front of the fireplace. "Someone is going to have to dump him." He turned to the taxi driver. "You. Where's a good place for a body around here?"

The taxi driver went another shade of pale. "I'm not dumping anyone. I don't want to be mixed up in this." He stood up straight and walked past Yuri to the door. "You can forget the one-way fare," he said as he went out the door.

Yuri watched him go and then turned to me. "OK, it's just you and me, Mr. Moto. Grab your end of the rug. We'll dump him in one of the machine shops and then figure out what's next."

"I didn't shoot him," I said. "He's not my problem."

"He's not my problem either. He shot himself. But having to explain a corpse will be a complication I don't need. Do you?"

"No, not really." I picked up one end of the rug, Yuri picked up the other, and we marched out of the house to the closest factory building, which from the looks of it was built into the side of a small hill. We passed two guards along the way. They watched as we went by, lugging the rolled-up rug with the bulge in the middle, but neither of them said anything.

"This is the calibration shop," Yuri announced when we reached the doorway. He set his end down and fished in his pocket, finally producing a key ring with five or six odd-shaped, variously colored keys on it. "One of these fits."

It better, I said to myself. The second guard we passed had turned around and was coming back our way. "Get a move on or we'll have to deal with that guard, who has just unbuttoned his holster."

"Never mind him," Yuri said. "Just look unconcerned. Let me do the talking."

The guard stopped about a meter away and surveyed the scene. He looked at Yuri, at me, at the rug, and then back at Yuri. "What's the deal? You have authorization to go in there?"

"The boss wanted us to put this mock-up in the freezer."

The guard looked puzzled. "There's a freezer in there?"

Yuri pulled a cigarette from his shirt pocket, struck a match against the doorjamb, and then blew it out. "Almost forgot," he said. "No smoking in the facilities."

"Yeah," said the guard. "No smoking. And no bringing in food from the outside either. I heard the machinery is sensitive to breadcrumbs."

Yuri started to toss the cigarette away, but then stopped and offered it to the guard. "Here, it's Turkish. Very mild. Be my guest."

The guard hesitated for a moment. "You're the butler, aren't you? But who is this guy? Why doesn't he have a pass to be out here in the shops? This is a special zone. He needs a blue badge. I don't see one."

This was the sort of question that usually deteriorates into the sort of confrontation that the training manuals told us over and over to avoid. I started to say something, but Yuri interrupted. "Never mind that." He drew himself up to his full height, which was impressive enough under the circumstances. "This gentleman is with me. I am following the orders of the boss. And you? You are who? A guard? And you are guarding what? If I tell the boss that you got in our way, he will say you are a burro, and he will kick your ass something good. So get moving."

The guard looked annoyed, and then confused, and then very uncomfortable. "Just checking, that's all." He motioned toward the door. "Use the green one on your key chain. One turn left, one turn right. Once it clicks, you turn it gently a little more to the right. The lock needs oiling or something, so don't turn the key too hard or you'll break it."

Yuri nodded, selected the green key, and gently turned it until the lock gave way. "Very good," he said. Ignoring the guard, he nodded to me while he nudged the door open with his foot. "Pick up your end, and let's get this where it belongs. We'll find some graphite for that lock later. There must be some around here somewhere."

"Can I help?" The guard reached for the carpet. "It looks heavy."

"Leave it be! It's heavy and it's very, very intricate. Lots of little pieces. If you pick it up the wrong way and shake something loose, the boss will break your neck. Just get the hell back to doing whatever you get paid to do." Yuri waited until we heard the guard mutter a Spanish curse under his breath and walk away. "A genuine мудак." He shook his head. "Well, let's get this thing stowed away and then we'll have a little chat. I need to know who you are, more exactly. In fact, very exactly."

We hauled the body into a dark, narrow factory shop, maybe four meters wide and twenty or twenty-five meters long. The place had a peculiar odor, very unpleasant. There were small emergency lights along one of the walls every two meters or so. They must have been on a motion sensor, because the row of them blinked on a fraction of a second after we entered and then off again. Yuri found a switch that turned on three overhead bulbs in glass fixtures, each filled with dead bugs. The bulbs were low wattage and gave just enough light to cast shadows into the darkness. The ceiling was low, half rounded. I've never been crazy about confined spaces, and I couldn't imagine working in a place like this.

"Odd place," I said, dropping my end of the carpet.

"By design." Yuri dragged the carpet to the base of one of the machines. "It's supposed to replicate an underground factory so they can test how the machines stand up to humidity, how they function sitting so close to one another, vibrations, noise, that sort of thing."

"You know all of this?"

Yuri shrugged. "A good butler knows lots of things."

"Undoubtedly. Like where to hide the body of his employer."

"You have a deeply suspicious mind," he said. "What if I told you I am not a butler?"

"What if I told you I was the man in the moon?"

Yuri held up his hand. "Shhh." He took a rather large pistol out of his pocket and motioned for me to get down on the floor. There was a good chance he would shoot me in the head as I lay there, but the odds weren't much better if I rushed him. On the other hand, if I rushed him he would certainly shoot me and tell the guards I had attacked. If I stayed on the floor, however, there was at least some chance he had something else in mind. All of this went through my brain, but it wouldn't have made any difference if I'd decided differently because by the time I finished the thought, I was already on the concrete floor, once again cursing Luis. It was a bad way to go, I thought to myself. After all of these years of life, now I was in the dark, in a city I had no wish to visit, on a continent that was not mine. Mournful thoughts about bookcases I'd left behind filled my mind such that I didn't feel it the first time Yuri nudged my elbow with his foot. The second time he was more emphatic.

"Roll over behind that machine," he hissed. "Do it now." He disappeared in the half-light. At that moment I heard a key in the lock and then the sound of metal snapping. From outside, there was a muffled shout.

Yuri appeared again, smiling. "That's one for us. The guard snapped the key. They won't be able to get someone to drill the lock until tomorrow morning."

"Perfect," I said. "We sit here in the dark and cold with a corpse rolled up in the carpet and then what? Yawn and stroll out like a band of monkeys when they open the door again? We're trapped. Who the hell are you, anyway?"

"I didn't think you'd be one to give up so easily, Inspector." He watched me closely. "You see, I already know who you are. I'm just not convinced you're here for the reason I was told to expect you. And you were getting to be trouble. Too many people around here were getting suspicious, and we wouldn't have wanted them to put the final pieces of the puzzle together, would we? It would have blown the whole operation. Luckily the Spaniard fell on his own pistol. It saved me from having to do it."

No one had told me somebody was already on the inside. Of course, no one had told me very much at all. This Russian might be an ally. He might be a snake. It could be fatal to agree with him too quickly. "First of all, I don't know what you're talking about." I stood up and brushed off my clothes. "I'm here on business."

Yuri leaned against one of the machines. "Yeah, I suppose you could put it that way. Look, we're on the same side. I'm here to figure out how to slip something small but very destructive into one of the dumpling machines. That won't be easy now." He pointed at the bundle of carpet. "Or actually maybe it will be easier. With the boss disappeared, the third in command will take over."

"What about the second in command? The man with the gray suit?"

"He'll be in the hospital for a while. The guard and I had a serious talk with him when he insisted on leaving his office."

"What makes you think he won't tell the police what happened?"

"He's not saying anything to anybody for a while, not until they teach him to talk again through a hole in his throat." Yuri began pressing his hands against the ceiling at intervals. "Ah," he said at last, "here it is." He jiggled a ceiling panel loose, took it down, and unlatched a trapdoor. "Perfect," he said, and lifted himself into the space.

"You going to leave me here?" I crawled over to see what he was doing.

"No, it's where I left some things I figured I'd need." He pulled a small bag down and unzipped it. From there he pulled out another pistol, two blocks of what I assumed was a type of explosive, a couple of fuses, a small box of ammunition, and a flashlight. "Planning." He grinned at me.

"Things *you'll* need. What about me? Naturally there is nothing to eat," I said.

"We'll eat when we get out of here. Meanwhile, hold this flashlight on the door lock and be quiet for a couple of minutes. I have to think."

"I don't know who you are, and I don't take orders from you. Hold the flashlight yourself."

Yuri shook his head. "No, I don't think so. I think you're going to hold it because we need to cooperate for at least a couple of hours if both of us are going to get out of here in one piece. They will kill us both and chop us up for seafood chowder if they can. They do not play by any rules in this place except their own."

"And what would those be?"

"You already had a taste of them when you first got here." On reflection, I was glad I hadn't tried the soup. Yuri continued, "They are engaged in a dangerous business, high risk, high reward. They don't want anything to spoil it."

I looked down at the carpet, which had unrolled slightly to reveal an arm. "Does that count as spoiling it?"

"Only for him, and he was expendable."

"At your hands?"

"No, that wasn't part of my assignment. It doesn't help at all that he's dead, of course, but they won't worry about it too much."

"They, who is they?"

"I thought that was why you were here. To pull on that thread."

"Let's just say that this is not a well-briefed operation."

"Portuguese?"

"Never mind whose." Actually, I didn't know whose this operation was. Poor Luis—momentarily I sympathized with him—didn't know either. The fact that the conversation on the bench beneath the castle walls took place in Lisbon, I was suddenly convinced, was an accident of geography. They, whoever they were, needed to do it someplace close to Spain, and it had to be where Spanish intelligence felt comfortable.

"And never mind what I was supposed to do," I said. What I was supposed to do was something that had been left unspoken. Unspoken was good for operational security, but not so good for operational effectiveness. Dropping into the middle of something without knowing why I was there, what I was supposed to accomplish, and most important, how I was supposed to extricate myself—none of this was the normal way I had been trained to do business. I was used to darkness and fog, but this was already over the limit. It exceeded normal "need to know" requirements. As far as I could tell, what I lacked in terms of detail belonged in the "vital to know" column.

"Then what good are you?" Yuri mused over the question. "It turns out you're just an anchor, and I don't like to drag anchors."

"Listen," I said, "you want to get out of here. You won't be able to do it without me. They think I'm here to finalize a very big contract. They won't touch a hair on my head until they realize that's not true."

Yuri shook his head. "No good. They already know that." He nudged the rolled-up carpet with his foot. "He already knew that."

"Maybe so, but who is he going to tell? And you said you've taken care of the man in the gray suit. Who is he?"

"His name is Perez. He only got here a few months ago. I think the organization wanted to tighten things up here, and Perez was supposed to see that was done."

In other words, Perez almost certainly knew from the start I wasn't who I said I was. Big hole in the planning by Luis's friends.

"OK," I said, "so at this point all we have to do is get past the guards, who are, you will pardon me, a group of stupid Slavs."

"I wouldn't underestimate them."

"Or you, apparently. Are we working together or aren't we?"

"I have my doubts all of a sudden. What do you think?"

I do not like it when people answer a question with a question. It means they have something to hide, or are at least acting like an octopus and squirting ink to cover their escape. Luis would tell me octopus sautéed with olive oil and a bit of garlic is delicious. I was in no mood for recipes. I was also in no mood to think charitable thoughts about Luis.

"All right," I said, "for the sake of argument, let's suppose for the moment we are working together. What are we doing? I can't help it if I don't know what is going on." Exposing ignorance is always a good tactic; it makes the enemy think he has the advantage. In this case, I had to admit, I *was* ignorant and he *did* have the advantage.

"These"—Yuri pointed to three tarp-covered wooden crates— "are the sections to a new model of a flow-forming machine."

"I'm greatly impressed," I said. "Would you care to squeeze out a little more in the way of explanation? I am supposed to be the moneyman, not a technical type. It never hurts if I know what I'm paying for."

"They didn't tell you? Flow-forming machines are crucial in making centrifuges. With one of these machines, every year you can make a thousand cylinders."

"And? So what?"

"The cylinders that are the basic building blocks for centrifuges." Yuri paused. "Before you ask, we're talking about a capacity to produce a lot of highly enriched uranium."

"Not dumplings?"

Yuri gave me a quizzical look. "I don't think so."

"Why?"

"Why what?"

"Why centrifuges?"

Yuri's neck muscles tightened slightly. He was suddenly very suspicious. "They spin, they spin really fast, and if you want to make nuclear bombs, that's good. The more centrifuges you have, the more bomb fuel you can make."

"And the more bomb fuel you have . . ."

". . . the more bombs you can make."

At that moment, most of what I needed to know clicked into place. That's why people far above Luis wanted me in the middle of this. They thought the so-called dumpling machine was meant for North Korea. The factory pretended not to know, though the man at the oak table seemed to have a pretty good idea of where the machine was going. Maybe others did, too, despite the smoke and mirrors meant to hide the actual buyer. Transportation, obviously, was key. You could hide a lot through paperwork, but sooner or later, you had to deliver. The transport route had to be closely held. Everyone involved was suspicious of everyone else because someone's intelligence service—Luis and his friends on the bench beneath the castle walls were only foot soldiers—had partially penetrated the network involved, and they had made some efforts to sabotage the factory. That's why the factory's special section had been created, with highly paid technicians who were kept isolated from the rest of the workers. I had probably been recruited because someone had concluded I could get into the factory and slip past the elaborate security once I had convinced the management that I was the new representative sent by the buyer to finalize the deal.

One big problem—no one warned me about Yuri. I ought to have known someone was working on the inside. He knew about me, why didn't I know about him? It struck me that Yuri didn't seem to have all the pieces to the puzzle either. He knew what these machines were, but he didn't know for sure where they were going or how they would get there. And despite what he said, it wasn't clear whether he was sure his job was to send them on their way or prevent them from moving. The death of José, if that was his name, was an accident, so that didn't lead me anywhere. The fact that Yuri was working undercover, disguised as a bumbling butler, could put him in either column—move the machine, in which case we were working against each other, or stop it, in which case we were on the same side. The key piece of evidence was going to be whether he killed me, in which case I would be ill placed to act on my knowledge.

In effect, Yuri had the same problem that I did. He wasn't absolutely sure whether I was here to finish the deal or disrupt it. Someone had alerted him that I was arriving, but that someone didn't seem to know the details. It could have come from someone at the hotel in Lisbon who had seen the call to the factory listed on my bill. It could have come from the Spanish couple in the room next door once they got out of the tub. It could have come from someone in Luis's group. Or, and this would definitely not be good, Yuri could have learned from Perez. There were a lot of people who didn't seem to trust each other on this peninsula. Maybe there was something about having the ocean on three sides that made people suspicious.

I wasn't sure about Yuri, and he wasn't sure about me. That would have made it a standoff, except he had a gun—two guns, actually—and I had none. He was also taller, heavier, in better shape, and younger than I was. He could move faster, see better, and had probably been trained in killing arts I preferred not to dwell on. But all of this meant I had one advantage. He thought I was not a threat. I was a mouse; he was the cat. He could bat me around in his paws, toy with me, watch me try to run and pull me back until, when he finally tired of the game, finish me off—if that was what he wanted to do. Only I was smarter than he was—I had to believe that—and I had instincts he couldn't even imagine as long as he thought I was a mouse.

"But the contract only calls for one of these machines," I said. "There are three of them." I pointed at the crates.

Again Yuri looked at me quizzically. "No, this is one machine.

It's been specially engineered to be shipped in three sections for easier handling."

I realized my mistake. I should have guessed that. The best way to compensate for a fatal error is to laugh, which I did. "Yes, easier handling and in smaller separate shipments, which will be easier to get through customs. But I was told the disassembly would take place in my presence, so I could double-check. That's what has me confused."

"You're an engineer? Funny, I didn't have that impression. You just said you were only the moneyman." Yuri's Slav eyes narrowed, so he looked more like a wolf than an undercover butler. He pulled his main pistol from his belt. "I wasn't sure where you stood, but I think I figured you out."

"And what would that be?"

"You're here to interfere with this shipment."

"And you're not? You just told me you were supposed to slip something small into the machine to keep it from working. Well, there's the machine. Why don't you do your job?"

The barrel of the pistol described a small circle. "Because I don't have what I need with me. It's in the butler's pantry. I didn't think I'd get into this area so soon. I needed to find out a few things first. So yes, I'm here to make sure it doesn't work, but for different reasons than you."

"What makes you think you know my reasons?"

"Because you are Japanese."

This annoyed me, and so I clenched my fists at my side. Yuri stepped back, apparently alarmed, or perhaps to get a better shot, and struck his head on the open hatch door to the ceiling. It must have been made of steel, or maybe the back of his head was unusually soft, because he staggered, his eyes rolled back, and he collapsed to the floor.

"I am not Japanese," I said as I knelt and removed the big pistol from his hand, and then the smaller pistol from his belt. "And you think so at your peril." I rolled him partway over to get at the keys hanging from the other side of his belt. "I think it was the green one. One turn left, one turn right." I stood to go but then remembered the box of ammunition. I do not like carrying boxes, so emptied it into my jacket pocket. For a moment I thought of taking the explosives, but figured that would be overkill, especially if they went off in my pocket. Instinctively I pulled the ID from the chain around Yuri's neck. If it had to be read by a machine, no doubt it would sound an alarm, but if I merely had to wave it, the chances were good it would be enough. Guards are supposed to check passes. They rarely do, not carefully anyway, especially near the end of their shift.

Before leaving, I decided I needed to look at the dumpling machine. I lifted the covers on each of the three sections. The center section seemed to be the most important, but I had no way of knowing for sure. There was a thick notebook hanging from a hook attached to the end of the right section. It might have been an instruction manual, but I didn't have time to read anything complicated. I flipped through and in a flap attached to the last page found what looked like a shipping document. I folded it and put it in my pocket. I replaced the covers, extinguished the lights, and turned the key, hoping the interior lock would not have been jammed by the broken one on the outside. It wasn't.

"Adios," I said, and let myself out the door.

3

Good to his word, once I strolled out of the gates past the guards, waving Yuri's pass to the desired effect, the taxi driver stood behind a tree smoking a cigarette. "I wondered if you would get out," was all he said.

"Very kind," I said. "Your steed is nearby?" I patted the tree. "Oak." I looked up at its thick boughs. "Very ugly."

The driver flicked the end off the cigarette and put the butt in his shirt pocket. "Parked beyond those trees. You hungry? We could stop for dinner. Or do you need to get back to the airport right away?"

"Actually, I don't since I don't have a ticket. I also don't have a hotel. You know of one that might still have room at this hour? Something out of the way, off the normal track so to speak."

"So to speak," he said. He drove for about a kilometer without any lights along a dirt road. "The cameras at the gate won't have spotted this car, and they won't have seen me either. All they'll know is that you disappeared behind some big trees. They'll look there, find tire tracks and try to follow them when it's light enough to see at dawn."

"And what will they see?"

"Different people will see different things. The federales from Madrid will see one thing, the locals will see something different."

"Who will carry the day?"

He laughed. "No one. They'll argue until noon, when they'll break for lunch. Besides, these tires don't belong on this model car."

At this point, there seemed a pretty obvious hole in the operation's planning, and it looked like someone was going to fall through it—namely me—if I didn't point it out. "What about a lookout at the airport? They'll have a watch on for me, won't they?"

"Perhaps."

"Maybe that's good enough for your sleepy culture, but I need precision, in fact, a lot more precision, on something like this. 'Perhaps' doesn't work."

"They'll circulate your picture from the surveillance cameras in the building, no doubt. They'll see an elderly Japanese gentleman. Can you look less Japanese?"

"I hope so. How should I look?"

"Have you ever thought of having white hair, cut short, bristly, like a kung-fu instructor?"

"I haven't." It hadn't occurred to me, but it obviously already had to them. This was the first reassuring sign I'd seen. It's one thing to have an operation mapped out in advance, it's another to have exits prepared along the way in case something goes wrong. And something always goes wrong.

"Well, think about it. There's a kung fu delegation in town putting on a demonstration. We'll say you have to leave early to make preparations for the next stop, in Portugal."

"Two questions."

"I'm listening."

"Why are you so helpful all of a sudden? I thought you were going to be sick after you saw that body in the dining room. You left in the hurry. Now you're fine."

"What's the second question?"

"How come you know so much?"

"This is not a simple operation, Inspector. It's been years in the planning."

So there was some planning to this thing after all. Years? So far it didn't seem that intricate. If there were layers to it, they only wanted me skating on the surface, which was not a good place to be. "Did you know Yuri?"

"Who?"

"The Russian butler who was in the dining room. OK, maybe not really a butler. But I take it you know Luis." The driver must have known who I was from the beginning, when he first picked me up at the airport. He drove a taxi, but he wasn't really a driver. The fact that he hadn't left the cigarette butt on the ground meant he wasn't just fussy about litter.

"I don't know anyone." He looked in the rearview mirror. "I don't know you."

"You never had an uncle either, I take it."

"I did, but he died ten years ago."

"From his injuries at the factory? And you, you worked at the factory? Or was that just a story?"

"I did, actually, but not for very long."

"But long enough to know the layout." I sat back. "You have a place already picked out for me to stay, I'm guessing."

"It wasn't part of the plan, but we adjust when we have to."

4

The next morning, when I climbed into a taxi, a different one from the night before, I had white bristly hair, a canvas carry-on bag with the logo of a Korean kung fu federation, and a plane ticket to Lisbon purchased by the Barcelona Sports Exhibition Alliance. The driver, different than the one I'd had before and not the least interested in his passenger, didn't even bother with a word of greeting. As soon as the rear door shut, we pulled away from the curb and drove in silence for the next forty minutes. At the airport, the taxi stopped long enough for me to get out and then was gone.

No one looked twice as I went through security. There were no old ladies seated in the waiting area, and no women with tight skirts either. As far as I was concerned, that meant I was being watched from somewhere else. I did a couple of kung fu moves that I remembered from years ago, bought a bottle of water, and spent the time looking out the window, waiting for the Spanish police to ask me to come with them, if that was going to happen.

5

At the bottom of the ramp at Lisbon Airport, Luis waited with two other men. They had pasted-on bored looks around their mouths, but their eyes were alert and worried. Luis nodded slightly when he saw me, no sign of surprise at my white hair. The three of them formed a triangle around me, and we moved smoothly through the terminal and out the door to the curb, where a small blue car with bald tires waited. Luis held the rear door open and indicated I should get in. Up till then, no one had said a word.

"No one asked if I needed the restroom," I said.

"Not interested," Luis said. "Get in before you get shoved in."

One of his tight-lipped friends climbed in the front passenger's seat. The other one stood next to Luis, scanning the scene.

"OK." Luis slammed the door and tapped on the roof of the car. "See you around, my friend."

There was a click as the driver locked the doors from his control, and we moved into traffic, out of the airport onto one highway, then onto another that passed through open countryside. No one volunteered anything from the front seat, and I decided they probably didn't know very much anyway. Whatever was going to happen would wait until we got to wherever we were going. Agonizing over a future no more than an hour or two away wasn't worth the trouble. The sky broadened as the road turned toward the ocean, climbed a steep hill, wound through a tiny settlement of several worn houses and what looked like a small restaurant with a few tables out in front, and then into an open field. The driver stopped, got out, and opened my door. The other man rolled down his window and lit a cigarette.

"End of the line," the driver said.

Behind him I could see the land fall away. From the sound of it, waves were crashing on rocks below. There was no one else in sight.

"Nice place," I said.

The driver walked me to the edge of the cliff. "See that?" He pointed to a spit of land off to our left. "You know what it is?"

"I have no idea." The breeze had picked up, and I was suddenly very hungry. "I don't suppose there's a place to eat. There was a restaurant back there. Why don't I buy you some lunch?"

"This is Cabo da Roca. Right over there"—he pointed—"is the farthest point west in Europe. You could swim from here to New Jersey." He grinned.

I took a small step away from the edge, nothing too obvious, but enough to give me a margin for error. "Very impressive," I said. "But first, why not get lunch? We can swim later." I took another small step back.

A big car drove up. Luis emerged from the passenger side in front. He moved quickly to open the rear door, then stepped aside. A tall man in a white suit got out and looked around. The wind played with his hair for a moment before he ducked back into the car to retrieve a hat. He nodded at Luis, who pointed at me. The man smiled. "Inspector," he said. "I am glad to see you."

"We haven't met," I said. "But I'm sure the pleasure is supposed to be mine."

The tall man turned again to Luis. "You'll excuse us for a moment? The Inspector and I have a thing or two to discuss. We'll walk along the cliff. You"—he pointed to Luis, then to my driver who had been standing off to the side—"and you, leave us alone for about fifteen minutes."

When the two of us had walked about twenty meters without speaking, at a point where a sheer cliff and the Atlantic seemed to be locked in a constant battle, the man stopped. He looked past me, out toward the ocean, facing into the wind. "Your stay in Spain," he said, "it went well?" His English was heavily accented. It had a Russian tread to it, though nothing else about him struck me as Russian. Maybe he was German, originally from the east.

"We still haven't been introduced," I said. "I don't know who you are, why you brought me here, and what you think I'm going to do tomorrow, other than get on the next flight home."

"Home," the man said. "Where would that be, Inspector? A mountaintop? Do you think you are Zarathustra?"

"People have been cute with me about that already," I said. "You want me to recite the opening line in German? I can, you know. *Wenn ich*—"

"Never mind that. How about the little house in Yanji with your nephew, the illegitimate son of your despised brother?"

"Big deal," I said nonchalantly, though I felt my stomach tighten. "Someone handed you a file. You skimmed it. Does it have pictures? I would love to see them."

The man shook his head. "No filthy pictures, Inspector. You live like a monk, it seems, or most of the time, anyway. That's not the point, is it?"

"Go on."

"The point is, your stay in Spain didn't go well at all. I've seen the reports. You did only part of the job you were sent in to do.

That is a disappointment. It also puts you in a bad place. You know enough to be a problem, but you haven't done enough to be paid."

"Paid?" I was only a few hours back from Spain, and the man had already seen reports? Either it was a much better network than it appeared, or the man was lying through his teeth. "I get paid?"

"In a manner of speaking."

"You wouldn't happen to know Yuri, would you? Sure you would! He's your boy, isn't he? Did he send you a report?"

"Very funny, Inspector. Yuri is dead. That's not good. It's not good for you. And it's not good for us. Yuri was inside, very well placed. It took a lot of doing."

"I hate to tell you, but your Yuri may not have been as much on your leash as you seem to think."

The man rubbed his chin. "And what makes you think that?"

"Just a hunch. He kept going out of focus, if you know what I mean."

"I guess I don't know what you mean. What I do know is that you seem to have screwed things up, exposed him somehow, maybe trashed the whole operation."

I was standing on the very edge of the cliff, my back to the ocean and also the wind, which was picking up. In front of me, off in the distance the sky was still brightly lit, but black clouds were rolling overhead and piling up inland.

"No," I said. "I didn't expose Yuri, and I didn't kill him if that's what you're about to say." I decided to leave out the part where he bumped his head and I took his keys. "He was in good shape when I left him. In fact, we had worked out an agreement. He wasn't sure of me, and I wasn't sure of him, so we compromised."

"Compromise. Not always smart."

"In this case, it was." I didn't like standing so close to the edge of the cliff. It made my ankles twitch. "We agreed he would remain behind and continue to watch things in the factory. I would get out and report what I had seen. Of course, I haven't had time to write a report. Do I send it to you after I have a chance to do that, or just leave it under a rock?"

The tall man shook his head and motioned to his driver to bring the car. He got in just as the rain started. "Someone will pick you up and drive you back to your hotel, Inspector. Think about things while you're waiting, will you? The wind doesn't play around out here. Neither do I."

The other car started and fell in behind the white one. The two of them bounced across the field onto the road and roared off. Being left alone on the far edge of Europe wasn't much of a plan. It was storming too hard to stand around thinking. I spotted a building about half a kilometer away, on the far edge of the field, and with no thought other than to get out of the rain, I set off for that.

Chapter Six

It's near the beach." That was all the driver would say when I asked where we were going.

The ocean was on our right once we got down from the hills, so I figured we were heading south. The rain had let up a little by the time we got to a town. As we slowed at a roundabout, I caught a glimpse of a long beach with a line of orange umbrellas, but the place was deserted. No one likes the ocean on a rainy day.

"Gloomy," I said to the driver. He looked at me in the mirror, then back at the road. A few minutes later he turned onto a street lined with tall trees, swung through a short alley, and stopped under a covered entrance of a hotel. An elderly porter held the front door open. He glanced at me, and then quickly turned away. The place was fancy enough so at the front desk they pretended not to notice that I was soaking wet and had no luggage. The clerk silently handed me a room key, and a woman in a pale yellow blouse and tan pants walked in front of me up half a flight of stairs and down the hall to my room. As I put the key in the lock, she reached down and retrieved an envelope that was partially under the door.

"Have a pleasant stay, senhor," she said as she handed me the envelope. "Breakfast is downstairs at seven A.M. The bar is open until midnight. The weather is supposed to clear by tomorrow afternoon, but until then I'd stay off the balcony if I were you."

I opened the door and looked inside. The room had a high ceiling with tall windows offering a view of a fashionable group of palm trees that looked as if they were vacationing together. The bed was huge; the furniture had been picked to look expensive. The walls were hung with watercolors of country scenes. It didn't feel like the places where I normally stayed.

The woman looked me over. "You might want to take off those wet clothes. There's a bathrobe in the closet. If you call housekeeping, they'll pick up your shirt and trousers to dry them. If you want the pants pressed, they can do that, too." She pointed at my pants. "I think you might want to try that."

"That's fine," I said. Just before she turned to go, I held up the envelope. "You sure this is for me?"

"I'm sure I don't know who it's for."

"My wallet must have fallen out of my pants when I got out of the car," I said. "Otherwise I'd give you a tip."

She bowed slightly. "We are here to serve our guests, senhor, not to collect money. I'll tell the doorman to look for your wallet. Will there be anything else?"

"Just out of curiosity, are you from around here?"

"Press three-zero for housekeeping," she said, and after a few steps down the hall, disappeared into a doorway.

In the room, I stripped off my wet clothes, put on the bathrobe, and went to the glass door leading to the balcony. It was raining hard again. Down below, I could see that a few of the chairs by the pool had blown over in the wind. I called housekeeping, gave the girl at the door my clothes, and sat down on the bed. It was clear to me that whatever was in the envelope would only complicate my life. Whatever it was could wait until I took a nap, had some dinner, and found my way to the bar. They were unhappy with what happened in Spain, but so was I, and I didn't like being told it was my fault. José, or whatever his real name was, had been a dangerous character, like a spider with a smile drawn on its face. He wasn't in charge, though. Someone else was running whatever went on at the factory. Yuri had said it was nuclear. If he was right, and I had no reason to believe anything Yuri said, that might explain why no one would tell me what was going on. My guess was it was something else. And whatever it was, it was enough to get several noodle eaters killed half a world away.

2

The hotel dining room was dim and completely empty. The waiter told me that since it was off-season, the menu was restricted to pork cooked with little clams, or fish cooked with bits of pork. Both came with a choice of potatoes or some sort of squash. There might be a serving of grilled octopus left over from the meal the chef had made for the staff, the waiter said, but on checking it turned out there was none. I could have as much red wine as I liked, with olives and bread freshly baked in town. Dessert was up to the chef, who hadn't committed to anything yet so we would all be surprised, the waiter said, and chewed his lip for a moment. "The chef is from France," he said at last, and rolled his eyes.

I had the pork with little clams, half a bottle of wine, a small plate of olives, and two baskets of bread. I told the waiter I didn't need the surprise dessert. When it came time for the check, the waiter told me it was already taken care of.

"Did you find your wallet?" he asked as he cleared the table.

"No. You looked in the kitchen?"

"So that means no tip." He shrugged.

"I thought your purpose was to serve the hotel guests."

"That's what the bell staff likes to say. They are like snakes. Do you think I can live on what they pay me here?"

"Apparently not."

"That's why I have to hold down more than one job." He lowered his voice. "People tend to talk a lot at dinner."

I looked around. "I suppose they do. When they show up. You have other diners?"

"We get enough. A couple of times a year there are car rallies.

Sometimes there is a busload of tourists who stay here to gamble at the casino next door. You gamble?"

"I don't have my wallet."

"The better for you. Anyway, like I said, I listen and learn." He leaned over and pretended to straighten the tiny salt and pepper shakers. "Listen and learn, you know what I mean?"

"Good for you," I said as I pushed back my chair. "If you'll excuse me, I think I'll stroll around the hotel."

"The bar doesn't open for another hour. You could sit in the meeting room if you like. The couches in the lounge area aren't very comfortable. Mostly for looks, but that's a matter of taste."

The lounge area was dark, except for some flashes of lightning from a storm that didn't seem far off at sea. The door to the bar was locked. I decided to go back to my room. On my way to the stairs I passed a room with a glass door. I looked in and saw a long table, bookshelves covering all the walls, and a floor lamp that cast its light on a man sitting with a small notebook on the table in front of him. He was watching the door, and as soon as he saw me he motioned that I should come in.

"Sit down, Inspector," he said. "Shut the door behind you."

"Don't tell me," I said. "You found my wallet."

"Your wallet?" He looked puzzled. "No, I've been waiting for you. Didn't you read the note I left under your door?"

"Forgive me, but it slipped my mind." I took the envelope out of my coat pocket and tore it open. "You can understand, I'm sure. We've met, by the way?"

"In a manner of speaking. My name is Tomás." He bowed his head slightly and then looked at his watch. "We don't have much time. A car will be here to pick you up in an hour."

"An hour? I just arrived. I was looking forward to breakfast."

"Well, it can't be helped. Plans have changed. You have to go back to Barcelona."

I stood up. "No. I don't have to go anywhere. Where is Luis, by the way?"

"Luis is busy. We're all busy thanks to you and your sloppiness.

Sit down, Inspector. I'm not here to argue. You were told on the bench in Lisboa that you could choose not to take part in this, but you declined that offer. So you're in, up to your neck. And so is your nephew."

I took a step toward the door. It was amazing, beyond belief actually. These people didn't have the slightest idea how to run someone in an operation. They were constantly threatening, and when they weren't threatening they were being obscure. If they had studied anything about me, they'd know I didn't respond well to threats. Luis would have told them that if they'd bothered to ask.

"Let's leave my nephew out of this," I said. "As far as that goes, leave me out of it, too. If you think I've been sloppy up to now, you won't want to see what's coming."

Tomás laughed. Then he pulled a pistol from his coat and laid it on the table. "I am not aiming this at you, Inspector, because I like you. But I want you to see that it is present and available."

"I'm impressed," I said. Idiots! Who would point a pistol at someone whose help they wanted? Not only wanted but needed. It was becoming clear that for all their lolling and complaining and pretending to yawn, for some reason they needed me. "You always do this with people on your payroll?"

"The one thing I don't care is whether you are impressed, believe me. I tell you plain and simple, if you take another step out the door, I will shoot you in the back. The hotel staff will tidy up. They are very good at what they do. Your body will never be found. Actually, no one knows you are here. You never signed in. There are no other guests. Come to think of it, maybe neither of us is here. An illusion, perhaps?"

I edged nearer the door. "Maybe you have mistaken me for someone else, because you're right. I'm not here. I'm in my room." I had my hand on the door handle. I should have just followed my instinct and left. Instead, on the craziest of impulses, I turned and said, "Good night."

"Sit down, Inspector, I beg you, and make things easy for both of us. The hardest part is over. The next time you are in Barcelona, it will be much more pleasant, believe me. Much better than a bullet between the shoulder blades."

I thought it over. Tempting fate at the right moment was something I had done more than once in my life. But this wasn't the right moment. "All right." I returned to the table and sat down. "I don't believe a word you say, other than that you will shoot me in the back. Mr. Big said Yuri is dead. I don't care about Yuri, but if anything has happened to Luis, you will wish you had never dragged me into this crazy operation."

"Mr. Big?"

"The man who met me on the edge of the cliff."

"Oh, Vincente. He's tall, not big."

"He speaks like a Russian tank tread going over a kitten."

"He's not Russian."

"I didn't say he was. All I said was he sounded like one. He left me in the rain. I take it you don't like him either."

"You are jumping to conclusions, Inspector. Vincente and I work together."

"Lots of people work together. It doesn't mean they like each other. He seems more in charge than you, if you don't mind my saying."

Tomás smiled. "Believe what you wish. Just pay attention to what I am about to tell you. It is the only time you'll hear it. I don't know why it wasn't made clear to you before. Of course you're annoyed. How can you take part in an operation if you don't know what it is about? This isn't the first time we've had this sort of breakdown in communications. The results are not pleasant. I've been trying to remedy the problem."

"Good. Nice to hear. But you have a ways to go."

"Tell me, what do you know so far about the operation?"

I froze. Was this how they ran things in the West? "I have no idea who you are," I said. "No idea how you fit, or even whose side you are on, assuming there are sides to this thing. And you expect me to tell you what I know? Not likely. Let's try it the other way around. You tell me what you know about the operation. I'll decide if it fits with what I know. If we have a match, we can both relax."

The man who wanted me to call him Tomás looked at his watch again. "I don't give a damn who goes first, Inspector. But we are running out of time. I'll start if you like, it makes no difference. In some circumstances I might applaud your caution. Not now, it wastes the tiny opportunity we have. If we squeeze our options any more than they already are thanks to your bumbling, we'll likely never recover."

"My bumbling? First it's sloppiness, now it's bumbling. Everyone is moaning about my performance. Let's get things straight, you sent me on a mission with no information, no backup, no communications, not even a shred of an idea of left from right."

"May I remind you that you accepted?"

"I played along, all right? I needed a change of scenery. That's different. Now I've had enough." I stood up again.

"Sit down, for the love of God, Inspector."

I sat again. The more I thought about it, the angrier I got. Walking out would mean they had won, that they'd worn me to my limit. I wasn't going to give them that satisfaction.

"That's better. You're in, and you know it. You were selected because you have worked with British intelligence before."

"What?" I bolted out of my chair. "Who told you such a thing?"

"Sit down, will you! Twice, three times actually, you worked with them. Twice in Prague, once in your capital."

This time I decided not to sit. It was time to show that I didn't have to listen to everything they told me to do. Actually, it was past time for that. I paced around the table. "Did you pay for that information? I hope it was not very much, because it's wrong, completely wrong. I never worked for the British. Never, ever, and I'm not going to. They tried a recruitment once, in Prague. It didn't work."

The man picked up the pistol. "I said sit down, and I'm serious. Believe me, the file is thick, Inspector. I know all about Prague."

Thick? That was hard to believe. Where would they have collected so much information about me? I thought back to trips overseas. Prague, Helsinki, Budapest, Macau, Geneva. There would be wisps of scraps they might pick up from receipts here and there, but not much more.

"Don't spend time wondering how we collect what we collect. Believe or not, we are efficient, and everything has been checked, double-checked, and triple-checked. I wouldn't expect you to admit anything. Anyway, it's not important." He looked up and pointed the pistol in the general direction of my head. "For the last time, will you sit!"

"Not important to you, maybe. It is to me." I sat down in the chair closest to the door. I wanted to hear more about what they thought they knew about me. It would be laughable.

"Ah." Tomás tapped his forehead lightly with the pistol. "I see the problem. Notice, Inspector, I didn't say you worked *for* the British. I merely said you worked *with* them. That gave us an idea."

"Where does Luis come into this?" Luis had been the bait, the long line, the procurer. From what I had seen of him in Macau, he didn't seem to fit any one of those assignments. If I hadn't been his friend, and owed him a favor, he would have been the most inept recruiter I'd ever seen. I kicked myself. That's why they picked him. They knew enough about me to bet that I'd see through his story but come along anyway.

"Luis is a good man." Tomás looked at his watch and frowned. "He has small needs, understands the world as it is, and best of all, sits in Macau out of sight and mostly out of mind."

"He doesn't have an uncle in Harbin. He never did. It was a lame story. Incidentally, you might want to put the pistol back on the table. I don't like having a discussion when I have to watch a trigger finger."

Tomás shrugged and put the pistol down. "Yes, the uncle. Perhaps it was a lame story, but then again, we never thought it would have to hold up to much scrutiny. It only had to do what it had to do. Actually, to his credit, Luis didn't like it. He said you would never buy such a tale."

"I didn't."

Tomás smiled. "But he also said it wouldn't matter. These are only details. Like it or not, the fact is you went to Barcelona, and you got into a factory."

"No thanks to you that I got out again. I'm too old for those sorts of beatings. Besides which, I don't know anything about nuclear weapons. By the way"—I reached in my pocket for the page that I'd taken from the notebook hanging on the machine—"you might like this." I put it on the table. "Maybe it says something about building nuclear bombs."

"Nuclear bombs?" The man's tone was exceedingly casual; he sat back too casually, with every muscle in his face held to a mask of unconcern. "Why would I be interested in such a thing?" He didn't wait for me to answer. "And who told you that's what the machine was for?"

It was suddenly clear that I wasn't supposed to know what I knew. They had wanted me blindfolded, spun around, and then pushed toward the target. They figured I'd do what I had to do, that I was enough of a machine to go in the direction they pointed me without asking why. The game had suddenly become more interesting. Still irritating, slightly more dangerous, but much more interesting.

"Yuri and I became fast friends," I said.

"Yuri, eh? If I were you, I wouldn't believe anything Yuri said. Did he give you a crash course on making warheads?" He smiled, but I knew he didn't expect a smile in return. "Never mind. It's better for you if you don't know." He paused. "I take it you saw the dumpling machine." He looked quickly at the paper and then pushed it aside. "This is worthless."

"Maybe, maybe not. I saw something in three parts. Your boy Yuri said it was a flow-forming machine, and it was in a test facility, a tunnel built into a hillside. Something about humidity."

Tomás sat up. "What about humidity?"

"How should I know?"

Tomás picked up the pistol. It wasn't pointed at me this time, but it wasn't too far off either. "What else did Yuri say to you? The fool always talked too much, more than he listened. Did he mention where the dumpling machine was going?"

I weighed my words carefully. "Not much beyond what I just told you. I had the feeling he didn't know for sure, though he seemed to think he did, or wanted me to have that impression. Anyway, we were a little busy trying to figure out how to save our skins for a lot of discussion."

"You saved yours, obviously. Yuri didn't, from what I hear."

"Apparently not. The big man told me Yuri was dead. Hard to believe, tough guy like that." Either they didn't know exactly what had happened to him, or they didn't care. "If he's gone, what does that leave of your operation? It looks to me to be in pieces, a lot more than three."

"No, it's fine, Inspector. It's perfect if we look at it in the right light. Sometimes it's better to trim a tree than cut it down." Tomás smiled at me, and this time he waited for my reaction. "It's the sort of thing your grandfather might have said, don't you think?"

3

Before I could reply, there was a knock at the door to the library. Tomás looked at his watch, swung the pistol toward the door, and motioned for me to move to one side.

"Come in," he said.

"I'm going to open the door slowly." It was a woman's voice. I recognized it immediately as the bellhop's, the one who had led me to my room, only when she walked into the library she wasn't wearing a hotel uniform anymore. She had on something of brown linen, with broad shoulders and a wide white belt. She looked taller than I remembered until I realized she was wearing spike heels— tan with deep red on the toes. They made it look like she had dipped her shoes in a pool of blood.

"There's a car outside, waiting," she said, "for him." She didn't look in my direction, as if the word was more than sufficient to indicate whom she meant. "They're in a hurry. The motor is running. Our man is fidgeting in the rear seat, and I'd say he isn't too happy."

She talked as if she frequently entered rooms where people were pointing weapons at her. It was something about the way she stood; nothing aggressive, just self-assured.

Tomás grunted. "If he did a better job pulling things together, he might be happier. Tell him we'll be five more minutes."

"I'll tell him," she said, "but he won't like waiting. You of all people should know that by now." At last she acknowledged my presence. "See you in Barcelona, Inspector." She did a quick turn. "Like this better than the bellhop outfit?"

After she left, Tomás pocketed his pistol, smoothed his hair, and stood up. "Yes, you are going to Barcelona. So is she. See? I told you it would be more pleasant this time."

"We'll see," I said. What was she going for? To keep an eye on me? I didn't need a minder, and I don't like people tagging along. A little help might be nice, but it didn't immediately come to mind how she could do that.

"One word of caution. She's Vincente's girl."

"And so she shall remain. I'm too old for that sort of thing."

"Not from what it says in your file, Inspector."

"So the file does have pictures after all? I asked the big man already, but he said there were none."

"She's smarter than she looks. By which I mean, she's very smart." He looked sharply at me. "And very crucial to this whole effort. That's why she's part of it, and that's why she's traveling with you. Understand?"

I didn't, but he wasn't going to tell me any more, so I nodded.

"Oh, nearly forgot. I do have something of yours after all." He reached into his coat pocket. "Your wallet. You left it in the car from the airport." He threw it on the table.

I picked it up and quickly went through the contents. There was considerably more money in it than I recalled. Also, anything with identification on it—all of it false anyway—had been taken out and new pieces put in, nicely aged, all with a Japanese name, Tamada Hiroyuki.

"You were born in Kobe two months after the war ended."

Tomás didn't bother to refer to notes. "Your family moved there from Tokyo after the firebombings in 1945. All the records were lost in the inferno. Your father was in the Imperial Army, a communications specialist as it happens, and died on Okinawa. Your mother died of TB when you were three. No siblings. No relatives at all. Uncles and aunts were all killed in the war, either fighting abroad or minding their business at home. When you were fourteen, let's see, that would be 1959 or 1960, you fell in with a gang."

"I'm not chopping off a finger, not even my little one if that's what you're thinking. And, no, definitely not, I will not pretend to be Japanese."

"Don't worry, you're not pretending. Pretending is bad, it gets discovered. For the next few days, maybe a week, you *are* Japanese, top to bottom, inside out. And you get to keep your fingers." Tomás looked at his watch. "Time's up, we need to get rolling. Who was head of your gang family?"

"How should I know?"

"Good, exactly what we want you to say. You never learned his name. He was a shadowy figure who operated out of a restaurant in Osaka. There were rumors that he was Korean, but no one knew for sure."

"Don't tell me, it was a dumpling restaurant."

"Very good, Inspector." Tomás smiled broadly as he opened the door for me. "You can remember what I just told you? Nothing too complicated for Mr. Tamada."

"Do I have a passport? One of the details, you know."

"I thought you already had one of your own—phony, which is all the better. Keep using it. By now it has all the stamps you need to travel around, and you're comfortable explaining its oddities to any immigration officials who examine it more closely. Even the ones who aren't old classmates of Luis."

I frowned and shook my head.

"Now what is it?" Tomás was getting impatient. He looked at his watch for the third or fourth time.

"First of all, all you've done is dance around the main point.

What is this operation about? I got beat up pretty bad last time I was at the factory, so I get to ask that sort of thing."

"You know what it is about."

"It's one thing to know, it's another thing to get a briefing that lays out where I fit, how I fit, and why I fit."

"OK, that's first of all. What's second of all?"

"How many times do I have to tell you people that I don't like pretending to be Japanese? I can't do it anymore. I won't. We're not interchangeable toys for Westerners' convenience. We don't look alike. We don't think alike. We have different moral compasses. No. Forget it."

"Yes, well, you did fine a few days ago. Just stick with it a while longer. You can mentally hold your nose if you want. Sort of a self-loathing thing, eh? It might be very effective, given the circumstances."

I didn't have any idea what he meant by the circumstances. "Why Barcelona again?" I asked, though I already knew the answer. They wanted me back in the factory. The minor details of why and what I was supposed to do apparently were not mine to inquire about. To hell with that. I was going to find out, or I wasn't going to Barcelona.

Tomás indicated I should walk out the door ahead of him. "Why Barcelona again? That's someone else's job to explain on the way to the airport. I wish you good luck, Tamada-san." He pointed down the hall in one direction, waited a moment, and then walked the other way toward the bar.

4

The car was waiting out in front with the motor running. It was not the same car the man called Vincente had arrived in the first time I saw him, at the cliff. This car was smaller, also white but respectably dirty. I climbed in the back, as the doorman indicated I should. Vincente leaned over and shook my hand.

"Ah," he said, "Mr. Tamada, I presume."

Vincente's girl was driving. She looked in the mirror and smiled. "Off we go," she said. "The regular driver took sick while we were waiting for you. Something about his girlfriend's cooking, he said." She winked at me. "We made a quick switch."

Vincente leaned forward and patted her shoulder. "You drive," he said. "I'll explain things to Hiro. Can you do something about that perfume?"

"Too much?" She waved her hand in front of her face and laughed. "Vincente is nervous when I drive. He thinks it isn't lady-like."

"She takes turns too fast," Vincente said. "Especially when she's not paying attention."

"There's not much traffic. We'll be at the airport in under an hour." The woman turned onto the main road at a high rate of speed. "Hold on to your hats."

Vincente shook his head. "She was supposed to do the briefing, but she can't do both."

"Sure I can," the woman said.

"No, I'll do it. I may be a little rusty at this sort of thing, but since it's my operation, I know the details as well as anyone. You just concentrate on the road." He turned to me. "Tomás filled you in on part one. I'll give you part two."

"Tomás doesn't know part two?"

"No one knows part two, not all the details, anyway, except me, Rosalina, and, by the time we get to the airport, you."

I looked at the driver. It had a pretty ring to it, but Rosalina couldn't be her real name. Tomás hadn't made much clear, but he'd left no doubt that she and Vincente were more than colleagues. More than that, he'd underlined that she was crucial to the operation. In case Tomás hadn't already made that clear, now Vincente had confirmed it. The woman was going to Barcelona with me, but to do what? Maybe that was part three, if there was one. It was worth asking.

"Is there a part three?"

The big man laughed, a soft laugh, but it had something bitter on the edge of it, like it was kept too long in a dark place and had spoiled. "Rosalina—you recognize the name, Hiro?"

"Shakespeare," I said. "And don't call me Hiro."

The driver gave a tiny beep on the horn. "Score."

Vincente sat back. "My, my, I wouldn't have thought . . ."

"Could be *Romeo and Juliet* to be specific, but I read it a long time ago. Surprised?"

"No, I meant I didn't think you'd be so negative about a Japanese identity. We hoped you'd find it ironic. As for Shakespeare, Tomás no doubt mentioned that we know a lot about you. Actually, based on what we know, nothing about you would surprise me."

"Don't be too sure," I said. "Sometimes I surprise myself."

Rosalina tapped on the horn. "Score."

"All right, let's hear part two," I said. "After that, you can go on to parts three and four, if there is a part four. I assume you had to do some fast reshuffling to the plans now that Yuri is dead. Maybe part five?"

Vincente sat back and rolled down his window slightly. "Rosalina, why is the AC not working in this damned car?" He watched as she fiddled with the controls. "Never mind! Keep your eyes on the road." He rolled his window down the rest of the way and closed his eyes as the wind blew in over his face.

"He gets carsick, poor baby," Rosalina said. "Can you believe it?" She looked in the mirror. "Chew some gum or something."

The big man was silent for a couple of minutes. Then he took a deep breath and sat up again. "Let's just say that at this point Yuri was no longer going to be central to the operation. Eventually we would have had to get rid of him anyway. You were right, he wasn't totally on our side. He thought we didn't know it, and so he had convinced himself that he was using us."

"I take it he wasn't. I also take it he didn't know anything that could compromise things."

"You mean, pose a danger to you? Not likely."

"Not likely. Easy for you to say."

"As it happens, we could have used his bulk a little longer, given how things have developed, but we can make do without it. You'll just have to substitute wile for bulk. You can do that, I'm sure."

"Do that for what? First you tell me you had a double agent in your midst, then you dodge the question of whether I'm stepping into a trap, and now you want me to be wily. Before we get to the airport, I need clarification. Believe it or not, some people work better when they know what they're doing and why."

Vincente looked bored. "You are one of those?" He searched his pockets.

"I am. In fact, I don't get on a plane unless I do know what I'm doing and why. You may think I'm bluffing, but page fifty-six in your file will probably make clear that I don't bluff." Putting together what I'd heard from Yuri and then from Tomás, I already had a pretty good picture of the why, but I wanted to hear the details straight from Vincente.

Rosalina beeped the horn again. "Two to nothing so far, Vincente."

"Three," I said. "That's three."

"We'll take the why first. The what flows from that." He put a piece of gum in his mouth and chewed it furiously for a moment. "OK, don't ask questions until I'm done. It all fits like a Persian glove."

5

By the time we arrived at the airport, I knew a few more things than I did before. I knew what my mission was, more or less. I knew I had been right that someone didn't want the dumpling machine to reach its destination, and that I was the one who was supposed to stop it. But I also knew there were still a couple of key details they were keeping from me. They had kept Yuri in the dark, too. That hadn't turned out so well as far as I could see. Although maybe it had, if he had a foot in both camps, whatever the camps were. On reflection, it made sense that they were keeping a few things from me for the same reason—they couldn't be absolutely sure of my reliability, file or no file. That was their problem. Mine was staying alive. There were plenty of minor questions that occurred to me as well, but we were already approaching the passenger terminal.

When Rosalina pulled up to the curb, Vincente took a small piece of paper from his jacket pocket. "These are the numbers to call if you run into trouble. They all reach Rosalina. Memorize them and then get rid of the paper. It dissolves in your mouth; don't throw it away." He reached into his other pocket. "And here is the number of the bank account you give them if things reach the point where there is a final transaction. They know they're not going to get full payment until the merchandise reaches the buyer, but there's a thirty-seven percent down payment when it's shipped from the factory."

"Thirty-seven percent?"

"Odd number. They figure only someone in the deal would know it. You give them the account number, they transfer the funds, then you get out. The funds won't actually transfer, but their account will think they have. Some computer magic or something. That's not your concern. What you need to do, if you have the opportunity, is to put this chip in the machine." He handed over a tiny plastic bag, not as big as the tip of my thumb. "Put it somewhere you won't lose it and they won't find it if they search you."

"I can only think of a few places."

"Yeah, well, it's up to you. We thought Yuri might do it. Actually, it was a test to see where he stood."

"I suppose it's the same for me."

"Not really. If the machine is already broken down into several parts for shipping, you might not have a chance. In that case, the key becomes finding out the transport route. That's critical. We'll do the rest. Clear?"

"How do I find out the transport route? Why wouldn't we already know it?"

"Because they are very secretive bastards. You'll find out how secretive. That's why we picked you, because we knew you could do work in that atmosphere."

"Don't fuck with me."

The big man smiled. "There's a transportation specialist in the factory. We don't know his name, but we know he's there. He arrived only a day or two ago. Listen, if we knew everything already, we wouldn't be here right now, we'd be having a nice dinner. You have a reservation on the eight o'clock plane. All you have to do is show your passport at the checkpoint."

"My passport isn't Japanese. It isn't for someone named Tamada. It's my old one."

"Didn't Tomás tell you that's no problem? We made arrangements. Most important, it will help reinforce your story when you get to the factory. If all you had was a genuine passport, they would be suspicious. They'll be suspicious of a phony one as well, but less so. It's Costa Rican, right? Let me see it."

"Passports are headaches." I handed mine to Vincente. "Better to come ashore from a submarine. I did that once, but they make you wear black clothes. I don't look good in black."

Vincente raised his eyebrows. "Sorry to be so traditional, going such a mundane route. We didn't have a submarine handy. Don't worry, no one here in Portugal will look twice at yours." He flipped through it before handing it back to me. "It won't be a problem, not even going through security. There's a suitcase in the boot; you can check that at the ticket counter. They don't like passengers without luggage traveling on an evening flight. It rings bells in the system. Bells we don't need."

"Besides," Rosalina said, "you can use a change of clothes. I picked out a nice shirt and a blue tie. Nothing black. You'll like it."

"You sure I have a seat on this flight?"

Rosalina turned around. "We are sitting next to each other."

"Am I supposed to know you? Or is that part three?"

"Only casually." She turned and looked at herself in the mirror. "But who knows where things could go?"

Vincente grunted. "Good luck, Hiro. Bon voyage. Have a pleasant flight. Oh, here, something to remember us by." He handed me a tiny cloth bag with a drawstring. "For you. We'll be in touch."

The suitcase in the boot was an overnight bag, a Louis Vuitton that wasn't cheap, unless it was counterfeit. It wasn't heavy; in fact, I had a feeling it was almost empty. A shirt and a tie wouldn't weigh much.

"The plane isn't full," the woman at the ticket counter said. "You can take that bag on if you want. It will fit in the overhead. If you check it, it's liable to get beat up. Looks expensive."

"No, I'll check it. You mind?"

"Makes no difference to me." She looked at my face, then at my passport, then back at me. "Plane boards at eight fifteen. Security is that way. You'll have to hurry."

A few seconds after leaving the counter I looked back. She was already on the phone.

Chapter Seven

As she said she would be, Rosalina was seated next to me. I was in the window seat; she was on the aisle, which meant I had to climb over her. It was a short flight, so we didn't have much time to talk, and anyway I didn't think it was a good idea if we appeared to know each other. Vincente hadn't been specific on that, and Rosalina had only passed it off with a wink. I was getting used to their idea of what made for a good operation—leave most things vague and hope for the best. So far, there didn't seem much to recommend that approach.

"If you'd like to put your bag in the overhead before you climb into your seat, there's room up there." She pointed.

"Thank you. I checked my bag."

"Interesting," she said. "Most people carry their bags on, especially if they aren't very big." She paused. "Sometimes they disappear if they're checked."

"I see," I said. "You have a point. Unfortunately, it's too late now." If they had wanted me to carry it on, they should have told me. I smiled at Rosalina. "Excuse me, but I have to get to my seat."

"Going far?" Rosalina asked while we waited to take off. She was wearing sunglasses. I thought that might attract attention she wouldn't want, but it wasn't my operation so it wasn't my place to say anything. Maybe they were banking on the idea that if people focused on her, they would be less inclined to pay attention to me.

"Not far," I said. "Only as far as the plane is going. And you?"

"I love Barcelona." She was pretending not to listen. "Beautiful city, graceful people, good food, a nice breeze off the Mediterranean. Have you been there?"

I considered this. She knew I had been there, but we were just making up conversation. "Once or twice," I said. "Maybe we could have a cup of coffee in the city. Do you know a good coffee shop?"

She patted my hand. "That would be nice, but I'm afraid I'm terribly busy. I have to go to a conference."

"Oh? Something interesting, no doubt."

"Yes, it is. It's a conference on nuclear engineering. A lot of people from all over the world. Austrians, Poles, Japanese, Israelis, quite a mix. You're not a nuclear engineer by any chance, are you?"

"Me?" I noticed the man across the aisle leaning slightly in our direction. "No, I'm just a businessman, a buyer of trinkets."

"Trinkets?"

"Machinery, actually. That sort of thing."

"Well, you never know, we might run into each other on the street. The conference only lasts a day. Then I want to do some sight-seeing. Have you seen the Gaudí yet? If I were you, I'd stay away from the Gaudí."

"The what?"

"Gaudí. He was an architect. The Catalonians are crazy about him. I think he's a little overdone. I prefer things more subtle. How about you?"

"I do," I said. "I mean, maybe I'll have a glass of water."

2

After standing at the baggage carousel for twenty minutes, after all the bags from the plane had gone around the belt and been taken away, I went over to the baggage desk.

"My bag is missing."

"It happens. Describe it."

I realized I hadn't paid much attention to its appearance. "It's small, a carry-on."

"Looks like you should have carried it on. Make?"

"A Louis Vuitton, I think."

The man whistled. "You think. Must be nice, having expensive luggage and then forgetting what it looks like."

"I need it."

"Sure. Everyone does. Let me see your ticket and your passport."

"Why?"

"Because I need to fill out a form. The form goes to the baggage department. They run it through the computer. The computer coughs once if it recognizes the description."

"I have a baggage claim ticket. That should help."

"It should."

I handed it over. The man looked at it carefully. "We'll give you a call when we find it. Got a phone?"

"I do." Actually I didn't have one anymore, but someone walking around without a phone was sure to raise flags. "Unfortunately, my phone was in the bag."

He nodded. "Hotel? Or was that in the bag, too?"

"Never mind," I said. "When you find the bag, just set it aside. I'll pick it up when I come through the airport on my way home. It will only be a day or so." I figured I could do without Rosalina's shirt and tie for a couple of days. If there had been anything important in the bag, they would have told me. Or at least, in a normal operation they would have told me.

"Have it your way," he said.

3

The same burgundy taxi was waiting in the queue outside the entrance to the terminal at the Barcelona airport. Vincente had told me to take the same cab as before. He said that the taxi driver would take care of me again, but he hadn't gone beyond that. It was clear what he meant, so I didn't ask what or why.

Rosalina had left me as soon as we walked off the plane. She had squeezed my hand when we landed, but otherwise, there were no farewells, none of the "nice talking to you" chatter that ends a flight. I stopped to look into a couple of shops in the terminal so she could get ahead of me. Running into each other at the exit would mean having to exchange more pleasantries. At that point, I wasn't feeling pleasant.

In fact, I was feeling unpleasant because I was pretty sure this couldn't end well. It occurred to me to find a plane to China and go back to my nephew's, but I knew I couldn't. I'd never left in the middle of an operation, even a poorly planned one, and I wasn't going to start now. I reached into my pocket and found the tiny bag Vincente had given me. It contained a small piece of wood—beech, the sort of wood my grandfather insisted was loyal beyond imagination. "Beech doesn't waver," he'd told me. "Everyone might desert you, leave you naked in front of howling enemies, but beech will stand firm at your side. No one ever accused a beech of betrayal." He had clenched his jaw. "A turncoat can get you killed," he'd said. "Beech will save your life." When I asked why, if beech was so loyal, there were no beech trees around our village, he looked at me silently for a long moment, and then walked away.

I smoothed the little piece of wood with my fingers. If I ever put stock in omens, I might have done it now. But an omen was like a coincidence; it could only get you so far. Beech—maybe Vincente and his friends had done more research than I'd realized, or maybe it was all they could find. I put the wood back in my pocket. Since I didn't know who was on which side, it was going to be tough to figure out who was loyal to what. It wasn't my business, anyway. Somebody wanted a dumpling machine that made fuel for nuclear bombs not to get wherever it was going, and they thought I was just the fellow to stop it. No one had told me, but I had a pretty good idea where they thought it was going, and if I was right, it was starting to be clear what had happened to those unlucky diners in Yanji.

As I climbed in the back of the cab, the driver looked at his watch. "You got a bag? People don't usually travel without a bag."

"I had one, but they lost it."

"You checked it in Lisbon?"

"I did."

"Mistake," he said, and looked a little worried for a moment. "Nothing fatal, but it's probably being given a complete physical. They won't bother to put it together again either. You know what was in it?"

Funny question, unless he already knew I'd only received it at the last minute.

"Not really," I said. "Do we have a problem?"

"I don't. You might." He took out his phone and dialed a number. After an exchange of a few words in Spanish, he put the phone away. "The usual from Rosalina, just a shirt and a tie. Well, maybe that will keep them guessing." He smiled and looked a little relieved. "Actually, it might be good. They'll spend a lot of time worrying whether the bag was checked just to throw them off, or whether it got checked by mistake and there is something in it they ought to be able to find."

"I take it this is not just the baggage people you're talking about."

He nodded. "You remember the green van? The one parked nearby when you were first here?"

Connection points started lighting up. He knew Rosalina. He knew about my first trip here with Luis. This thing was better organized than it first appeared. Better organized, or maybe less secure.

"It's the same people," he said. "They're not sure of anything yet. What they most want is to get you on the rack."

"More training from your Inquisition?" I looked out the window at the crowd waiting for cabs. "Hadn't we better get moving?"

"You're early." The driver pointed to his watch. "I thought you'd be on the ten o'clock plane."

"Who told you that?" I don't like scheduling mistakes. They can end up being fatal—wrong place, wrong time.

The driver ignored the question. "We end up having some time to kill. I can take you downtown. Maybe we can find another bag. After that we'll walk around the Gaudí cathedral."

"Let's skip the church. Someone told me to avoid Gaudí."

"What? Who would say such a thing?" The driver started the engine, listened to it for a moment, then pulled into the airport traffic. "You can't understand the Catalonian mind if you don't see this church, my friend. And who knows, it might come in handy, understanding the Catalonian mind."

"Why, it's unique? No frontal lobe?"

"None at all." The driver turned off the main road onto a small street. He pulled over for a minute, then sped down the street. After two quick right turns he looked in the mirror and said, "All sacrificed in favor of the creative portions, with the remainder given over to pleasure and rebellion, in equal measure."

I looked behind. "Green van?"

"No, not green." He pushed a button on the steering wheel; a tiny red light flashed a couple of times. "Pleasure and rebellion," he said. "What would life be without them?"

"No room for discipline?"

"Ha! Just the sort of thing you'd ask," he said. "Believe me, once you see Gaudí, I'll have to drag you away."

During my first visit to Barcelona, with Luis, there hadn't been a chance to see much. The second time here had been no better. Now I had a couple of extra hours. Rosalina had warned me against going to see Gaudí, but she hadn't bothered to explain, and a little peek couldn't hurt, especially in the dark.

"All right," I said, "as long as we won't get off schedule." I hadn't told the driver where I needed to be, or when. Presumably he already knew, assuming they hadn't misinformed him on that as well.

"Stop worrying. Besides, you never know when you'll need a mental map of a place."

"How do we know the van people won't be with us?"

"That's my job. As of right now, they're arguing about who lost us. Listen, it's a nice evening, and as long as you're here there are a few places you ought to see."

He drove down quiet streets. The stores were all closed. "Mostly dark buildings," I said. "That should help with a mental map."

"Are all of your people so dour?"

"Not dour, just practical."

I thought of what my grandfather would say when I complained he was always negative. "Being positive doesn't get you across the river." He'd look up from the piece of wood he was measuring. "Being positive wastes time. Do you think birch trees spend their time running about with smiles on their faces? They do not, boy, and neither will you when you realize what life is about."

"Dour is Seville," the driver said. "Dour is the mind that ran the Inquisition. Dour was Tomás de Torquemada."

"Friend of yours?"

"Tomás de Torquemada? Not in this lifetime. He was the Grand Inquisitor, a monk if you can believe it."

"His name was Tomás?"

The driver turned around. "Not an uncommon name," he said slowly.

Thin ice, I thought. For some reason it was OK for him to mention Rosalina, but not Tomás. But it was clear the driver knew Tomás, or at least knew of him. That would make sense if he was more than just a local hire. I sat back to think. Looking at dark buildings wouldn't improve my mood. What I needed was a quiet place where I could lay out the holes in my knowledge about a few necessary facts—who did what, who knew whom, and where did I fit? The closer the time got to going back to the factory, the more I felt this was a deep hole, and it was going to be fatal to someone.

For one thing, I didn't want to stroll around in plain sight. "Won't it appear strange, the two of us together? An Asian and a

European walking around at night? Maybe if we were a couple of businessmen it wouldn't stand out, but you don't look like a businessman. Pardon me, but you look like a taxi driver. Why don't we just find somewhere to sit and relax?"

"Do you people worry about everything? Cheer up, we can have a bite to eat at a place I know. No one will give us a second glance. Then we'll get you up to the factory in plenty of time. You're supposed to be there just before midnight, right?"

The man knew something about the operation, at least the logistics; he knew Tomás, he knew Rosalina, he probably knew Vincente. The possibility began dancing at the edges of my sudden paranoia that he knew more than he was supposed to. It was even possible, I thought glumly, that like Yuri he was playing both sides of the street. Maybe that's what Rosalina meant when she warned I should avoid Gaudí.

"Yes, before midnight," I said. "Who picked that time? It's a lousy time of night to show up at that place."

"That's why we need to tire you out with a little sightseeing around here. You're supposed to look weary from travel."

"With this back and forth to Lisbon, I'm already tired. Don't I look it?"

The driver glanced at me. "No, you still look too fresh. When we're walking around, just pretend I'm your guide. Can you gawk like a tourist? Too bad you don't have a camera."

"Maybe we should buy an orange."

The driver grinned. "That's the spirit," he said.

He knew plenty.

4

Once we got downtown, we drove up and down some smaller streets with Chinese grocers in front of their stores smoking, a few taking the fruit in from the sidewalk displays; past a bakery with a few cakes still in the window; by apartment houses with ornate balco-

nies and orange awnings; past sidewalk cafés with old men sitting
under large umbrellas sipping coffee from small cups. The driver's
phone rang once and then stopped. A minute later he pulled into a
narrow, dark alley and parked. Dark alleys, dark buildings, dark
rooms with dark portraits—the clouds of gloom around me thick-
ened.

"This is good," he said. "We can walk from here to Gaudí's mas-
terpiece, and from there to Avinguda del Paral·lel to look around.
From there it's a short walk to the Jewish Quarter. It has tiny
streets that wind around. The place is rarely crowded, especially
this time of night. That's where the restaurant is. If there's time
after we eat, I'll take you to the Roman ruins. They look terrific in
the dark."

"The Romans were here? In Barcelona?" I asked to be polite. I
didn't care about the Romans. Europeans talked as if they were the
center of civilization. It was annoying. "What about the Mongols?
I don't suppose you know if they were here as well?"

"Never thought about it. Maybe a few horsemen, but as a group,
no. Why?"

"You might not understand. If I'm farther west than the Mongols got, that's something. I'm not so interested in the Romans."

"The Romans were everywhere, my friend. Have you looked at
a map of ancient times?"

"As a matter of fact, I've looked at plenty of maps. You Europeans give too much credit to the Romans. I once showed a map of
the Mongol conquests to a Swiss businessman. He was in Pyongyang looking at factories, but something about him wasn't right, so
I was supposed to keep an eye on him."

"Really? Swiss? What kind of factories?"

I didn't like the question. What happened in Pyongyang wasn't
his business. And I sure as hell wasn't going to tell them anything
that might add to the file they apparently were keeping on me.
"Dumplings," I said. "He was looking at dumpling factories."

"Sure, everybody goes to a dumpling factory in Pyongyang." He
laughed. "That's what I would want to see if I went there."

Rosalina would have tapped on the horn and given him a point. I decided he deserved it.

"So what did this Swiss businessman who was not quite right say about the Mongols that annoyed you?"

"He wasn't impressed, as I recall. All he said was that the Romans were better."

"And you disagreed."

"Listen, the Romans may have thought they conquered the world, but there was a lot of the world they never saw. Europe is not the center of the universe, not even close."

"OK." The taxi driver was surprisingly agreeable, nothing unctuous about it, just agreeable as if there was no reason not to agree, and disagreement would almost always be a waste of time. "That may be so. They may not have been everywhere, but they were here, and you can bet they enjoyed themselves."

"Did they get to Portugal?"

"*Dios mio!* Of course! Why, did Luis tell you they hadn't?"

Who said anything about Luis? For some reason that bothered me. Even if he knew about the green van, he didn't have to know Luis, or at least to know Luis by name. Surely they used different names for the operation. Rosalina wasn't the woman's real name. I doubted Vincente was the big man's real name. The last time I talked to the driver, when I'd asked him if he knew Luis, he had ignored me, as if he didn't know whom I was talking about.

I already knew for sure the man wasn't really a taxi driver, and that at least some of the story he'd told me when we first met was bogus. He was a more important part of Vincente's operation than I'd first thought, seemed to know more about it than I did, and now appeared to know more, or was willing to talk about it more openly, than seemed to me to be wise. It was one thing for Vincente to brief me. He was in charge. But this driver didn't necessarily know what I had learned, how much I was supposed to know, and how much had been withheld. That he openly admitted he knew Luis was only a single leaf on the tree, but it made me think the operation might be lashed together in ways that made it vulnerable.

That led to only one conclusion. If the operation was vulnerable, so was I.

I stopped to look in the window of a darkened candy shop. "Does anyone have lights around here? Very nice, very neat window display from what I can see. I wish they would be so tidy in China."

"What about Tokyo, that's full of neat and tidy stores, isn't it, Señor Tamada? And Kobe, they are neat there, as well?"

"Do all cab drivers in this city know the names and history of their fares?"

"No, but guides do. And since you contracted with me to give you a guided tour, I needed to know your name, which you graciously provided, and even something of your life—your hometown, for instance."

"In that case, no doubt you gave me some information about yourself."

"Very good. Please call me Salvador, Salvador Mercador. I am a licensed guide, having been born in a small town in Catalonia, its name will mean nothing to you, and graduated from the University of Barcelona with honors." He bowed slightly. "Here's a tiny guidebook of the city to make you look authentic. Put it in your coat pocket."

"I already have a guidebook. I don't need two, do I?" The book was very light, even for something so small. I looked at this man, this Salvador.

"It has a passport inside," he said quietly, "your Japanese one. They decided after you left Portugal that it was a mistake for you not to have one. They put it together in a hurry, but it will do."

" 'It will do' is a phrase usually meaning it's fucked up but we can't fix it."

Salvador pointed to a building, as if giving me some information. "If anyone is curious, you can say it's newly issued, that's why there are so few stamps. You were once in Finland, right? That's what your file says. So we figured it was safe to put a Helsinki airport stamp in. The Finns don't mind, they're happy for visitors, even notional ones. You can come up with a story of what you saw, what you ate, the usual. The other stamp is for Malaysia. Shouldn't be hard to produce a story for that. It's very hot there. Maybe you stayed in your hotel the whole time so didn't see much. You can mention the Indian cab drivers. Also spicy food. Oh, and you went to a factory there, something related to this current deal. You don't have to say much, better if you don't. Plead the need for security; be mysterious."

"Did you really work in that factory? You seemed to know the owner."

"Jobs are scarce for history majors, my friend. Besides, the factory had a glorious history, or it did until recently."

5

We walked a few blocks in silence before Salvador resumed the conversation. "Let me explain, as every good guide should. At one point, in 1936 when the workers seized the factory, the one you're going back to, they named it Fábrica Roja de Trotsky. It was not a very imaginative name, but they didn't have much time to think about it, and anyway the name had to be voted on by all the workers, like everything else did. A lot of voting, a lot of speeches, a lot of excitement but not much getting done. Production went down as zeal went up. Some people who knew better warned them that Trotsky was on Stalin's bad side and wouldn't like the name, but most of the workers thought Stalin was bullshit and didn't care. Trotsky had been here in Barcelona in 1916, and the workers thought he was a great friend of theirs. Actually, Trotsky didn't see much of the city when he was here. Little did he know that the man who would murder him someday was here at the same time, though was only a child in 1916."

"Trotsky!" I stopped walking.

"What's the matter?"

"The man follows me everywhere. I was once arrested and beaten because someone drew a straight line between Trotsky and a Kazakh woman I had bumped into. My shoulder still twinges when the weather changes."

"Because of the woman?"

"No, because of the beating. I didn't even know that Trotsky had been in Kazakhstan."

"Neither did I. But he was here in Barcelona, that I can tell you. It was only for a few days before he was put on a ship and sent away by the authorities, maybe at the behest of British intelligence, which thought he was nothing but trouble. British intelligence is sometimes effective." He paused, but I left the bait on the hook, so he continued. "I often wonder, did he pass that young boy who would someday murder him? Maybe they went into the same candy store. Maybe the one we just passed."

I looked around and spotted a young Chinese woman standing in a dimly lit doorway across the street. "And who have we over there, do you think? An outpost of the Celestial Empire? What should we imagine she is doing here? A Chinese maiden, working for whom? To accomplish what task? Perhaps she is here to murder me."

"I hope not. What a mess that would be." Salvador clapped me on the shoulder. "Just stick close." We walked another block, where he stopped and pointed across the street. "Here we are. The Gaudí cathedral. The most wonderfully imagined building in creation."

The structure he pointed to took a moment to register in my brain. Even if it had been full sunlight, I would have had no idea what I was looking at. It defied description. It was, as far as I could tell, a waste of good resources. It made no sense at all in its lines— too many towers and too many angles. It looked like nothing nature would ever permit even in the worst of times. Evolution would have killed it off at birth. Against the night sky it crouched like a wounded beast.

"Well," said Salvador, "was I right?"

"And they think we're crazy," I said softly. "If this thing were in my country, foreigners would fall down in hysterics and say it showed what fools we are. But here, you people worship it. It must be the Catalonian brain."

"Don't speak." Salvador held up his hand. "Silence! Just walk with me around the perimeter. Look at the shapes, look at the forms, look at how it encompasses space and reaches upwards. It is whimsical but serious at the same time, wouldn't you say? It is like life itself. You can't see many of the details right now, but all the better for you to understand the basic structure, the essence of its being."

"How long have they been wasting their time building this thing?"

Salvador suddenly grabbed my arm. "Enough," he said. "Let's walk. Look at your watch, then take the map out and study it. There, very good, you see? It's nearly dinnertime. Shall we head off?"

6

When we'd walked for about fifteen minutes, Salvador slowed his pace. He stopped once, ducked down a narrow passage, waited several seconds, and then resumed. He had long strides, but I had a lot of practice keeping up with foreigners with long strides so I stayed right on his heels. At last we emerged onto a broader road.

"Here we are on the Avinguda del Paral·lel, a street that has seen better days." He looked carefully both ways. "Early in the last century, it was a center of bohemian life. A distant relative on my mother's side was much attracted to it, as were many young women of the time."

"Why did we rush away from that building?"

He shook his head. "Nothing to worry about. Just something I noticed. Where was I?"

Our abrupt departure combined with Rosalina's warning did not strike me as nothing to worry about. "You frequently notice things in the night that scare you?"

"Forget it." The driver took another quick look up the street and then down. "An old lover, just someone I prefer not to run into. Painful memories." He shot me a pained look.

Amazing, what they thought I would believe. It wasn't an old lover, that was for sure. I hadn't seen anything, but I hadn't been paying attention to the surroundings as I should have been. That was a mistake. All right, I vowed, no more gawking at the sights, no more distractions.

"I think you were telling me about your relative," I said.

"Ah, yes. Early in the twentieth century. She was Cuban, had fiery blood, I guess. Her marriage was not to her liking, and she raised one of her sons to be a Communist."

It was clear Salvador was relieved I hadn't pressed the point, though I was pretty sure he didn't think I had accepted his story about an old lover.

"Interesting," I said. "We've had similar problems in my country."

As we walked along the street, I paused a few times to look in dark windows, hoping to get lucky and spot who might be following us. Dark windows are not the best for that, but there wasn't much else on this gloomy street. "Not much to see," I said. "Just old stores."

"Oh, there is if you use your imagination." Salvador was suddenly animated, whether by the pictures of the past that ran through his mind or by something else I couldn't tell. "Look hard enough and you'll see cafés one after another filled with beautiful young women, poets sitting in the calm of dusk drinking until they can barely keep from sliding under the tables, dancers with long legs and burning eyes hurrying across the street to get to the theaters for the nightly performance."

"I should have known." I shook my head. "You're a romantic. That only happens in books. I'll bet you there was murder, intrigue, and betrayal all around."

"Yes! Exactly! Something to stir the blood!"

"Lucky Trotsky."

"No, Trotsky didn't stay around long enough to enjoy it. He left on a ship."

"For Kazakhstan?"

"No, for New York. Eventually he went to Mexico. A Russian agent drove a pickaxe into his skull."

"Someone from Barcelona, I gather."

"Yes, that boy."

I considered this. "And you have some connection with him?"

"Why would you ask?"

"A whim, perhaps. Or maybe because you are so focused on the story."

"It was a cousin, a distant cousin. The son of my great-great-aunt on my mother's side."

"Your great-great-aunt, a woman whose marriage was not to her liking. Imagine, if her husband had pleased her, Trotsky might have died of old age, and the rest of us would have been left in peace."

7

Service at the restaurant Salvador had picked for dinner was slow, but there were few customers, and no one followed us in. Someone could be lingering outside in the narrow, dark streets, but Salvador didn't seem concerned. He ate a big dinner of roast octopus and fish stew, with a plate of grilled vegetables, half a loaf of bread, and most of a bottle of wine. I wasn't hungry, but had a plate of chicken to be polite. I would have preferred pork, but it wasn't on the menu. Salvador insisted we have dessert, an assortment of sweet tarts. I offered him mine, but he seemed offended, so I ate two of them.

By the time we finished our meal there was no time for the Roman ruins, so we walked quickly back to the cab. Salvador motioned for me to stand to the side. From his pocket he took a small flashlight, which he used to inspect each wheel. Then he slid under the rear of the car. When he emerged he was holding a small black box. He indicated I should stay silent as he tossed it farther up the alley, over a wall that leaned toward the building it was meant to protect.

"I was waiting for that to happen." He motioned for me to follow. Fifteen meters up the alley was a black Mercedes taxi. He did a quick check under the hood; then we got in and backed up at a high rate of speed. "It was either going to be that or a parking ticket." He spun the steering wheel and shifted into drive. The tires squealed, lights went on in several apartments overlooking the street, and we sped away. "Actually this was easier." He turned to me and smiled. "Tickets are getting harder to fix."

As we headed out of the city, I thought I'd ask, since the answer probably had a bearing on my safety, "Who left you that present under the car? Friends of Gaudí? Old lover with a grudge? What is it this time? And don't tell me not to worry. You said that they wouldn't know you had picked me up at the factory last time." I paused. "But then again, they'd know that you dropped me off."

"Yes and no. Don't worry. It's my problem, not yours. For now, they're out one tracking device. And they won't know this car. It's a game they play."

"That's supposed to be an answer?"

"Take it for now. We can go into detail later."

While we raced past dark fields and an occasional house on the road up the mountain, Salvador didn't say much. I used the silence to go over in my mind the different scenarios Vincente had laid out during the drive to Lisbon Airport a few hours ago.

The first scenario, the most likely in his eyes—and the least likely in mine—was that things would proceed as if nothing un-toward had happened. The reason I didn't think this was likely was because two people had died just before I had disappeared into the woods on my first visit to the factory. It was hard to believe that everyone would have amnesia and welcome me back without the slightest ripple of suspicion that I had been involved.

"It's a matter of perspective," Vincente had said when I looked unconvinced as he went through this scenario. "Turn things around for a minute. Yuri shot the owner, whose time was nearly up any-way, and then you killed Yuri. Yuri was already suspected by José and his friends, and that you killed him puts you on the right side of the street."

"But I disappeared."

"Sure, but even more important, you are appearing again. And you'll be carrying instructions to order more machines, though the terms will be tougher this time because of the delays in shipping the original order. These people want to protect themselves, they are intensely suspicious, but most of all they want money. You are their pot of gold. They'll overlook a lot if they have to, as long as you don't go over the line."

"What line? What if you're wrong?"

"I'm not wrong. And I have good reason to be sure that I'm not. Besides, do you think I'd send Rosalina into something if it had failure written all over it?"

From what I'd seen, Rosalina wasn't one to worry about failure. And I wasn't worried about her; it was my skin that concerned me. "What is this magical line of safety I shouldn't cross? They thought I was Japanese. I told them I was Korean. Is that over the line?"

"Don't worry about that. They don't know the difference, and they don't really care. I'm telling you, they care about getting paid. In fact, it's good if they are confusing the two. Anything that gets them edgy or suspicious, you can tell them it's because of Korean culture."

"Meaning what?"

"Calm down, will you? Meaning whatever you want. Their heads are filled with nutty things about Asians. You can use that to your advantage." Vincente gave me a sideways glance. "Listen, we can scrub this whole thing right now if you're worried. I can't have you walking in there with a shred of doubt hanging off your shoulder. They'll sense it. In or out, let's settle it right here. I have a backup waiting; it will delay things a day or so to work him into position, but he might even work better than you, now that I think of it."

"You have a backup. And this backup of yours has been fully briefed with the same care and precision that I was briefed, I suppose. Water bottle, phone numbers in underwear drawers—the whole brilliant scheme. Of course he'll work better than me. A trained monkey would do better than me. Here, take this ridiculous passport. Give it to the monkey." Vincente didn't have a backup; that much was obvious from the way his jaw was set as he looked at the passport.

Rosalina started humming. She lowered the window and rested her arm on the frame. We'd left the highway and were driving through countryside, oak trees overhanging the road and clumps of small houses in the distance.

"I thought we were heading for the airport," I said.

"We are, but I didn't like the car that was behind us." She glanced in the mirror. "It was red and too clean. It had special tires on it, too."

I turned around to look out the rear window. The road was empty.

"Don't worry, he didn't turn off when we did, so maybe I was just being overly cautious. Or he radioed ahead and they think they'll pick us up when we get off this road and back on the highway. Never mind, this is better than the highway, and I know a way to go so it only adds a few minutes to the drive."

"OK." I turned back to Vincente. "That was scenario one. Nothing happens. For laughs, let's hear number two."

Vincente eyed the passport, which was still sitting on the seat between us. I'd made no move to pick it up again.

"The second possibility is the opposite of the first, but with caveats. You walk in, they're suspicious, they drag you down to that room and push you around a little, but not much. Maybe some light slaps. They can't afford to make a mistake. What if you really are the customer of their dreams? They'll be careful not to do anything that they can't fix later. After they're done, when they're convinced you're OK, they'll pretty you up, invite you to dinner, toast to your health and ask if they can send you cards of greeting on holidays."

"I'm supposed to be reassured? I had dinner there once already. It was not among my favorites." I picked up the passport and put it back in my pocket. "Lucky for you I owe Luis a big favor."

"As you wish, Inspector," Vincente said briskly.

I noticed that Rosalina did not honk the horn.

8

The taxi pulled up in front of the factory at about eleven forty-five. Salvador let me off directly at the entry gate.

"I'll be back to pick you up at two thirty tomorrow afternoon. Might be another car. I'll wait fifteen minutes, maximum. If you're not here, either you're already dead, or you soon will be. Good luck, my friend."

The black car pulled away, barely waiting for the door to shut. I was left alone in the dark for a few seconds before three bright spotlights hit me from three different angles simultaneously. For a moment I couldn't see, but I could hear the whir of a camera being moved to focus on me. From a loudspeaker off to the side I was commanded not to move.

"Do you want me to put up my hands?" I looked around, squinting to avoid the light, which was painfully intense. I felt like a bug.

"I said don't move." The loudspeaker crackled and then threw a high-pitched squeal at me. "Don't move means exactly that, don't move."

"All right," I said, not moving. "But I'm expected here. I have an appointment, and if I have to stand in this spot all night blinded by this light, your boss won't be happy with the consequences."

PART III

Chapter One

Once I was inside the front gate, the spotlights stopped following me and went off. Waiting for me was a woman whom I did not recognize, though I was familiar with the type. She was slightly stooped, frowning, clutching a clipboard as if it was a weapon. Instinctively I knew I did not want to be around her any longer than necessary. She stood in the dim light of a tiny bulb illuminating the area just outside the entry hall, saying nothing, but observing me closely. Finally she turned her head slightly and spoke into her shoulder. As she did, I could see she was wearing an earpiece.

"Have I passed your scrutiny?" I unbuttoned my jacket and turned around slowly. "Because it is late. I'd like a shower, a bed with crisp clean sheets, a bite to eat, and a glass of vodka. I assume we will talk in the morning."

The woman shook her head. "No time for anything so civilized." Her voice was perfection. If I closed my eyes, I thought I could listen to it forever. That would be a mistake, I knew, but it wouldn't be my first.

"Follow me," she said. "We have business to conduct."

2

When I came to, I was in a different room than I had been the last time this had happened. I was on a bed, not a dirt floor. Two pillows were behind my head. My tongue, again, was like a board, and my head hurt, but Vincente had assured me that at the end of this would be a meal and something to drink. If he was wrong, I would never get to tell him. Aside from my tongue, it didn't feel as if I had been beaten, nothing beyond a couple of knocks on the head. Maybe they'd given me a drug. I listened for the lovely voice of the woman who had put me here, but heard nothing and soon enough fell asleep.

When I awoke again it was because someone was slapping my face. Contrary to Vincente's assurances, they were not light slaps.

"Stop," I said, moderately pleased that my tongue was back to normal so quickly. "This is a hell of a way to treat a big-spending customer."

"Mr. Tamada, we are deeply, deeply apologetic. This is such a horrible mistake. Shall we call a doctor? You can tell him what ails you, and he will know what to do. He is very good." It was the same woman's voice, though with a half-note of concern that was as thin as the wing of a dragonfly.

"I don't suppose you have water?" I kept my eyes closed. "Something cold?"

"Of course. You had a terrible fall and a bad night."

"I fell?"

"But of course. You don't remember? What a shame. Why don't I call the doctor? Then you'll feel better, ready to fight the bulls in no time. *Olé!*" She gave a short, sharp laugh.

"No, no doctor." I opened my eyes. She was swaying over me, like a cobra. "I'll be fine. Are we going to eat something? I think food would be good. Doctors only prod and probe. No need for that now. Can you help me to my feet?"

"Here, close your eyes. That way you won't be dizzy."

As soon as I stood, I knew it was a bad idea and sat down again on the bed. "Perhaps all I need is food. Just a bite."

"Of course, why not? You are Japanese, a delicate creature, not like the men here. But I'll tell you, exotic things are tiresome when you have them two days in a row. Hold still." She stuck a needle in my vein. "This will make you drowsy again. Maybe a little giddy.

Mostly you'll answer questions with an ease that will surprise you. It usually wears off in a day, two at the most, so don't worry. It's rare anyone has a bad reaction. All right, open your eyes."

I did, but there was nothing. My eyes met nothing but the blackness of death. "You've blinded me," I said. It was not pleasant, so I said the only thing that came to my mind. "The deal is off."

"Don't be hasty," she said. "It's completely normal. Sit still, the injection goes into effect more smoothly if you don't jump around. Now, I'm going to ask you some questions. They are simple, so the answers should be simple, and when you've given me the answers, we can have some food. Is it agreed?"

"I'm blind, you fool. I don't want food. I want my sight back, and I mean now." If they were going to save the blindfold and shoot me like this, I saw no reason to be polite.

"No, don't worry, it's just the way this stuff works, a side effect. Some people see odd colors. Others see nothing. We think it has to do with personality, or maybe it's a form of cultural bias. Japanese tend to see bright reds. Koreans don't see anything. Of course, it was a small sample; there's much work left to be done in this field. Are you sure you don't see bright red?"

Why did she keep saying I was Japanese? Hadn't I told José I was Korean? With great clarity I recalled the room; I vividly saw the oak panels, the dark portraits on the wall. I even thought I could hear the air move as Yuri leaped across the table and landed on José. Of course! José hadn't had time to tell anyone. With what seemed to me an audible click, my mind moved from the past onto the present situation. "You mean you've done this before?"

"Oh, my, yes. It's the only way we can stay in business. So many people sneaking around the place, trying to interfere. You're not trying to interfere, are you?"

I had to marvel at her voice. The tissue-thin concern of a moment ago had turned into mockery heavy enough to sink a battleship.

"What are you talking about?" I didn't have to pretend to be upset; it was all I could do to sit still, I was so angry. Panic was the farthest thing from my mind. I was actually furious, and I knew I had to play that to the maximum. "I come here to make a purchase, and the next thing that happens I'm beaten up and blinded."

"Where were you born?" Leaden, serious, just this side of deadly.

All right, I thought. Here we go. I remembered what Tomás had told me so clearly I was convinced it was true. "Tokyo. During the war, if you want to know. It was not a pleasant time." If the shot was some sort of truth serum, it didn't seem to be having the effect they wanted.

"Not pleasant," she mimicked me. "Wars never are. Your parents?"

"They died during the war or soon after. All my relatives perished."

"How convenient."

"Well, it wasn't convenient for me. I lived out of garbage cans and slept in broken buildings, those that hadn't burned to the ground in the American bombing. It was a bad time."

"Common enough. Next you fell in with a gang, I suppose."

"Nothing of the sort. I became a servant in the household of General Douglas MacArthur, polished the silverware, and was promoted three times." This blew a hole in the story Tomás had given me, but I could tell that for some reason the woman seemed to know bits of the story already, so I decided to alter a few details. "That job disappeared when MacArthur was dismissed, and then I fell in with a gang."

The woman grunted. "You didn't know the name of the gang leader."

"Of course I knew his name. It was Shin. He was Korean."

"As are you. We don't like to dance around on these things. It wastes time. We need to know exactly whom we are dealing with. If that bastard whom you killed told you differently, he was an idiot. Let us be frank. We think you are Korean, and you want to purchase these machines for your ridiculous regime. We could care less, believe me, who purchases what and why. But we are ready to crush double-dealers. They are dangerous; they are slime. If you tell us you are Japanese but you aren't, what are we to think?"

"Think whatever you want. What difference does it make? I could come from Mars for all you care. I hand you what you want, you hand over the merchandise, deal done. Since when do we go through a questionnaire on country of origin? I'm not applying for a visa, I'm buying machinery. Are you selling, or aren't you?" Problem—how did they know I wasn't Japanese if José had died before he could tell anyone? The oak table was so ugly, no one would have noticed a couple of wires.

"Relax," she said. "You don't make the rules here, we do. I asked you a question."

"Yeah, well, I have one for you. When do I get my sight back? And I didn't kill that bastard. Your man Yuri did. Surely your cameras told you that."

"That's your story." She sounded amused. "You have a lot of stories."

I decided not to argue about Yuri for the moment. "When do I get my sight back?"

"When I say so." It was firm and thoroughly unpleasant. I decided that despite an occasional laugh, she was basically sour on life.

I heard the door close and was left alone. There was nothing to do. The blindness forced me into a bank of memories that I'd locked up years ago. I sorted through them, put each in a folder, and built a mental bookshelf to hold them. Eventually, it would be tomorrow, unless it already was. Salvador would wait fifteen minutes as he said, and then he and his taxi would roll back down the dirt path to the main road. He'd report to someone, maybe Rosalina, that the plan hadn't worked. Then they would go out for a drink. It didn't bother me. All I wanted was some sleep.

When I woke, I went through a list of all the trees I knew and what my grandfather thought of each, and then got up and walked around the room, feeling the walls and trying to locate a window. There was only one, and it was high up on the wall. Eventually, I sat down and waited. Finally, there was a knock at the door. I heard the faint sound of a key in a lock.

"I knocked so you would not be alarmed or surprised." It was the same woman's voice. "Here is some food. When you finish that, you'll get another injection that will give you back your sight. It takes several hours to take hold, and sometimes there are side effects."

"Like what?"

"Perhaps nausea. Perhaps dizziness. Perhaps dryness of mouth. It is rarely fatal."

"Rarely" was not a word that carried much reassurance on its back at the moment. "I'm pleased," I said. "I often beat the odds."

"Here's the tray with the food." I heard her move across the room. The next time she spoke, she was very near. "I'm putting it on a small table against the wall. There's a chair beside it. Let me help you find it." She took my arm. "You are a bad boy, you threw your pillows on the floor. If you sleep without the pillows after the injection you might be dead when you wake up. Something about your air passage getting closed off. No oxygen. We don't want that, do we?"

After she'd put me in the chair, she put her face next to mine, very close again. "There is fruit, bread, cheese, and a glass of good wine if you don't spill it. I'll put it here, beside you, to your right. I'm not paid to feed you, but I know you can manage. You are a capable man, very masculine." She purred this. "Very sexy."

"True," I said, "but let's hold that for now. The prospect of being nauseous and dizzy makes me uneasy. When I'm uneasy I'm not in the mood for women, however pleasant their voices."

She laughed. "As you wish," she said. "I'll be back in about thirty minutes with the needle. I have to give it to you in your backside, so don't think I'm being forward when I tell you to lower your trousers."

The fruit consisted of oranges, cherries, and slices of overly ripe pear. I don't much care for cheese but nibbled at a piece. The odor was familiar, but I couldn't place it. The wine was not very good; I guessed it was red and raw, maybe something local. I drank it anyway and wished for more.

A few minutes later, the door opened. "Ah, good, at least you ate the fruit. The cheese is from sheep's milk, aged in a cave for around a month. Some people don't like how it smells. It's strong at first, but it fades."

The odor finally made the connection. "You age it in the cave with the dumpling machine?"

"So, you were there with Yuri? We thought so. The guard wasn't forthcoming, and Yuri wasn't speaking." She laughed gaily, like a spider noticing a new bug in its web. "As far as I'm concerned, we should get rid of all of them, worthless Slavs. Anyway, for purposes of cheese, a cave is a cave, is it not? The wine is not paired well with this cheese. I apologize. It should be red, but all we had was this white from Tarragona. It's too silky for my taste. Tell me, did you like it?"

"I prefer vodka, actually." Silky? My grandfather would have refused to remove paint with it for fear of destroying the wood underneath.

"All right. Stand up, lower your trousers, and bend over."

"Is this necessary?"

"If you want your sight back, I'd advise it. After that, you can rest for a few hours, and then we'll be ready to discuss business. We talked it over, made a few phone calls, and I can tell you we are now largely convinced you are who you say you are, that you are not from Mars but a gentleman from Japan. Please excuse my suspicions to the contrary."

I heard voices from outside the door, and then I sensed someone step into the room. It was a woman. She had on delicate perfume.

"Just a minute." The first woman moved away, and there was a whispered conversation. In less than a minute, she was back in front of me. "What we need now is to finalize the transaction and arrange the transportation for the merchandise immediately." She'd lost some of her sense of command.

"Something the matter?"

"Something is always the matter in this business. Bend over."

3

Never in my life have I been so sick. At one point several people stood over me and murmured in worried voices. It developed into an angry exchange and seemed on the verge of getting physical until I groaned and turned on my side. Then they quieted down again and the room was still.

When I woke, I was glad to find I could see light and dark, though still nothing distinct. I held my fingers in front of my face, but only blur registered. Outside the door, I heard voices conversing in Japanese. The door opened, and I could at least make out that a shape was standing in front of me.

"You had a bad reaction to the shot." The woman sounded concerned. She wasn't, but it was a good imitation. "Apparently you're past that stage and through the worst of it. We've consulted some knowledgeable people, and they say it may be another few hours before everything is back to normal."

"Meaning what? I can have more of that cheese in the meantime?"

"Meaning your sight will be back. The delay is not good."

"No, it's not."

"I meant for us. We can't afford it. We're running out of time. If you're not ready to complete the transaction by three P.M., all hell will break loose."

"What time is it now?"

"About ten thirty in the morning."

"Well, don't blame me. In fact, when I tell the organization what you put me through, I doubt if they'll be interested in further purchases."

"I'll be back at noon. If you can't see by then, we'll have to reconsider."

"Any chance of something to eat?"

"I'll check, but people are busy packing right now. You've caused a lot of problems."

They were in a rush, packing, she'd said. I knew the machine was already crated, so they must be packing something else, like files. And I was excess baggage, except they thought I had what they needed—the money. Vincente had given me a phony bank account number to use for the advance payment, 37 percent. When they asked for that and I handed it over, that would buy me some time.

A few minutes later the door opened.

"We didn't know you would be so difficult, or we would have selected someone else." It was a man's voice. He spoke in Korean, but it was clear from the accent that he was Japanese. He was a dark shape, nothing more.

"You have an advantage, whoever you are." I twisted my head from side to side, as if trying to get a fix on his location. "Come back when I can see."

"No time for that, as the prickly woman explained. I need to know if you have the final transportation arrangements, Route Victor, according to the agreed plan."

I had no idea what he was talking about. I was supposed to find out the transportation route from them. They thought I had it?

"Of course I do," I said confidently. "But nothing happens until I can see."

"We can't wait for that." The man should have been calm if he hoped to be in charge. Instead he was shrilly impatient. "My bonus is at stake, and probably your life." He took a breath, as if he realized he had made a mistake. His tone softened. "If we work together, maybe we can get out of this, each with what he wants."

Even though I couldn't see, it was clearly a transparent lie. "And you are who?"

"You can call me Kame. I handle transport."

Bull's-eye! I was with the man who handled transport, only he didn't know what he was supposed to know. I weighed where this left me. Kame couldn't be his real name. The word means turtle in Japanese. Who would give that name to a transportation specialist except maybe a gang with a sense of humor? On the other hand, maybe it was his real name; maybe he had drifted toward that profession in subconscious reaction. He had probably heard every bad joke about the name already. I let it go; no sense rubbing it in at this moment. Besides, he sounded nervous, and with nervous people, sometimes it's best to say nothing. It often makes them more nervous.

I was right. This one couldn't stand even five seconds of silence. "You may not have heard of me," he said in a low voice. Before I could reply, he pressed on. "I'm not supposed to have revealed myself to you, but things being what they are, we have to bend the rules. Anyway, you can't see me, so it's as if I don't exist."

I instantly liked this logic. It meant as long as I couldn't see, he assumed I didn't exist either, not enough to hurt him. It was similar to what I had heard from Tomás in the hotel. Personally, I always felt that cosmic questions about existence were a distraction. If I wasn't here, then why did my head hurt? If I was here, how did I get into this mess? For now, the sense of my existence racing parallel with my nonexistence seemed perilously hooked to the fate of a phony dumpling machine.

"Listen," I said, "you want your bonus, but you can't get it if you don't come in and knock me around. Am I right? They need to think you beat it out of me."

"A good point," he said. "Not unreasonable. I need to know the transport arrangements. You must have been entrusted with them. They'll be suspicious if you just hand them over without a fight." He waited a moment, and then repeated what he'd said, as if to convince himself. "You must have been entrusted with them."

"I must have been."

"Who are you?" He hissed the question as he grabbed my hand. "You have all your fingers. Where are your tattoos?"

"Who am I? Funny, I have the same question—who are you?" I pulled my hand away. They still thought they were dealing with the Japanese mafia. "I also have clean fingernails. Care to see my feet? You think I'm going to give you any information when all I know is that you claim you're in charge of transportation. I can't see you. You said it yourself, maybe you don't really exist. You want a bonus? Then you better start talking, fast."

"I got here yesterday," he said. "How come I don't know you? How come no one told me to expect you? I thought I was supposed to work through that Russian fellow, Yuri." The turtle sounded off balance, which is what I needed. If I was going to get out of this room, I was going to have to be the one in control of our encounter.

"Yeah, well, things changed," I growled. "They do that sometimes. And we adjust, don't we? How come you don't know me? I'll tell you why—because they've tightened up on security. Too many things have been going wrong. Too many threads leading to too many other threads. Yuri's dead, hadn't you heard? Broken thread. The deal is through me." Considering I could barely see shadows, it was not a bad foray.

"The plans for Route Victor, where are they?" The turtle had suddenly regained its balance and was getting annoyed. "No games on this, whoever you are. The others have convinced themselves that you are Japanese. Of course you aren't. Any idiot could sense that. Doesn't matter anymore, because we are nearly out of time. Everything has to start rolling in less than an hour."

I could barely see, and I didn't know where I was in the factory. I also hadn't learned what I had been sent in to find out—how the dumpling machine was being shipped. But I had established one thing beyond doubt. They were all sufficiently crazy that anything was possible, all of which gave me added incentive to get out and away from them as soon as possible.

"I need back my sight," I said, craning my neck. "As soon as I can see, I can sign the necessary papers, you'd get your bonus, and we'd all part friends." It didn't sound very convincing once I'd said it, maybe a little too subservient. It was immediately clear that it wasn't convincing to the turtle at all.

"We don't need you to sign anything," the man said, his voice shaking in anger. His Korean was in shambles. "That's a stupid formality. I'm surprised you don't know that. They'll burn the paper as soon as they have the money. They're not keeping any paper, nothing."

If money was so important, then I might as well retreat behind those walls. It was my last chance. "I can't release funds without a receipt."

A solid whack on the back of my head threw me to my knees. "Maybe you are Japanese after all," he screamed. A second whack on the head was more vicious than the first. "There are two receipts. Want another?"

I was stunned for a moment by the blows. When I finally raised my head, I could see again, better in one eye than the other, but this was no time to insist on perfection. I couldn't let on that my sight was coming back. As long as they thought I couldn't see, I was relatively safe. If they really needed the transportation details from me, it wouldn't do them any good to kill me. That made sense to me; I had to hope it made sense to them, too. Vincente had emphasized that they wanted one thing—money. If they were greedier than they were crazy, that gave me a margin of safety I might be able to use.

"Don't do that again," I said. "You'll dislodge my memory. Do you think I was stupid enough to put anything on paper? You think I like paper any more than your friends do? The transportation schedule is up here." I tapped my head.

The woman who'd given me the injection burst into the room. "We have to move," she shouted at Kame. Her voice was a notch above a high-speed saw cutting through metal. "Find out what we need from this donkey's ass and then get rid of him."

"How?" Kame sounded as if the idea had never occurred to him.

"Are you kidding me? Out back, same as always." She seemed to be in a terrible state of confusion. She ran to the window, stood on her tiptoes to look out, then turned and ran out the door.

"I need the transportation route," Kame screamed at me in English. "Route Victor! V Victory. Now! And when I say now, I mean now." Then he repeated it in Korean, then in Japanese, and finally, for some reason, in German.

"If you kill me, you won't get it. The dead don't talk, or haven't you heard?" I cocked my head as if I still couldn't see and was straining to hear what was going on. "I'll make you a deal. Get me my sight, I give you the information."

"I don't know how to fix your damned Korean eyes."

"It's easy. The lady explained it to me." I stood up.

"Don't move, you bastard." He was off to my right, backing away slightly.

"Look, I'm not doing anything, just getting onto my hands and knees, see? Here, come over and put your hand on the back of my head."

"What if I slit your throat instead?"

"A lot of blood, and you'd probably slip on the floor running out, at which point you'll realize that you don't have the transport information and you've blown the chance for a bonus. Go ahead if you're going to, we haven't got all day."

He moved behind me and put one hand on my head. I could feel it was missing a fingertip.

"Both hands. Hurry up, will you?"

He complied, and as soon as he did, I grabbed both of his arms, lowered my neck, and threw him with all my strength across the room. His body somersaulted and hit the wall hard. I heard something crack, and then he slid to the floor. I waited for someone to come through the door to find out what had happened, but no one appeared. When I crawled over to Kame, he wasn't moving. His neck looked broken, and he didn't seem to be breathing. A quick check proved he wasn't armed. The threat to cut my throat had been a stupid bluff. His wallet had a few euros and twenty thousand yen folded under a flap, but no identification other than a business card covered with phone numbers. I put the wallet in my pocket, checked one more time to see if he was as dead a turtle as he looked, and carefully stepped into the hall.

I figured I had two options at that point—find a way out of the factory right away, or postpone that until I located the dumpling machine and figured out a way to disable it, even if it was already in three parts and crated. If they still lacked Route Victor, the machine must still be here. And if it wasn't, there seemed little chance at this point I'd make any progress on discovering the transportation plans.

The first option, getting out of the factory, was more inviting, but after all I'd been through, I was determined to come out with something to show for my trouble. I needed to find the machine. According to the plans Vincente had shared with me, his preferred choice had been that I "reprogram" the machine. He wouldn't say what that meant, only that it would be a simple task, so simple even a baby could do it. At that, Rosalina had softly tapped the horn, so I figured Vincente had scored a point. Vincente had smiled to himself and then leaned toward me. All I had to do, he said, was insert what he called a "gizmo" into a slot. That's how it was explained to me as he handed me the very tiny plastic bag with the even tinier object in it. The slot was supposed to be on the left side of the machine, and if it wasn't there, it was on the right side. Find the slot, slip in the gizmo, and the job was done. Only no one had considered the possibility that the machine would already be crated. Vincente had admitted that much. It would make using the gizmo more difficult, but if I could find the machine, maybe still not impossible.

The fallback in case option one didn't work was also so simple even a baby could do it (again, Rosalina tapped the horn). That was to discover the transportation route so the shipment could be intercepted. Simple, except it turned out that no one at the factory knew the routing. They all thought I had it. And why was the turtle talking about a bonus? If he got the routing from me, whom was he going to tell, and what were they going to do with the information? Sell it to an interested party, someone connected with Yuri? And who might that be?

4

The last time I had seen the dumpling machine it was in a tunnel about five hundred meters from a heavy oak door that opened to the outside from the kitchen. Even if I found the kitchen and got out that door, I didn't have the key I'd taken from Yuri, the one that he'd used to get into the tunnel. The key must still be on the bedside table in the fancy hotel near the beach in Portugal. There had been no chance to return to my hotel room to retrieve anything after that not-very-informative session with Tomás. It didn't matter; the key probably wouldn't work anyway, since when the factory guards repaired the lock they would have replaced the cylinder.

The hallway outside the room where I'd been for the past day or so was dark, with soft blue lights hanging from the ceiling every ten meters or so. The passage was only about a hundred meters long. At the end was an elevator, which opened silently when I approached. There were no buttons to push. The doors closed as soon as I stepped in, and the elevator went down. When the doors opened again, I was in another corridor, this one with no windows but the same blue lights. It had the feel of an underground passage, the more so because of the series of pictures on the walls of lean young men and women doing exercises in a sunlit meadow. All were wearing clothing, but not much. They were the sort of pictures that were supposed to convince the observer that he wasn't really underground, and distract him long enough to find the way out before claustrophobia set in. Years ago I'd been in a long tunnel in an East German secret police training camp that had a similar air about it. I didn't like it then, and I didn't like it now.

The corridor lights were on a motion sensor, but there was a delay, so I was always stepping into darkness. Maybe 250 meters down the corridor there was a Y intersection. I make it a practice to go right when I'm not sure. Sometimes that doesn't work, but this time it did. Two hundred meters farther on, there was another elevator.

Again the door opened as I approached. This time there were two identical buttons side by side on a metal panel, with no indication what they were for. In the upper left-hand corner of the elevator car, I spotted a tiny camera disguised as a ceiling light. I grinned at it and punched one of the buttons. The doors closed, but nothing happened. After a minute, the lights went off and so did the ventilation. A tiny red light blinked from the camera, so I figured it was still working, maybe monitoring what I was going to do next. There wasn't much I could do, so I leaned against the back wall and closed my eyes. That seemed to be the right move, because the car started to move again, inching its way up. At one point things jerked to a stop and I could hear the whir of a motor as if the cable was old and catching its breath. The car moved again, jerked one last time, and then the door opened into a brilliantly white room, white marble entrance, white carpet, white walls, a white leather sofa, and stark white chairs. The effect after the darkness of the elevator was blinding, as it was meant to be. I was in no mood for a merry chase, no mood for an interrogation, and too old for a seduction. I blinked once, looked at the dimmest corner to give my eyes a moment to adjust, and stepped into whatever waited.

5

Across the room was a white teak desk, and behind the desk was someone in a chair facing away from me, looking into a garden of oak trees and a riot of red flowers. My footsteps on the carpet were silent. I coughed softly, and the room swallowed the sound. White room, no sound, very appealing view of a garden—I braced myself. This was the sort of place you walked into and were never heard from again. If there had been another chair near the desk, I would have sat down without being invited, but there was nothing, so I stood and waited. The person in front of me didn't turn around. It was a woman with long brown hair. Her blouse was blue, almost sheer, and she had on a scarf that, at least from the back, looked expensive. I waited. The view of the garden was nice, but I didn't think it rated complete concentration. Finally, I walked around the desk.

It was Rosalina. She was perfectly dead. Her lips were pale, her eyes open, her body slack but more like someone resting for the moment instead of forever. There were no wounds I could see, but I had a feeling the death certificate, if it got to that, wouldn't say "natural causes." Apparently, she hadn't been to a nuclear engineering conference. Instead, she had briefly been in the room where I was being held. I was pretty sure the perfume was hers.

I spent a moment looking out at the garden, wondering if she had noticed something before she was killed. When I turned around, two men were standing inside the doorway across the room. One of them was tall, thin, with hands like hammers, heavy hammers, not the small lightweight ones for tapping in brads. His shirt wasn't tucked in, not that I cared, but it looked like he had dressed in a hurry. The other man was immaculately groomed. He was what you might call little, and he was holding a small pistol pointed directly at me. Even across a wide room, you can tell something like that.

"We knew you were a problem," the small man said. "But she said she could handle it." He waved the pistol at Rosalina. "She was wrong. Dead wrong."

The other man laughed. It was the sound of a heavy sledge breaking a boulder. He took a step toward me, but his friend muttered something and he stopped.

Normally, someone—even someone so short—who has a pistol conveys a certain air of confidence, which is usually a good thing because confident people don't pull the trigger by mistake. This man looked confused, nervous, like a sparrow that thought everything that moved was a cat. His eyes darted to the garden, back to the body, and then back to me. There seemed to be a lot of nervous people in this factory.

"I think you have this wrong," I said calmly. No sense in shouting at a nervous, twitchy person with a gun. "I walked into the room, and she was already like this. I assume the place is wired." I looked into the corners of the ceilings for a camera. There were two. "You can check the tapes yourself. And, no, I'm not trouble. I am just trying to finalize a business deal." I shook my head, slowly. Sudden movement is only useful sometimes, and this was not one of them. "Never had anything quite like this deal. Almost too much trouble." I nodded slightly in Rosalina's direction. "I don't even know who she was."

It was easy to sound convincing on this because it was actually true, even truer now that I'd found her like this, dead in an office that looked to carry with it some weird authority, and seemingly a colleague of the nervous man with the pistol. I doubted she had anything to do with the little man's ragged friend, but you could never be sure in these sorts of operations. For a fraction of a second it occurred to me that he was her killer, but then I realized that for hammer-hands to do anything so delicate as to leave no visible trace was unlikely. If Rosalina, or whatever her name really was, had been mixed up in this dumpling business, seriously mixed up in it, that raised the question of Vincente's role. And that, in turn, raised questions about what I was doing here. Decoy? Bait? Sitting duck?

None of these sounded appealing, but on second thought, none of them rang true either. Unless this was the most brilliantly conceived double operation I'd ever encountered, it made more sense that I was supposed to do exactly as I'd been instructed, and that Vincente, along with Rosalina, without telling me, had been running something parallel in support. Nice plan, if that's what it was, but it had come to a bad end. Rosalina, it seemed likely, had convinced the shrill lady that I really was connected with a mysterious buyer and thus not to do anything to make sure I woke up dead. The fatal flaw for Rosalina was that somehow her part in this shadow operation meant to keep me safe had been compromised, and now her misfortune or missteps were about to drag me down with her. Who had compromised her? My first hunch, based on nothing, was that Salvador had said something to the wrong person. Sometimes even a little can be too much.

This was a lot of thinking and supposition to run through my mind in a few seconds, but the room wasn't that big, and the space between me and hammer-hands would diminish rapidly once he was told to start moving in my direction. I had to think fast.

"As I just told you," I said, "I have no idea who she is." Delay seemed the best option. Starting a lengthy conversation wasn't in the cards, but a few back-and-forths might buy me a little time.

"Was," said the man with the pistol. "No idea who she was."

"Was." I nodded. "You're right about that." I glanced at the body. "I don't know what she thought she could handle, or had to handle, or might have handled. I'm just here to finalize a deal." I started to reach inside my coat pocket to produce some papers to wave in the air. I knew they didn't like paper. Maybe it would distract them.

"Don't move. Do not even twitch." The voice was nervous, and the fingers on the pistol tightened. This is never a good sign, so I relaxed my posture slowly, easily, and let my hands drop to my side.

"Paper," I said. "I have the original contract in my pocket, and if someone would sign it we could clear all of this up. Are you authorized to sign?"

The man with the pistol smiled, only it wasn't really a smile. "Sign? Why would I want to do that?"

"Well," I started, but he cut me off.

"Why would I want to do that?" The expression on his face was fixed now, cemented in place. He raised his hands, palms up, and shrugged his shoulders, holding the pose. "Why"—his voice crept up onto an annoying plateau—"would I want to do that?"

"If you'd let me finish, I could explain to you why." I watched the hand holding the pistol as it completed part of an arc and ended up pointed at me again.

The little man seemed a little calmer, even thoughtful. "You might start talking and then this pistol might go off. What then?"

Hammer-hands was edging to the side. That meant, I had to

hope, that they didn't want to shoot me, not really. They'd rather knock me out.

"Look," I said. "The contract is for the shipment of one dumpling machine." I grinned. Grinning throws a lot of people off when they're holding a gun on you. "It's worth big money if it ends up in the right place, in the right condition. Anyone who facilitates that outcome gets a bonus, that's in the contract. Anyone who gets in the way . . . well . . . you figure it out."

"You think you can scare me?"

"No, I just thought you had a healthy regard for money, like a lot of people I've met around here. The organization knows what works; that's why it usually gets what it wants." I was hoping the word "organization" would put a mental foot on the little man's brakes.

Before either of us knew what was happening, the door behind the little man opened and three people poured through—Vincente, followed close on his heels by Salvador and a compact fellow I didn't recognize. Vincente, in a pretty good imitation of an aging tiger, leaped on the back of the little man, grabbed his pistol, and used it to slug him twice on the back of the head, to good effect. Salvador and the other fellow tackled hammer-hands, who would have put up more of a fight if they hadn't rammed a hypodermic needle in his neck. He gurgled and relaxed, gurgled again, and then stopped moving entirely.

"Where is she?" Vincente stood up and straightened his tie. "Where is she? And don't say you don't know."

I pointed at the chair. "She was already there when I came in."

Vincente walked over to the desk, moving as if there was nothing urgent about seeing a figure that sat motionless, its back to us, ignoring everything that had just gone on. He stepped around the chair, put his hand gently on Rosalina's throat, then her neck, and then looked into her eyes. "She's dead. Couple of hours, maybe more. I don't think she died here." He turned to me. "You know who she was?"

Had I or hadn't I sat in the car as she drove the two of us—Vincente and me—to the airport? Had I not climbed over her to get to the window seat? Had she not squeezed my hand when the plane landed? Were we back to the existence-nonexistence wind that kept blowing over this operation? "I don't know. Do I know her? Is that a trick question?"

"No tricks. No jokes. Nobody left on base."

"Am I supposed to get what that means?"

"It's baseball, and you're about to lose the game if we don't move you out of here in a hurry."

Salvador knelt down and put another needle into hammer-hands's neck. "OK, Viktor, he's gone."

"Viktor?" I moved back around the desk so I was closer to the door. "Viktor? I thought your name was Vincente."

"Depends," said the man I didn't know and who had been watching everything closely.

"Depends on what?" The turtle had said the routing for the machine was called Route Victor. My head started buzzing, like it does when there are too many things going on at the same time. "Like depending on what?"

"On location. Where you saw him before, maybe he was V1. Here he is V2."

"No V3?"

"You don't have to know. Get back on the other side of the desk."

"Shut up, both of you." Vincente closed Rosalina's eyes and looked at her one last time. He frowned. "Somebody take care of the one by the door. Then we move." He took a piece of paper out of his pocket. "This sketch says we can go out the garden, through the second gate on that side by the tree, and then work our way along the perimeter wall until we get to a fire ladder that takes us up and out of here. It better be right."

We watched while Salvador put a needle into the man who'd held the pistol. The little hands clenched once or twice, then went limp.

"Done," said the taxi driver.

"Stay close," said Vincente, and the four of us went out in single file.

6

All of the trees in the garden were oaks, except for one noted on the sketch. When we got to that tree, we stopped. The gate that was supposed to lead us out was locked. It was a big lock, and it was rusted shut. Vincente looked at me. "Do something."

"Me? What do I know about rusty Spanish locks?"

"It's not Spanish. It's Chinese. Who do you think owns this place? Fix it, and do it now. We have four or five minutes at the most. There were no alarms—Rosalina turned them off—but it won't be long before someone will check the monitors for what is going on in the white room. Then they'll come looking."

"I'm not Chinese."

"I don't give a fuck what you are. Fix the lock."

The tree next to the gate was a linden. My grandfather thought lindens were very smart trees, smart and honest. "They don't put on airs," he would say to me as we stood outside his workshop in the morning, watching the sun rise. "Honest as can be, reliable, and friendly. They grow as they will. You can't prune a linden," he'd say. "They grow according to their own sense of the world. Don't forget that. And they can help. If you're sick, you want a linden nearby. Listen to me, boy. You get sick, you just need to find a linden. Don't bother with those doctors they send around these days. They were all trained by the Japs."

In those days, there weren't many lindens in the countryside. There weren't many trees at all. Most of those that had survived the Japanese occupation had been chopped down for firewood during the awful winters during the war, either that or bombed to splinters by American planes whose only purpose seemed to be to pulverize the land. Miraculously, there was a linden that had somehow survived near my grandfather's house, and after the war he fiercely protected it. Everyone in our village knew to leave it alone, but people passing by only saw it as wood that would burn and give them heat in the winter nights that seemed to be getting worse every year. Some nights I'd wake to the sound of my grandfather chasing people away, whirling a big axe over his head.

I must have been staring at nothing, remembering my grandfather's voice when he was angry, because Vincente snapped his fingers in front of my face. "Stay with us. You on drugs?"

"No, just thinking."

"Christ, don't think. Fix the lock." He looked at his watch. "I'll give you two minutes."

"This is a linden tree," I said, suddenly drained of energy. "Good place as any to die."

"Nobody dies," said the man who still hadn't introduced himself. "We're supposed to deal with that dumpling machine shipment, and we can't do that if we're dead. We also can't do it if we stay arguing under this tree. I don't know about you, but I'm not waiting for a Chinese lock to get unstuck. I'm climbing over the fence."

It seemed like a bad idea. The fence was at least four meters high. It was made out of big stones for the first three meters or so, then changed to thick boards that were fitted tightly together so there was no way to get a foothold. At the very top was a roll of razor wire. At some point, the big oak trees in the garden had been trimmed back so that none of them hung over the fence. The trimming had been brutal, huge limbs hacked away so that the trees were disfigured. It was surprising that all of them had survived. The linden, for some reason, had been left untouched. It had grown with a mind of its own so that its upper branches leaned toward the fence.

"Well, if you're going to do it, do it," Vincente said. "Here." He took off his jacket. "Wrap this around your arm so you can get over that wire. Or better, lay it on top so we can follow you. Up, quick. They'll be out here any minute."

The man was up the tree in a few seconds. He found his footing on the first thick limb, lifted himself to a second, smaller one not far above, and then crawled out so that he had bent the branch almost to the point of breaking as it hung over the top of the fence. He dropped the coat on the razor wire, lowered himself onto it, and then, with a wave, jumped down on the other side. The branch sprang back again.

"Your turn." Vincente pointed up the tree. "Get up and over fast. Don't look back. The two of you have a job to do. We're not going home until it's done."

I'm not as agile as I used to be, and my hands didn't give me the grip I needed, but somehow I didn't fall. When I reached the limb that led over the fence, I looked down. Vincente stood below me, calmly lighting a cigarette. He looked up and nodded. I heard a shout from the white room, Vincente ducked out of sight, and I slipped off the branch onto the coat that covered the wire. A second later I slipped off that and fell four meters onto a large, unyielding azalea bush.

"You hurt?" The man who had gone first was brushing himself off. "You almost ruined that azalea. It's fifty years old, maybe more. One of the few charms of this place." He put out his hand to help me off the bush. "Call me Yakob. That's my name here. You run into me somewhere else, you don't call me Yakob. You don't know me. Understood? Come on, we can't afford to stand around."

"We aren't waiting for Vincente?"

"You mean Viktor? No, he has to stay to handle things from inside. Too bad about the woman. You knew her?"

Vincente already knew the answer but had asked me the same question. Why? Salvador already knew where Rosalina fit. That left this fellow, Yakob. He knew, he didn't know? He was testing me? I decided to go with Vincente's warning, if that is what it was.

"No. Never met her," I said.

Yakob was already heading down the gravel path. "No matter, it's done, finished, the whole fucking operation is busted except for the one thing left for us to do." He looked over his shoulder at me. "Once we find the machine, we fix it, then we never see each other again. You clear on that?"

"Don't worry. I'm not looking to make new friends." I stopped. "Wait a minute. What about Salvador?"

"Who?"

"The one with the hypodermics. He drives a taxi, but that's not his job, I gather. He seems to have some connection with Trotsky."

"Never knew that. Never knew his name. Maybe he went back to clean up the white room. Don't worry. He seems to know this place even better than I do. We'll probably meet up with him once we're outside. Let's move. You know where the machine is, I take it."

"Last I saw it, I was with your pal Yuri in a tunnel not far from the door to the kitchen."

"The workers' kitchen or the bosses'?"

I made a note. He didn't react to the mention of Yuri. And he said "bosses." Maybe he was a secret fan of Trotsky's, too. Maybe this whole thing was part of a Trotskyite coup . . . I caught myself before jumping off that mental cliff.

"The kitchen was next to a dining room with a big, ugly table," I said. "I guess it was in the main house, if there is such a thing here. It didn't look like a place for workers, unless there's been a revolution." I threw that in to see if he'd respond. He didn't, so I moved on to something that was still needling me. "Why didn't anyone ever give me an overview of the place? How did they expect me to find my way around?"

"Maybe they didn't expect you to find your way around. How should I know? I don't set these things up. Planning isn't my business. I just grunt and tackle. You? One of those Asian-guru idea types?" He gave me the once-over. "Never mind that now. Listen closely. We're on the far end of the factory compound. The main house, the guest quarters, and the offices sit in a little valley behind that rise. That's probably where you were. One of the underground passages leads there, but we're not risking it underground. Can't see what's coming at us up top. The special machine shops are about a kilometer away. They're isolated, but it's not so difficult to get inside. The housing for the foreign machinists is in another compound. That's an overview. Satisfied?"

He seemed to know the layout pretty well. What else did he know, I wondered. "Where are the machinists from?"

"Not your concern."

A few days ago it wasn't my concern, but suddenly it was. "How many of these dumpling machines are there?"

"That's not your concern either."

"You have an annoying way about you, anyone ever tell you that?"

"Let's get to that dumpling machine you saw before it disappears. After that, if you want, we can compare notes on who is the most annoying."

7

We worked our way around the small rise and found the adit. No need for a key. The door had been pried open. Whoever did it must have used something heavy, because the steel frame bolted into the rock had been twisted. The tunnel was empty, stripped bare; even the lights had been pulled down and taken away. A tiny bit of daylight was coming in from somewhere, maybe an airshaft at the far end.

"So much for that." Yakob pulled down the trapdoor in the ceiling where Yuri had kept his cache of equipment. How would he know where it was if he didn't know Yuri? Trapdoors aren't thrown into plans for free, and they aren't supposed to be obvious to anyone who wanders by.

"What's that?"

"This? What does it look like? A cache. It's supposed to have a few things in it." He felt around. "Fuck me, all gone."

"Yeah, gone." I gestured around the tunnel. "Nothing here. So what's next?"

"They are a step ahead of us, which is exactly where we don't want them to be. The damned machine is already on its way, and now we have to find it. What's the routing?"

Why ask me, I almost asked, but something warned me to try a different tack. "Good question. I spent the last couple of days drugged, blind, and drinking bad wine trying to convince some-one to tell me the routing. They claim they don't know, and after what they put me through, I'm prepared to believe them."

"Then you're an idiot. Someone knows."

"The turtle didn't."

"Who?"

At least he didn't know Japanese. "The guy in charge of trans-port. He didn't know. If he didn't, who did?"

"Like I said, someone knows. Someone always knows. Other-wise, it would still be here. Someone who knows the routing put it on a truck. It had to leave here by truck. That much we can figure out by ourselves. That machine is too big for a bicycle, and too heavy for a wheelbarrow. So it left in a truck. And if it left in a truck, there is a manifest, no question about it. Truck drivers are psychotic in their need for manifests. They can drive without gasoline if it comes to that, but they have to have a manifest; otherwise they can't get past customs, and if they don't get past customs, they don't get paid. No one cares if the manifest is accurate or not; whatever it says, cus-toms needs it. At most seaports, you can ship an elephant as vanilla ice cream and no one in the customs office will blink an eye as long as there is a manifest and something in it for them. Airports are tougher, but they won't ship this machine on a plane. Planes crash sometimes, and if this shipment doesn't make it all the way through, there will be a lot of unhappy people in high places."

"And that would be bad?" The ambivalence embedded in this whole operation was getting to me. He almost sounded like he wanted it to get through to the buyer. "I didn't slip the gizmo Vin-cente gave me into the machine. Your friend Yuri didn't either, though he had the chance." I paused to give him time to say he didn't know what I was talking about.

"I don't know what you're talking about."

"Figures. I gather you didn't, maybe because you don't have a gizmo. That means the thing will work when it gets to wherever it's going, which I'm assuming is not what Vincente's or Viktor's, or whoever the hell he is, plans called for. So the next step, if I'm not assuming too much, is to intercept it, though you don't sound very keen on doing that. I'm even less keen on it than you are, mostly because it isn't my problem." And then, I thought to myself, there was the matter of Rosalina. Dead because why? She got in the way? Tried to help me? Figured out she was being used? Tried to double-cross someone who was already double-crossing her? I didn't know her very well, so it wasn't as if I'd lost anyone important to me. It's just that I didn't like finding people dead when they obviously weren't supposed to be in that condition. She was sitting in a big white office looking out at the garden. Why? She had turned off the alarms. How? She was important to Vincente; he was important to me. Her death had knocked something loose. The problem was, I didn't know what.

"One thing at a time." Yakob pushed the trapdoor back in place. "Forget about intercepting it. I told you, it's already on its way. So now, step one is to find the manifest. Otherwise we look for a planning memo. They're different, but they usually say the same thing. OK, so I knew Yuri, if that is what you've been fishing for."

He smiled. I smiled back. Two rats trapped in a box.

He continued. "Yuri was supposed to have made a copy of one of them, whichever one he found. There's always a planning memo attached to these things. Don't ask me why. Maybe it's because the Swiss are usually involved."

"The Swiss?"

"Yeah, who did you think was supplying the machine tools? The Algerian mafia? Listen, I'm not sure how much you know and how much you're supposed to know. No one introduced us, and no one told me you'd be here. So from this point on, we don't say a lot to each other."

At least he knew something about operational security. Nice surprise. "Fine with me," I said. "Here's what I know: nothing. I was bored at home so thought I'd have some fun and catch a plane to Barcelona, but this isn't what I had in mind. For one thing, I'm a man who likes noodles, not dumplings. For another thing, I'm through pretending I'm Japanese. You need anything more by way of introduction?"

Yakob led the way to the exit. "You don't know anything, you like noodles, and you aren't Japanese. Can we put that on your gravestone?"

"If it fits."

8

The first place to look for documents was obviously the factory's main offices, near the entrance where the taxi had left me off. After being slapped around, losing my eyesight, and winding through underground passages, my sense of direction was a little wobbly. Someone once told me I was like a carrier pigeon. Once I've been somewhere, I can find the route again even years later. The only way to hone that skill is to get lost and find your way out again, over and over again. For that, a GPS is a tool of the devil, and whenever they used to issue one to me at home, I always sent it back. I didn't need it—until now. Now I was lost.

Yakob seemed to know the place by heart, though, and we trotted along the gravel path, past a series of outbuildings with bars on the windows, and up a short flight of stone stairs under a walkway lined with enormous oak trees. These had been left unscathed. Any one of them could have supplied wood for the ugly table in the dining room where I'd sat with the factory manager. When we got to a narrow steel door, off a short path nearly hidden behind a huge iron vase on a pedestal, Yakob stopped.

"You stay out here and keep watch," he said. "This is the secure office area. From the looks of it, I don't think there's anyone left around here. I'll only be a minute. If the bill of lading isn't here, the routing instructions might be. If they're not here, I'll have to get fancy and get into the vault area for the planning memo. That won't be fun. If I need your help for some reason, I'll whistle."

"Good plan," I said. "Afterward, you can pat me on the head and feed me a treat. You want me to bark if I see someone?"

"Let's just get this done, OK?" He did something with a keypad on the door and disappeared inside.

A few minutes later he came out again. "Nothing. The computers are wiped clean. The file cabinets are filled with old cheese sandwiches."

"Don't tell me, but you found the routing instructions."

Yakob shrugged modestly. "Not quite. But I think I found the shipping company. It's Chinese, and it's based in a city called Barbin. The company is Bing something. Here's the business card. Heard of it?"

I took the card and studied it. Maybe Yakob was nearsighted. The city was Harbin. "No, actually, I don't know much about China," I said, turning the card over.

I was doing what I always told my nephew not to do—bet. I was betting that if this operation was dangerously loose in some aspects, it was unusually tight in others. Luis knew some things about it, but seemed not to know others. Salvador was harder to figure out. He pretended not to know much, but he was involved up to his ears. For one thing, he showed up in a cleanup crew with a hypodermic needle. Yakob really did strike me as a late addition, and someone who had been working on the inside, like Yuri had, without much knowledge of the overall scheme. Yakob was fixated on bills of lading. Everyone has a specialty. That was his.

"Really? You don't know much about China?" Yakob was looking at a small map he'd taken from his pocket. "I heard you and Luis were friends. He's Chinese, isn't he?" The map disappeared back into the pocket. Wherever he was going, he didn't need me to know.

Yakob knew Luis? This was a bad sign. It meant he was in deeper than I figured. I decided to push my luck. "I thought you said you didn't know about me. How do you know who my friends are?"

"What I said was, no one introduced us. And I didn't know you'd be here. That doesn't mean I don't know about you. You got suspicions about me? Tough. My list against you is getting longer every minute."

At least he could remember what he said. That could be good or bad. It depended on who was remembering, and what. In his case, I didn't think it was a plus.

"Actually Luis is only part Chinese," I said. "We met in Macau. Macau isn't really China. It is, but it isn't. If you've never been there, you might like it."

"No thanks."

"You sure this is the shipping company? All you have is this business card, and it looks old. Old and greasy."

"You'd look greasy too if you had been under a cheese sandwich for a while. Give me that card."

I held onto it. "OK, what if this card is right? What can you do about it?" I put a little barb on the end of the question. Not much, but enough.

"What can I do about it? Plenty, but first I have to climb out of here and get somewhere I can send messages."

He didn't say "we" have to get out of here. Years ago I learned to be really sensitive about pronouns in these situations. It was clear he was planning to leave alone; the question was, in what shape was he planning to leave me?

"Salvador has a taxi," I said. "It must be outside somewhere. We'll split up and look for it."

Yakob didn't seem to think that was a good idea. He frowned.

"Out of curiosity," I said, "why do you think these offices weren't guarded? Where is everybody? They just let you waltz in and look around? Does that make sense?"

"Simple. The two we got in the office were just a couple of thugs. They probably hadn't gotten the word yet that the game is over. The rest of the guard force, or at least the smart ones, have figured out they don't have anything left to guard. The guys in suits left earlier, once they smelled trouble. If the dumpling machine is on its way, and they wiped the computer files, the guards don't care anymore. Anyone left is scrambling to get out. They are only loyal to their own necks. The machinists know they'll be well taken care of. They're paid not to talk, and if they're deported, they don't care. They're too valuable for anyone to sacrifice. Too bad we won't get a chance to squeeze information out of them. Madrid won't want the embarrassment."

Madrid? Yakob was working for the Spanish? Somehow I doubted it. "What about the Swiss?"

"They'll tut-tut and arrest someone, but it won't amount to much."

"In the garden, Vincente said the Chinese run this place."

"Then he must know something I don't. I've heard rumors, but that's not my problem, and it's not your problem either. Now I have a question. You still have the gizmo Viktor gave you?"

"It's in my pocket."

"Give it over. You don't need it anymore."

"What if I run across the machine?"

"You won't. As far as I can tell, you're done." That didn't ring so well in my ears. "If Viktor needs you for anything else, he'll let you know. Your next move from here is down along that wall about five hundred meters. There's a big, heavy gate. It swings in. Once you're outside, you're on your own. There should have been a pickup car to meet us"—he looked at his watch—"two hours ago. It won't be your friend the taxi man."

"Should have been, as in, it isn't there anymore?"

"They wouldn't hang around forever, especially if there was no signal from us. Unless Viktor has been able to get hold of someone to reschedule, they are long gone. Best of luck, cowboy."

"Funny way to run an exfiltration," I said, "but then, everything about this operation has been funny."

"Your people do things better, I suppose."

"You know my people? They usually don't rely on 'best of luck' as the fallback. Listen, there's no sense getting bogged down in what went wrong and who screwed up worse. If there is nothing else, we might as well split up like you said. I'll give you a minute to move out, then I'll head down the wall as you said."

I wasn't going to argue with him. I also wasn't about to go looking for a gate five hundred meters down the wall if that was what he
wanted me to do. The opposite direction might not be any better,
but I doubted if it could be any worse. After listening to him the last
few minutes, I had decided that Yakob was not someone I trusted
with my life. If there was more than one way out of this place, I'd
find it once I was clear of him.

"A pleasure working with you," I said. "If I see you again I don't
know who you are, do I have that right?"

"Right." He paused. "The gizmo. Hand it over."

"Apparently, I don't have it after all." I made a show of going
through my pockets. "They must have taken it off me when I was
drugged up."

Yakob took a step toward me, then must have thought better of
it, because without another word he turned and walked quickly back
toward the main path. As soon as he disappeared behind the iron
vase, I started through the bushes, keeping to the wall of the main
house, going the exact opposite direction from what he'd suggested.
The bushes along the wall were old, with thick branches that refused to give way. "Trees have a sense of decency," my grandfather
would often tell me. "Bushes? Not a bit. They are selfish, devious
little things."

So they are, I thought, but I don't need warnings of that from
the grave. A few minutes later, out of breath, my legs heavy and my
heart pounding, I stopped and slid to the ground behind a big
juniper bush. Shouting, two guards ran past on the path, then two
more. Yakob was wrong. Not everyone had left. I heard gunfire.
Then it was quiet.

Chapter Two

It couldn't have picked a worse time to rain. The canopy of the oak trees kept most of the water off me, but most isn't none, and a little water can soak your shoes as much as a flood. I curled up under one of the azaleas, but that wasn't much good. The rain stopped and the sky cleared fifteen minutes later. It was long enough for the ground to have become soggy, and the bushes more devious. They grabbed for me at every step. Wherever the bushes retreated, the mud sucked at my shoes. At last I decided that if I didn't get back to a solid path, I'd collapse and be found weeks later, grinning at the sky, my bones providing extra phosphorous for these man-eating bushes.

The main path, I discovered, was only a few steps away, on the other side of a monstrous hedge of ancient Japanese yews paralleling the azaleas. I could see it through a tiny break in the hedge, which was too high to climb over, and so impenetrable that there was no way through. I finally crawled under it on my stomach, cursing the Japanese, cursing Luis, vowing never to eat dumplings again as long as I lived. When I emerged, the front of my shirt was mud-soaked, and the back of my jacket was in shreds, but I was away from the bushes and on a pathway that might get me to safety. It might also get me killed if I ran into those guards, but there was no time to weigh the odds. After about fifty meters, the path diverged. As usual, I went right, and there, in front of me, was a small iron gate. On the other side, leaning against a tree and smoking a cigarette as if there wasn't much else to do in the world, was Salvador.

"You'd better have a key to this thing," I said through the gate, "because I'm done climbing over, under, or around things."

Salvador looked over at me, ground out his cigarette on the tree—careful to put the butt in his shirt pocket—and opened the gate. "It's not locked," he said. "This is the one gate they never locked, don't ask me why."

"At this point," I said, "who cares why? Do you have something to drink? My nerves are shot."

"The taxi is over there. I was waiting for another fare, but I might as well take you. You look awful, by the way. Can you take off that jacket? I don't want to get mud on the upholstery. I think I have a bottle of brandy under the seat, if I didn't drink it all the last time Vincente nearly got us all killed."

"You've run this operation before?"

"No, not exactly, but something close. Similar outcome. It's getting discouraging."

"It was worse than that for Rosalina."

Salvador shut the gate behind me. "She wasn't one to make mistakes. Someone must have sold her out."

"I vote for Yakob."

"He say something to you?"

"Not exactly, but he uses the first-person pronoun too much."

"Well, he won't be using it anymore. Don't ask why."

"I'm not interested why. How come he doesn't seem to know you?"

"He didn't need to know me. But I knew him."

We got in the cab and drove slowly down a dirt path to the main road.

"You want to turn on the meter?"

"It's a flat fee," he said. "Let's throw your jacket away here. Go on, just throw it out the window. It's best if they find it. We'll get you another one. Do you like brown tweed?"

"Possibly," I said. "But only if it's three buttons."

2

I was exhausted, and after a few sips of the brandy that Salvador handed me, I might have slept. Salvador had other ideas. He wanted to talk, and he wanted me to listen.

"What do you think?" he said over his shoulder. He was driving faster than seemed to me safe on the winding road.

"I think you can slow down a little."

"Relax," he said. "I can drive this section with my eyes closed." He closed his eyes and smiled. "See what I mean?"

I took another swallow of brandy. "You know we missed the dumpling machine, and no one knows its routing. Yakob thought it would go by truck."

"Yakob knew exactly how it was being transported."

I should have guessed that much about Yakob. So why was he so intent on going through the act with me?

"I think Rosalina found out," Salvador said, "and that's why they killed her."

"She stepped in to save me."

"She what?"

When I'd explained what happened, he pounded on the steering wheel a few times.

"She knew that was forbidden. She wasn't supposed to have anything to do with you once you got off the plane. She shouldn't even have been seated next to you. That was a bad idea. Someone saw you. Even if they only spotted you getting off the same plane it would have been fatal. It took us months, almost a year, to get her on the inside. They left her like that in the chair because they wanted Vincente to see. I think they were going to take a photo. They hoped it would drive him crazy."

"Will it?"

"Probably. I don't think anyone should work with him anymore. He's going to take too many chances. He was already taking too many." The car sped up as we crossed the double line to pass a truck. The truck honked, and Salvador answered.

Once we passed, I looked back. It wasn't a big truck, but it was big enough for three crates. The license plate was covered in mud.

"If he was so close to Rosalina, why did he let her get so far inside?" The brandy was a couple of drops away from putting me into a deep sleep. "He must have known it would be risky."

"Brown tweed," Salvador said. "And a tie, maybe dark blue."

"Blue like the sky in summer," I said. I was fighting to stay awake, but Salvador had turned up the radio, and the battle was going against me. A woman on the radio was singing a sad song. I decided the brandy made me sad, too. I took another sip, barely twisted the cap back on the bottle, and fell into a mournful sleep. Linden trees receded on the horizon as I struggled against azalea bushes, monstrous things that pushed me again and again and again into a deep, greasy swamp of Chinese dumplings.

3

When I woke, I was sweating. Salvador was pulling onto a narrow road with no lighting and missing most of its pavement, so we bumped our way over a series of ruts in the dark until we came to an isolated warehouse. The entrance was nearly hidden, lit by a single bulb hanging on a long wire over the loading dock. It didn't look like a place that had seen a delivery in years. The loading dock sagged; so did the stairs. I couldn't see the roof, but a good guess was that it sagged, too.

"Home again," Salvador said. "You can pay me later."

I didn't move. "You go in, I'll just wait here."

"Nope. There are people you have to meet and forms to fill out. It won't take very long. They may even have a tweed jacket that fits. Then we'll find you a bed and an air ticket home."

"I can't get out of the car. I can't move. It's my back."

Salvador shook his head. "Don't be difficult. I've had a bad night."

"You've had a bad night? You've had a bad night? And I was at a carnival the whole time, is that it?"

"You'll get your money, don't worry."

"What money? You think that's what I'm here for? Keep it. You don't have enough to make up for what I've been through. Use it to buy Rosalina a nice funeral. I don't need anything but a ticket out of this madhouse."

"I'll help you ease out of the car." Salvador had opened the back door. "Just move your legs a little, and use your hands to push yourself along. You can lean on me once you're out."

"I don't lean on anyone. Not here, not anywhere. Get out of my way, and don't hover. It makes me nervous." My shoes were still wet from the rain, as were my trousers and my shirt. The night air was cool, and it carried the sounds of a guitar off in the distance. If I'd had the strength, I would have broken away and run into the darkness toward the guitar, but I was too exhausted, and my back wouldn't have supported me running more than a few steps. There was nothing to do but walk with Salvador, slowly, up the rotten stairs and through a door—it had once been red, I noticed—that opened as we approached.

4

Vincente looked up as we entered. The space had once been a storage area, but now it was empty except for six chairs arranged in a loose semicircle. Four of the chairs were occupied. Vincente sat in one. Next to him sat the man who called himself Tomás. Luis was in the third chair, looking unhappy; next to him lounged the man I'd met on the bench outside the castle in Lisbon. He nodded at me. Luis had pushed his chair back so he seemed part of the group but slightly apart. He avoided my eyes. Tomás pretended to be preoccupied with adding figures in a small notebook that he balanced on his knee.

Salvador sat down in one of the empty chairs closest to Vincente. I remained standing. If I sat down, I knew I wouldn't get up again without help.

"We don't have time to go through everything," Vincente said.

I couldn't tell if we had come in while a conversation was already under way, or if they had been waiting for us. Vincente sounded tired, none of the bravado that had been in his voice every other time I'd heard him. "Some of the planning worked, most of it didn't. Rosalina . . ." His voice trailed off.

Tomás coughed. "We disrupted the factory, that's worth something."

"It's worth nothing if we can't find the machine that got out. Someone please tell me they got hold of the routing." Vincente looked at each of us in turn. "Someone? Did anyone do what he was supposed to do? Did we at least disable the goddamn thing? Inspector?"

No one spoke. They were all looking at me.

"Listen," I said, "I was promised a brown tweed jacket. After what I've been through, it's the least I deserve. And no, I didn't fix the machine. It disappeared before I could get to it again. Here's the gizmo you gave me." I tossed it at Vincente's feet. "Yakob, or whatever his name is, tried to get it from me, but I told him I'd lost it."

"Well," Tomás said, "that's something. We should have gotten rid of that snake when we had the chance." He turned to Vincente. "I told you he was a snake, right from the start."

I expected Salvador to break in to say that Yakob had already known the routing, but he didn't.

"Enough," Vincente barked, "enough raking over bad decisions. We need to stop that machine. Inspector, you don't have any idea what the route was? You didn't hear anything at all?"

Again I waited for Salvador. I looked at him. He looked away.

This wasn't my operation. I was only something the wind had picked up and blown into the middle of things. "Yakob thought he'd found a business card," I said.

"Well, did he?"

"It was for a Chinese shipping company. I had my doubts."

"And why is that?"

"It was covered with cheese."

Tomás sat back and looked at the ceiling. "I think they're going to use a small port in Italy," he said. "One of the fishing ports. If they load the crates onto a fishing boat, they can transfer it to something larger later." He looked at his watch. "They may already be on the A9 in France."

"I don't think so," I said. "I think I just saw the truck on the road a couple of hours ago."

Luis smiled to himself. Salvador didn't change expressions.

"Well, we can alert the ports, but I doubt if it will do any good." Vincente waited for a moment for someone to contradict him, then went on. "If that's all," he said, "I have some phone calls to make. Tomás has the paperwork. Unless I hear differently, this team is dissolved, permanently, as of tomorrow at noon. Someone please find the inspector a place to stay tonight, and then get him on a plane and out of here as early in the morning as you can. I don't want any footprints. No breadcrumbs. Nothing. Luis?"

Luis shrugged. "There's a seven o'clock flight to Paris. He'll be on it."

"No, I'm not going to Paris." I had never been to France, and I was damned if this was going to be my first visit. Not with the crummy passport I was carrying. The French have sharp eyes and short tempers when it comes to official documents. I'd never had to deal with it myself, but I'd heard the stories. "Find something else. Get me to Prague. I can get home from there by myself."

"Jesus," the man from the bench muttered.

"All right, we're done." Vincente opened his jacket and pulled a holster off his belt. "This has two rounds missing." He handed the pistol to Tomás. "I know we're accountable down to the penny, so I'll pay for them with Yakob's money. He won't be needing it. Any objections?" Tomás said nothing, but Vincente hadn't waited anyway.

Tomás pocketed the pistol and shook his head as Vincente walked into the shadows. "The man said we're done. That means we're done. I'll get you the necessary paperwork tomorrow. *Adeus.*" He looked at me. "You need to get cleaned up." He disappeared toward the back of the room.

A minute later, the man from the bench stood up. "I've got a plane to catch and a lot of reports to write. Good night, all."

As soon as he was out the door, we heard a motorcycle engine start. The driver let it idle for a moment and then pulled away with a terrific roar.

Salvador waited another minute after that, as if this was a familiar ritual always to be honored before leaving. "Luis will find you a change of clothes and a hotel," he said to me. "If you ever get back here, we'll go to the Roman ruins."

"I'll buy dinner," I said. "Something from the sea." We shook hands quickly, and then I was alone with Luis.

Neither of us said anything. Finally I decided that one of us had to break the silence or we'd be there all night.

"I guess I don't owe you anymore, Luis. We're even, wouldn't you say?"

Luis stood and paced slowly around the room. "This was a surprise to me, my friend," he said. "I thought it would be something easy, like in Macau. But they chew up people here like they're a plate of mussels." He stopped. "Are you hungry?"

"I'm not," I said. "But I'll watch while you eat. Maybe I'll join you in a glass of wine and a few pieces of bread. Listen, I hate to keep asking, but can you find me a jacket and some trousers first? I could use some dry shoes, too, if that's not too much trouble. If I stagger into a restaurant like this, they'll send me around to the kitchen door."

"One thing," Luis said. "No questions during dinner. That's the rule. When an operation is over around here, it's done. No one has a rearview mirror. Straight ahead, that's the game. Not like in Macau. We practically walk backwards after an operation trying to figure out what went wrong."

"A good way to end up in the swamp every time," I said. "I mean, either way it doesn't work. That's why at home we used to look where were going, and look where we'd been at the same time. We couldn't afford big failures in those days. I don't know what is what anymore."

"You might like a shirt, too." Luis had a yellow tape measure out and was measuring my arm. "Stand straight," he said. "You're slumping."

5

The restaurant was all candlelight, which was good because the only pants Luis could find were too long.

"If we were in Macau, I could have had those fixed in twenty minutes," he said. "The tailor down the street from my office is a Malaysian who works for the Singaporeans. We help each other out. A little information goes a long way in Macau. Your people used to go into his shop, but they stopped a few years ago."

"Tailored suits? My people?"

"Oh, sure. Some of them, anyway. Good suits, though their taste in ties wasn't always the best. One time they went into the shop and bought fifty silk ties. Not real silk, of course, but they didn't care. The main thing was the color. They all had to be red and black stripes."

"Only that?"

"That's what the tailor said they told him, only that."

"Who came in the shop next, did your friend tell you?"

"Yeah, it was a South Korean. Two of them, actually."

"Let me guess. They wanted ties. Had to be silk. Had to be black and red stripes. Not the other way around, right?"

"The tailor said he told them he had just sold the last one. They weren't happy."

"Of course not. They never are." I took a piece of bread and broke it in half. "Why do we do this, Luis? Maybe I should switch to washing dishes and sweeping floors."

"Well, it makes no difference to me." Luis examined the wine bottle in the candlelight. "I'm staying in Macau from now on, no matter how many offers they send me from here, and no matter who signs the papers. I'll clean tables in Lulu's restaurant, and then I'll sing to her at night under the stars. Come and visit us, Inspector. Don't come back here." He filled my glass and then his own. "There's not much to toast, I guess. *Saúde.*" He tipped his glass and drained it. "You sure you won't join me in dinner? Maybe an appetizer of artichoke and ham? Or the goat cheese and figs?"

I shook my head. "Do you think they have any vodka?"

Luis picked up the menu. "Russian?"

"Russian, Finnish, Mongolian, and Polish, exactly in that order."

Chapter Three

By the time Luis got me to the hotel, I was singing an old song about a fisherman who fell in love with a wave.

"It was all we could find on short notice," Luis said as he helped me up the stairs. "Very small rooms and very thin walls, but it will do for one night. The bathroom is at the end of the hall. You're supposed to have a sink in your room. We'll see."

The room was so small the bed barely fit. The only other furniture was a tiny table with a lamp that didn't work.

"They've hidden the sink," I said, and collapsed on the bed. "Tell them you're taking it off the bill."

"The car will pick you up at five A.M., Inspector. Don't worry about the airport; you'll get through the security check with no problem, and I'll make sure you have a seat on the plane. It's a propeller plane. I hope you don't mind. Some people think they're dangerous."

"Speaking of dangerous, what about the new Inquisition?"

"Don't worry. By now Vincente will have pounded on a few desks in the local security offices about the factory that was operating here under their aristocratic noses. They won't want any trouble while they figure out how to dodge this. They'll ignore you. Shall I hang up your jacket?"

"There aren't any hangers." I shut my eyes. "You can't even hang it over a chair."

Luis reached into his coat pocket and took out a brown envelope. "This is fifteen thousand euros. It's yours, don't argue. Take it home; maybe you can use it to buy some exotic wood for a bookcase. I'll put it next to you, here, on the pillow."

"I'm going to ask you a question, Luis. Just answer me straight out, OK? And don't say it depends on the question."

"It always depends on the question, you know that."

"Do they know where that machine is going? Do they know who bought it?"

"That's two questions. But there is only one answer, so you can apply it to both. They think they do."

"But they don't know."

"It doesn't matter, does it? If they think they know, that's all they need. Anything else would just get in the way."

"My regards to Lulu," I said, sitting up out of respect to a departing guest. "*Adeus.*"

"Five o'clock, Inspector. Have a safe journey home." He patted my shoulder, backed out the door, and turned to go down the stairs. Suddenly he appeared again with a tiny bottle in his hand. "It's Mongolian vodka," he said. "It's the biggest bottle I could find."

2

The plane left late, at 7:45 A.M., which was just as well since they stopped me at the security checkpoint and wanted to know why I had no luggage. It turns out it wasn't a propeller plane, but that didn't make me feel any better when we went through a storm that threw everyone else's luggage around the cabin. In Prague I ran to catch another flight, this one to Germany. The Germans scowled over my passport at the control booth but waved me through anyway. The next flight, overnight and crowded with Chinese who talked the whole way, got me as far as Beijing, and from there it was easy enough to find a plane to Yanji. I bought a red and black tie at the airport in Germany to help me convince my nephew I'd spent the last week visiting friends in Berlin.

There isn't much else to do on an airplane but think unless you want to sleep. I did, but the Chinese didn't, so I went over things in my mind. Luis had said there was no rearview mirror for the operation, but we were flying into the dawn, so I figured that counted as looking ahead.

There were enough facts jumbled together from the past week to support at least five different explanations. I decided to leave aside the characters in the drama for the moment and concentrate on the main events. My being recruited from northeast China to an operation in Spain wasn't easily explained, unless they—I was going to have to work my way to who "they" were at some point—were more interested in nationality than personality. A particular flag had to be flapping in the breeze for anyone who was watching. As long as it was the right flag, it could have been anyone, and it turned out to be me.

If that was so, why the focus on dumplings? Japanese liked dumplings; so did Koreans, and so did Chinese. Then it occurred to me. They needed Mike, and the reason they needed Mike was they needed to point the way through Yanji. And they needed Yanji because . . . well, it was on the border with North Korea.

I stopped and chewed on that thought. Mike was a noodles man, so they made some noise that would leak into various channels that he was switching to dumplings. That would explain why a dumpling machine was supposedly on its way to Yanji. Only for anybody who saw even part of the trail, it wasn't a dumpling machine.

That was one big part of the puzzle, or at least a few pieces of it. So why didn't Luis's friends just jump in and take down that factory? They didn't like what it was producing. Why all this sniffing around? Why make something so simple into a dangerous high-wire act? It got Rosalina killed, and almost got me killed, too. If they didn't want that damned machine going anywhere, just go the hell into the factory and pull it apart! Why all the mystery about where it was supposed to be going? It was going across the river from Yanji. That's why I was pulled in. But if they already knew where it was going, what did they need me for? And why the shadow play about Japanese?

PART IV

Chapter One

The picture on the TV screen in the hotel room flickered briefly before it went blank. I felt Tuya shift her weight beside me.

"I thought this was an advanced country," she said. "I can't go to sleep without the TV on."

"It will probably be just be a minute. Maybe someone in the hotel plugged in an iron or something."

"Look out the window and see if this is the only building without electricity. *Affrettando.*"

I got up and pulled aside the curtains. The entire city for as far as I could see was black. The only lights were from cars moving through the streets. From below there was a screech of brakes and then a loud crash, then another, then yet another. Traffic lights were probably out as well. "I better call the office."

My cell phone was dead. I picked up the receiver on the bedside phone. It was dead, too.

"Nothing doing," I said. "It might be a few minutes more." I could hear emergency generators starting up somewhere, but not in the hotel. Fire engines and police car sirens wailed through the streets. When I went back to the window, it was like being in another century, darkness below and stars above. I wondered what Uncle O would say.

Tuya sat up and began breathing strangely. She gulped for air for a few seconds, then lay back against the pillows. "I need a cigarette," she said. "I tried to quit before I took this assignment."

"You smoke?"

"Pressure," she said. "If I don't smoke, I get headaches. You don't have to act so surprised."

"You? I thought your . . . you know . . ."

"Say it, go on."

"No, it's just that, I thought with your talent . . ."

"You don't think I'm normal? My 'talent,' as you put it, takes me out of the realm of normal?"

"Of course I think you're normal. I think you're better than normal. I just meant I thought because of the way you take care of yourself . . ."

"How would you know how I take care of myself?" She was sitting up now, pulling the sheet around her body in a good imitation of an unassailable fortress.

"You're in such good . . . shape. I mean . . . Never mind. If you need to smoke, by all means, go ahead and smoke a cigarette."

"I smoke two packs a day."

"Then I'll buy a lighter and a couple of ashtrays and we'll live happily ever after."

"You have matches? I'll smoke here."

"It's a nonsmoking room."

"Pardon me, Mr. Cop. You can arrest me after I have a cigarette, OK?"

"I don't have any matches."

"Shit," she said, and covered her head with a pillow. A moment later, she sat up again. "This isn't what I expected. It's my fault. We're supposed to be working. Let's work. That will make things easier."

"All right," I said. "You're my source. So tell me something."

She smiled and put her leg behind her head. I was ready to break a thousand regulations at that moment, but before I could move, she laughed and put her other leg behind her head. "You want to know about Mike, right?"

That stopped me in my tracks. "That was the idea, yes. You know something?"

"He's moved from noodles to dumplings. He says noodle shops are too much trouble, low return, not upscale enough. He calls the shop owners squirrels. He complains they hide the profits and he can't afford the muscle it takes to squeeze it out of them. So he's taken up dumplings, maybe hooked up with some big Japanese dumpling king."

"Japanese dumplings?" I sat down on the other side of the bed from her. That made me nervous, so I moved to the only chair in the room. "I don't like Mike doing business up here, and I'm going to throw him out, as far away as possible. When he shows up, there is suddenly too much money sloshing around. He brings nothing but trouble, and I don't need more trouble. I have enough to do watching the border."

"Well, that's not my concern," she said. "You're the one in charge of security, not me."

"True, but you're working for me."

"Yes and no."

"I forgot, yes and no. What is it right now? Yes?"

"Ask me another question about Mike, why don't you."

"Why dumplings?"

"That's exactly what we wanted to know."

"We? Who is we?" One thing I'd learned from Uncle O—pay attention to pronouns.

"You think Mongolians just sit around and do nothing all day long but watch sheep?"

"No, I do not think you sit around. I was just wondering."

"Tell me about those funny deaths, the ones in the restaurants. I assume you consider them germane."

"What if I told you it was a state secret?"

"But you wouldn't do that." She rocked back and forth. "Would you?"

"No." I took a deep breath. "We have to operate as one, no barriers."

"I suppose so." She unhooked her legs and brought them slowly off her shoulders. "Despite what you think, Mike is not key to this. He may not even know what is really going on, but I have a feeling he knows something that will put us closer to where we need to be."

I didn't say anything.

"You disagree?" she asked.

"No, I don't disagree." I put thoughts of where we needed to be out of my mind.

"Mike," she said, "we're talking about Mike."

"OK, what might he know? Like what?"

"Like why all those people died on the same night."

"Did he have anything to do with that? There's nothing he's ever done that suggests he is a mad dog."

"Not directly, he wasn't involved in the murders. At least, they weren't his idea."

"Indirectly, then."

"I figure he was given an urgent contract to fulfill and he was under a lot of pressure. Don't ask me who gave him the contract. I'm still trying to find that out."

"Mike doesn't do well with contracts, we already know that. Besides, who would give him one? He doesn't like working with the Russian mafia, so that's out. And he had a bad experience with the triads, a lot of bad blood. Not much left, except the Japanese mafia."

"Maybe your uncle knows something."

"Wait a minute. Are you the one who told him that Mike was in town?"

"No, I haven't seen your uncle since you two were in Ulan Bator. He must have talked to someone else who knew about Mike. If you can find whoever that is, maybe they'll be able to tell you who paid Mike to . . ." She paused, puzzled. "To kill seven diners? Makes no sense."

"Could be exactly that. If it makes no sense, maybe it's not supposed to."

"Random?" She shook her head. "That's hard to believe."

"Do you know anything about an explosion?"

"Where?"

"On the outskirts of town. The chief of police thinks it was a bomb, and that it killed an unknown number of people. Last I talked to him, he was going to gather up body parts and see if they could figure out how many. That was a while ago. Funny, I haven't heard."

"You think this has something to do with Mike? Bombs aren't his style."

"How would you know his style? Have you met him?"

She was silent, serious, and serene.

"Maybe Mike didn't have any hand in that bomb." I decided the Mongolians had a file on Mike that I needed to see. "It's still a good bet that he is connected to the other bodies that turned up all at once on that Thursday night."

"Maybe, maybe not. Don't get too sure too fast. We have a saying in Mongolia about certainty."

"I collect sayings, but let's wait on that."

"It's about a man and a woman on a lonely winter's night, moonless, with the wind blowing so hard the *ger* is trembling."

"What about the sheep?"

"Frozen stiff."

"You realize I think you are beautiful."

"Don't forget, buster, I work for you."

"You said yes and no. Which is it right now?"

She slid under the covers. "No," she said softly. *"Amoroso."*

2

The power came on again a little past midnight. Phone service was right behind. The hotel phone rang first; after that my mobile buzzed.

"Do something, will you?" Tuya reached for a bottle of water the hotel had put on the end table. "What time is it?"

"It's almost twelve fifteen. Which should I answer first?"

"You're a major, you decide."

I put my mobile phone under the pillow and picked up the hotel phone. "This had better be important," I said. "Who is this?"

"Major Bing? I am assistant manager Wu. You may remember that I helped you locate a swindler about a year ago."

"If I stick my foot out around here I trip a swindler, especially in this hotel. Never mind that. What do you want?"

"We were told that Beijing wants to speak with you immediately." The assistant manager was nearly breathless, though whether with excitement or fear I couldn't tell over the phone.

"Who told you that?"

"I'm afraid I don't know who it was. But they said it was urgent and that we should wake you. I hesitated, but then it did seem urgent. So I called."

"How do you know it wasn't a crank call? No one even knows I'm here."

"Well"—Wu's tone changed—"it looks like someone does, doesn't it? They asked for you specifically. At first we told them there was no such guest registered, but things got nasty and names were named."

"So, who specifically did this unknown urgent voice say I am supposed to call?"

"They said you'd know."

"I don't know, Wu. I don't know. Beijing is a big city. You realize that it is a big city?"

"I've heard it said, yes."

"Good. If you get any more of those calls, hang up. And don't bother me again. Am I clear?"

"I'll have to talk with my manager. We could lose our license if we get someone in Beijing mad at us."

"You think it will be easier if Beijing, a place far away, is angry, or if someone very close—very, very close—is mad at you?" I slammed the phone down. "You can't do that with mobile phones," I said to Tuya.

"Your pillow has been buzzing the whole time you've been on

the other line. Can't you find a better ringtone for your mobile? A lullaby or something? Wind chimes? Answer it, will you?"

"The phone is not buzzing. See? It's dead." I held it up for her benefit. "Whoever it was gave up."

"Don't be difficult. Look to see who called and call them back. Maybe it was your uncle."

I thought about it. "My uncle is in Europe. Why would he call me? Anyway, the number didn't register."

"Message?"

I looked. "Yes, there is." I listened to the message. It was scratchy, and there were clicks and whistles in the background. "You'll never guess who it's from," I said when I put the phone down.

"Mike."

"How the hell did you know?"

"It's obvious. He called the hotel, they wouldn't connect him, so he found your mobile number and called. Any crook can buy it. What's the message?"

"You wouldn't care to guess that, too?"

"He's telling you to back off, that there are bigger things going on than you could possibly know."

"Are you on his payroll?"

"No, I'm on your payroll, remember? I just know something about this character, that's all. He's feeling the heat from someone bigger and meaner than he is, and he's scared. Otherwise, why would he call you?"

"You tell me and we'll both know."

"Don't be sore. You're still my idol." She batted her eyes and smiled. "See?"

3

I arrived at the office later than usual to find a stack of phone messages, most of them from the chief of police. He wanted a meeting at ten thirty that morning near the fish place where we'd had dinner.

It had to be at ten thirty, not earlier and not later. And it had to be there, in the alley. All morning it had been raining hard, and I wasn't in the mood to stand around in the rain waiting for anyone. I tried calling back, but there was no answer. When I called the duty number at police headquarters, an answering machine said to leave a message, everyone was on assignment. That got me curious, so I went out to see if our duty officer knew what was happening.

"No, sir. Quiet as the moon reflected on Tianchi."

"Cut the sappy images." I rapped on his desk. "No one is answering at police headquarters. Find out what's going on. Or are they just having a party?"

"Right away. I'll get back to you."

"I have to go out. Call my mobile if you get something useful. If the chief of police calls, transfer it to me right away. Clear?"

"Yes, sir. Do you want your security detail? They're around the corner."

"No, once in a while it's good to go out by myself. It spooks the opposition. They can't figure out if I'm really alone, or if they can't see who is behind me."

4

It was almost ten thirty when I got to Fuzhou Alley. The rain had finally stopped, but it was still misting. A group of rats huddled under the shelter of a pile of broken bricks. The biggest one came out to look me over, but he went back under the bricks when the rain started up again. I waited ten minutes and was about to leave when the chief turned the corner. He took a couple of halting steps toward me, but as soon as he shook his head, I knew our meeting was off. There was a dress shop partway down the alley, a jewelry store that sold fake jade, and a furniture repair place that my uncle visited once in a while. The rest of the buildings were vacant. A few years ago the block had been set for a big redevelopment project planned by a South Korean with a lot of money, but the deal had stalled, and so the place was left to decay. The rats didn't mind.

The back door of the jewelry store was open, so I ducked in. The owner, a pinched old man named Liao with a history of helping whoever paid him, made a face. He wasn't happy to see me. He never was.

"It's jade," he said. "It may not look like jade, but it is. We get it directly from Burma. It's all completely legal. You want to see my import permits? They're stamped front and back."

"I don't care about your phony permits. I don't care if you are selling green bricks as jade. Since when do I worry about that stuff?"

"Look, Major, things aren't good these days. Business is off. First, all those people were murdered in the restaurants. Even a foreigner! Who murders foreigners? Nobody goes out after dark anymore, worried they might not make it home again. Then someone, never mind who, came around wanting payoffs to make sure our shops don't burn down. I'm just a merchant trying to make money for my family. I can't work if my shop burns down, can I?"

I laughed in his face. "You are a crook, a pedophile, and a security risk. I'm going out your front door, and if anyone asks, you didn't see me come through here. The next time I run across your name in any reports, they better be favorable. Otherwise, if I were you, I'd make sure I was in Burma, or as far away from me as you can get."

"I guess you don't want to hear about the mayor, then." For a jeweler, Liao had long nails. He tapped them on his workbench. "Just as well."

"Make it quick, Liao. Don't waste my time. What about the mayor?"

"He and Mike have been talking."

It shouldn't have surprised me, but it did. "How would you know?"

"Same as you. I have to keep my finger on what is going on." He waved the longest fingernail at me. "Lots of people come in this shop."

"I bet they do."

"Sometimes your uncle comes in." Liao gave me an ugly look.

"Never mind my uncle. What about Mike?"

"Upstairs." Liao pointed his nose at the ceiling. "A meeting. There were several people. The mayor and three others went up. Mike was already there. Listen, I don't own the building. People think I do, but I don't. So I don't control the room upstairs. People use it, they don't ask me."

"Names."

"I don't know, they didn't come in and hand me name cards."

"But you knew who they were. You saw them."

"Maybe."

"Liao, I don't pay for information, and you know it. The last time you tried this, you had a couple of bad nights in the hills with my people. Who was in that meeting upstairs? Was one of them from Xinjiang?"

The old man stopped tapping his nails. "What if he was?"

"Next time someone from Xinjiang is in town, you tell me. No exceptions."

"You already saw him? Why are you asking me if you already know who it was?"

"We had a quick conversation, that's all. He might not want to shake hands for a while."

"OK, one of them was a Uighur, so what? I don't like them. They're shifty eyed. But like I said, I don't own the building. The other two, I'm not sure. One of them might have been Russian, you know, one of those mixtures where you can't always tell by their looks. Kind of a wolf, if you know what I mean."

"The last one? Don't hold out on me, Liao. Don't even think about it."

"The last one? Well, he was real tall."

"Shoes?"

I could see he was thinking of a smart remark, maybe something like "Yeah, he was wearing shoes, what do you think? People go barefoot these days?" But halfway through he changed his mind because he knew I wasn't in the mood for playing games.

"I asked you a question," I said.

He settled on the simple answer, "Brown."

"Scuffed?"

"Yeah." He grinned.

I grabbed Liao's hand. "You need this. A jeweler needs his hands, even one who works with fake jade. Tell your friends, if you have any, that I'm not backing off. You want me to repeat that?"

"Major, don't twist it, OK? I heard you."

"And?"

"I'll put out the word."

"And?" I twisted his hand, just to the edge.

"I'll keep my eyes open!"

"Yes, you will. I think that's what you'll do, Liao."

5

This is how it always happens in these cases. Dead ends everywhere, then suddenly a window flies open, and if you climb through it, you come up with a few facts that you didn't have before.

New fact one: My deputy had already met with the mayor, probably even before he showed up at the office. New fact two: My new deputy had also met with Mike. I was willing to bet this was the "appointment" he was so anxious to get to when I stopped him in the hall. It might not be a bad idea to transfer him out right away, but for that I needed a reason. Citing a crooked jeweler as my source wouldn't get me very far. What I had to do right now was find out the reason for the big meeting. That was where new fact three might be useful—a Russian who looked like a wolf.

6

"Dmitri Alexandrovich," I said, "the next time I knock on your door, you should answer it nicely."

"The next time, Bing, you should knock politely." The Russian was clearly annoyed. "Who is going to pay for this?"

I'd kicked the door in, and it was hanging by one hinge. "Maybe you can dip into your rainy-day funds. See? It's raining again."

"What do you want? I'm busy right now. I was planning to invite you to tea sometime, maybe next week."

"I'll bet you were. You're always busy, that's why I admire you. I hear you had a meeting."

"I have a lot of meetings, Bing. People who sell insurance do that."

"Is that what you're doing these days? Selling insurance?"

"If you'd looked at the door before kicking it in, you'd have seen the sign. You want insurance? You'll have to make an appointment."

"Does the mayor need insurance? Is that why you were meeting with him?"

The Russian gave me a look like a wolf that had other things on its mind.

"The mayor," I said, "not to mention your old friend Mike, and someone else. A lot of insurance, is that it? Group insurance? Better rates?"

"Yeah? So? There was a meeting. It's not illegal to have meetings."

I laughed. "Dmitri Alexandrovich, you are such a funny guy sometimes. Of course it's not illegal to have meetings. It's also not illegal for me to take you up into the hills and handcuff you to a tree. I'll bet the bears would be interested."

"There are no bears around here, Bing."

"Dmitri, Dmitri, don't tell me where there are bears and where there aren't. Just answer the question. What is Mike doing back here? You don't like him, I don't like him, and he doesn't like either of us. But you were sitting together with him in a meeting with our mayor. I don't find that normal."

"Normal, not normal." The Russian shrugged. "Mike had a business proposition."

"Ah, good. I'm interested. You see my ears bending toward you?"

"That's it. He had a proposition."

"No, no, no. Dmitri Alexandrovich, haven't you and I been through this sort of thing before? Short answers are only good when

I ask for something along the yes-no axis. In this case, I want details. You aren't even supposed to be in Yanji. The last time you were here, I told you to get out and stay out."

"You don't own this city, Bing."

"That's true. But I run security here, me and no one else. If you think the mayor can protect you once I decide to toss you off a roof, you might want to think again."

"Like I said, you don't own this city." The wolf eyes narrowed. "I came here to help out. Mike said he had some business. Sure, him and me don't see eye to eye all the time, but business is business."

"Which was it, noodles or dumplings?"

"Huh?"

"You're all in the same room, Mike is switching from noodles to dumplings, he's opened a fish restaurant and moved in some tough lady from Harbin to run it and do whatever else he wants, and suddenly we have seven diners die all at once. Three of them in a noodle restaurant. Two more behind a dim sum place. You know anything about that?"

"Huh? I mean, you know me, Bing. I'm not crazy. Seven people? Why would I do something like that?"

"When you get credentials, you can ask me questions. For now, you answer. Here's where you are on the answer scale. Zero. You aren't scoring too good." I picked up a teacup and threw it against the wall.

"Hey, that was my grandmother's!"

"I believe you. Now, tell me, what was that meeting about? You, Mike, and the mayor."

"And the tall guy." The wolf grinned, just like Liao had, only with more teeth. "Don't forget him."

Chapter Two

Dmitri and I parted on bad terms. That was normal. What wasn't normal was that for once, he'd told me something that he hadn't meant to. The murders of seven people in one night had shaken him. He didn't know who was responsible, but he wanted to make sure I understood he had nothing to do with it. He was a crook, he would rough people up if he had to, he said, but he drew the line at murder, at least at more than once in a while.

"Very good," I said. "You have a moral center. So who did this? Would Mike?"

He thought about it. "No, Mike couldn't. It would take several people to do this. Murder isn't easy. Not here, anyway. It's not like we use car bombs."

"Bombs," I said. "You do know something about bombs, as I recall. Last time you were in town, we worked over your apartment. You had boxes of strange things in the closest. Timers. Wires. Cell phones. Ever made something small?"

"Never made anything, Bing. I was in sales then, I told you. It was merchandise, inventory. Strictly business."

"You are not a convincing personality, Dmitri. I'm beginning to think you have something to do with those murders."

"Bing! Listen! I was trained to work one on one. To do seven in one night, in different locations? Almost at the same time? It would need quite an organization, a lot of resources to do that. I don't have those resources. And Mike is a little guy. He talks big, but he is a tiny fish, a sardine. Maybe less than a sardine. He couldn't pull it off. You sure those murders are all connected?"

"I have no idea. You know I'm not a cop, Dmitri. You know what I want to find out. Let's forget about the murders. Let's talk about Mike."

2

On the way back to the office, I was thinking about what Dmitri had told me when I spotted the police chief standing on the corner near Fuzhou Alley.

"You still here? Why did you wave me off?"

"Sorry, I thought I saw the mayor's driver coming out of the furniture store."

"Maybe the mayor needs a chest for all of his money."

"Maybe. But I checked. It wasn't him. He and the mayor are up in the hills getting ready for another party. Anyway, we finally got the results from the coroner on two of the stiffs."

"It took this long?"

"The coroner left town the night we found the bodies. Vacation, he said."

"Paid for by the mayor, I'll bet. What's the verdict? If you can believe the coroner's reports."

"I don't judge either way. You want to hear?"

"Not really, but go ahead."

"The upscale diner died of unknown causes."

"Very useful. Not the sauce."

"And the blonde died of an overdose of something, and it wasn't happiness."

"What about the other five?"

"Nothing yet."

"And the bits and pieces from the explosion?"

"Not human. The coroner thinks it was a couple of cows. Someone who lives in the neighborhood says the farmers up there had a running boundary dispute, and one of them finally got fed up and threw a stick of dynamite over the fence."

"You believe that?"

"We're checking."

"Well, don't bother about the noodle shop corpses. I'm less sure about the ones behind the dim sum shop."

"You want to go sit somewhere and explain?"

"No, I have to drive to the airport. My uncle is flying in. He's been away."

"We figured he was either sick or out of town because he hasn't been wandering around. Did he go on one of his trips to Harbin for lumber?"

"He called from Beijing to say he went to Portugal but didn't like it so he took a train to Berlin to visit old friends."

The police chief didn't say anything.

"Well, I was surprised, too. But he used to get around a lot. Could be."

"Could be." The chief nodded.

"Anyway, the three in the noodle shop made the mistake of being there when Mike was making the transition to noodles."

"Mike is back?"

"You didn't know? Great bunch of cops you have."

"You can't expect miracles from the street cops up here. They don't get paid enough, not—"

"—not after all the deductions. I know. Never mind. Yes, Mike is back, and he's switched his focus to dumplings. In fact, he's hooked up with some big Japanese dumpling king, a sort of globalization. Mike must have figured the best way to move our local consumers from noodles to dumplings was to poison a few of them."

"Then why kill off two hookers who were sharing dumplings?"

"Maybe connected, maybe not. If you want a theory, it was in order to put the other dumpling shops out of business. That way there would be no competition. What a world, huh?"

"Yeah, what a world. I'm still stuck with seven deaths on my statistics for the month."

As soon as he said that, something clicked. "No, you're not," I said. "These happened on the same night, but they're not all linked. At least two of them are routine—the blue-eyed tourist died of a drug overdose. Not much you could have done about that, especially if she got the drugs from the mayor's Uighur friends. And the diner at the hotel restaurant, well, that's an expensive place. No one will want to pursue it too far. Maybe he swallowed the salad the wrong way. That leaves five that fall in the 'suspicious' column. The mayor wanted to pin them on me, the result of terrorism that he said I hadn't stopped. But now he can't do that, because I know he was meeting with Mike. Believe me, Beijing would love to pin something like this on Mike, doesn't matter whether they can prove it or not. It will help them close the file. And if my Ministry can use them to close the file, they don't go on your statistics."

"Thanks."

"Who knows, maybe this is even the hammer I've been waiting for to use on the mayor."

The police chief looked down at his shoes and smiled. "Yeah, well." He looked up again. "I guess I'm off noodles and dumplings for a while. But what about fish? You think fish is still all right?"

"You never know until you try," I said.

"I guess so." The chief thought it over. "And our fish lady? She's clean?"

"You said it yourself, she's too tough to be controlled. But her place is dark and out of the way, a good spot for meetings that you should be watching."

"Well, as a theory, it's not bad, Bing. It all fits."

"Yeah, it all fits. That's what makes me nervous."

I waited until the chief had disappeared around the corner, and then walked slowly a few steps down Fuzhou Alley. It was time to try some fish soup.

Chapter Three

Open the crate." I handed my uncle a crowbar.

"I can already tell you what's in there."

"Open it."

Inside was a large machine. An instruction book in five languages was fastened to one of the knobs. It promised that careful adherence to the instructions would result in perfect dumplings, "every time."

"Satisfied?" My uncle picked up some of the wood from the crate and examined it. "They ought to outlaw this cheap plywood."

I looked at the instruction manual and then turned a couple of the knobs. "What is this?"

"If you were a seabird, you might fly to a small port on the north shore of Hokkaido. You might circle and watch as a Russian fishing boat pulls in and unloads three crates."

"Dmitri," I said softly.

Uncle O pretended to look at the instruction booklet.

"Let me guess," I said. "The real one was being sent to Japan the whole time."

"It was."

"And you knew it?"

"Not at first. Luis, poor Luis, didn't know anything about it, and neither did that bastard Mike."

"Tuya?"

My uncle looked away. "What do you think?"

"I'll give you a theory. It's a new theory. I just threw away my old one, so I have to make this up as I go. You don't have to say anything. Just listen for a change, all right?"

"I'm listening."

"From the very start, the machine was to be shipped to Japan."

"That's all you've got?" My uncle snorted.

"No, I'd say they figured it couldn't go directly, or at least not without an enveloping cloud of misdirection. There had to be absolutely no risk that it would be revealed. To avoid that, the whole thing had to leak into the world in overlapping and almost impossibly contradictory layers. The layers were sticky. If you picked one up, it stuck to you and gathered stray facts along the way. Stray facts that had been spread around on purpose."

"For example?" That was exactly what my uncle would ask whenever he already knew the answer.

"For example, someone had the idea to make it look like your friends across the river were shipping in something highly sensitive under a false label. Then they layered on another cover story that was accurate as far as it went. The machine wasn't going across the river, but was actually meant to go to Japan, a special model ordered by the dumpling king. Only, of course, it wasn't ordered by the dumpling king. Anyone who got that far in pulling the threads would find a third layer."

"Which was?" Again, he was just leading me along the path.

"Which was that the machine—labeled as a dumpling machine—was really going across the river for your friends. The Japanese mafia was employed, a route to northern China traced out, that rat Mike was brought in to arrange transport across the Tumen River from Yanji to North Korea, and finally, there was a series of murders in Yanji to add to the story that something highly sensitive was going on. Mike didn't know for sure it had nothing to do with dumplings. And the Uighur with the limp helped out by inviting his relative up here for something big but mysterious."

"A lot of seams."

"No, once it was under way, it was easy to make the whole story work because it fit what everyone already thought they knew was true. Once an intelligence organization decides it knows what is going on, all the facts fit. Those that don't fit end up in the wastebasket. So all they had to do was feed in the pieces of the story in the right place, at the right time. The fish lady had been sent months earlier to begin to lay the groundwork. She was putting out stories to the girls on Dooran Street about unusual visitors to her restaurant. I put the question to her. She was the one who said she'd seen Mike before he crossed the river, and you helped spread it. You know the lady?"

"In a manner of speaking. But I didn't spread it. I told you, no one else."

"You could have told me who the source was."

"That would have violated our agreement. Your sources are yours; mine are mine. We agreed."

I thought about asking whether he knew Dmitri, but that would have drawn a blank stare, so I let it go. Instead I pushed a little on a different door. "They played you like a fish on a line, didn't they?"

If I had worried this might annoy my uncle, I needn't have. He was very calm, almost amused. "They thought so, yes."

His calmness touched a nerve. "Oh, no you don't, not this time, uncle. For once I can see through you. They needed to have it look as if that machine was going to the North, and what better way to do it than to get a North Korean involved?"

"Even me?" He smiled. It was his satisfied smile.

"Especially you."

"Good, you have a theory. You have leads. And now you have some proof. What are you going to do with it?"

"That's my problem. I'll do what I need to do. But right now I want to know, how did you figure it out?"

"Phony shipping company. They said it was going through a shipping company in Harbin—Bingwei Marine and Rail. There is no such company. And it never had business cards."

"How would you know?"

"We used to put that name on phony bills of lading sometimes. It's made up. If you want to know, my brother—your father—made it up. No one realized it at the time, but now that I think about it, it was a reference to your mother."

"My father? Why did he handle clandestine shipments?"

"Never mind what he did or why. That's past, and he's dead." Uncle O suddenly looked younger. He had looked old and tired at the airport, but now that had dropped away. It was as if recalling the past wasn't a weight but lifted him up. "You never saw a reference to that company in your files at work? No, maybe not. We stopped using it almost twenty-five years ago for shipments over the border. The point is someone in Japan who was connected with the dumpling machine operation found a reference to it somewhere, and decided it was just what they needed to throw anyone getting too interested off the scent."

"But it didn't work."

"Maybe if I hadn't seen the business card it would have worked, along with everything else they were doing. But if you ask me, anyone who puts Bingwei Marine and Rail down as their shipping company is not going through Harbin. They're certainly not planning to go across the river through any crossing point you or I know."

"How could you be so sure your friends didn't revive it and use it as a cover to ship in the nuclear dumpling machine for their program?"

"That would have been stupid. We're not idiots, you know."

"I know that, uncle." I figured he'd told me all he was going to about shipment, so I asked the next logical question. "What do the Japanese want with the machine?"

"You tell me."

"No," I said. "You tell me."

"OK, let's keep it simple. Let's not draw big, sweeping pictures in the air. I'd say they want to produce centrifuges, but they don't want anyone to know what they're doing. That's as far as I need to go. I'm retired. I have no reporting chain. No one listens to me anyway. The big brains will figure the rest out, or they won't. If anyone finds evidence at that factory—and the people who send Luis his paycheck will pull it apart from the ground up—that the machine was shipped to Asia, everyone will assume it went to bad people. Everyone knows the Japanese are good people. You can do what you want with the information."

I thought about it. Nothing had gone on here except that a dumpling machine showed up. Solving the murders was the responsibility of the police. If I filed a report on them, Beijing would ask why I was interfering in local affairs. The mayor was still a crook, and I still needed to get transferred. Meanwhile, I had to figure out how to get rid of Mike and my new deputy.

"Then that's that," I said. "What happens next?"

"I have an idea for a bookcase, nephew. It's for very tall people who don't like to bend down. I'll need a few special gears for the shelves." He peered into the crate. "I'll bet there are one or two in this thing."

2

At dinner, Uncle O was preoccupied. He stared at the bowl, picked at his food, selected a grain of rice with his chopsticks and examined it before putting it in his mouth.

"Something the matter?"

He looked at me as if in a dream. After a moment, he shook his head slowly. "I think I'll sit in my workshop for a while. You go ahead with dinner."

An hour later, he still hadn't emerged. I listened outside the door for a couple of minutes, but there were no sounds.

"Uncle, everything all right?" I knocked at the door. When there was no answer, I rushed inside. He was sitting on his high stool, writing.

"You had me worried," I said.

"Oh? Sorry, some lines of poetry were running through my head.

All of a sudden, they came to me. Do you know, nephew, I think it's time to go home."

"We are home."

"No, I mean across the river. I've been here long enough."

I hesitated. He'd fed me a line not so long ago about needing to go to Portugal. I wasn't falling for it again.

"No," he said, "don't worry. This is not some great revelation. Even geese feel the pull. I need to go home."

"But you can't go back." I couldn't believe I'd said that. "Your enemies are waiting."

"My enemies are all like me, they're old and toothless. No one cares anymore who we were or what we did. If I have any time left, I might as well spend it where I belong. I know the trees there. They are all strangers to me here. Besides, I can take that crate."

I realized what he meant. "You're going into the dumpling business?"

"Nothing big, just a small stand. I know the perfect place, near a little train station on the way to Pyongsong. By the time passengers get there in the afternoon, they're hungry. They'll devour dumplings by the dozen."

"You'll never get permission," I said. "Why not do it here?"

"Here? This is a big, grand country, nephew, but I can't breathe here. It's as foreign to me as the moon. Don't worry, I can get back on my own. You don't have to do anything, and when your ministry asks, you can say you didn't suspect I was leaving."

"They're watching. A lot of people are watching."

"You think I don't know? Every time I go out I practically stumble over them. They are sloppy. I could go anywhere I wanted, and they'd be left with their tongues hanging out."

"Yes, if you want to go back, I guess I understand. There are new buildings in Pyongyang, lots of more modern things than when you left."

"I don't give a damn about buildings. I want to go back to the mountains. I want to see the trees. I want to breathe clean air again."

"You really do have the soul of a poet, you know."

"No, I do not. I am just past the point where it is any use looking ahead. So I'll go home and settle into the compass headings that I knew best a long time ago. Before I die, though, I'd like to go to Kyongju. My grandfather used to tell me about it."

"How are you going to do that? Kyongju is in the South."

"I know that."

"Maybe I could help you get there. I can go easily enough. If you're with me . . ."

"I'm Korean, nephew, I don't need anyone to help me get around my own country."

He was being stubborn. Nothing would ever change that.

I tried a new tack. "My reports say they're cracking down again on defectors. It's ugly, and it's more dangerous than it has been for a long time."

"It's always more dangerous today than it was yesterday. It's one of the problems with being born, nephew. But I'm not a defector. I was on an extended vacation as far as they are concerned. I never spoke against the government, never benefited a foreign service, shared no secrets, collected no compensation from anyone. I know these people. New buildings or not, they haven't changed. They don't want to waste bullets on an old dog. It would serve no purpose."

"Revenge."

He thought about it for a moment. "Revenge I know something about. If it is meant to be, it will be. Why should it worry me?"

"They'll know you lived with a Chinese security official while you were here. They'll think you helped out with our operations against them. They'll want to find out what else you know. They won't ask politely."

My uncle shrugged. "I go back tomorrow. I'd like to take the machine in that crate. I don't think I can row it across the river."

There was no stopping him, no argument, no logic, no plea. He was my uncle, and he was determined to go. No one had to tell me what I had to do.

"I'll find a truck going from Tumen across the bridge," I said. "You'll need some money."

"I have enough."

3

The next morning, very early, a drab truck with no markings pulled up outside the house. The crate was wrestled into the back. My uncle climbed into the cab. He rolled down the window and leaned out. "Good-bye, nephew." He said it in Korean.

"I'm probably not going anywhere for a while, uncle, so I'll be here. Come back to visit. I'll keep your bookcases."

The old man smiled. "Sell what you can. I can always make more. I left you a poem on the workbench."

"Send me a postcard from Kyongju."

"I will."

He waved. I saw him watching from the window as the truck pulled away and disappeared in the dark.

4

I went back in the house and called the office. The duty officer answered on the second ring.

"Get me the mayor," I said.

"It's four in the morning, sir. He's asleep."

"I know what time it is. I have a watch. You have a watch. The mayor has a lot of watches. Get him on the phone. And don't let someone else answer and tell you he's sleeping."

"You're the boss."

"I am. Now get him on the phone. I'll just sit here picking my teeth. No, wait. Forget that. New plan."

"You're the boss."

"First thing, call the new deputy into the office. Tell him it's an emergency and he needs to get in fast. As soon as he gets there, strap him to a chair. Knock him out if you have to, I don't care."

"Your deputy, the tall guy?"

"You know another one?"

"OK, then what?"

"Then you get the mayor on the phone. This needs to be done in exactly the order I gave you, clear?"

"Clear."

"No mistakes. And get it done fast. Send my car for the bastard. Have them drive like crazy so he'll think it's really important. I'll keep this line open. If there's trouble, let me know. But I figure you can handle it."

About fifteen minutes later, the sound of the mosquito came over the line. "What the hell, Bing! You don't call me at four in the morning!"

"I do, and I did. Get dressed, Qin. We're bringing you in."

"You're what? Have you been drinking?"

"No, I'm very sober. You interested in the charges, or would you rather wait to hear them?"

"You've gone mad. I'll have your job. I'll have your head, that and the head of your crazy uncle."

"You threatened before to have my job, but here I am, still waiting. You are a disappointment, Qin. You are also sloppy. You had a meeting a while ago, upstairs in the jeweler's building. You remember?"

"I don't know what you are talking about."

"Good. You're on tape, by the way. Deny whatever you want; they love it when people deny things. It lets them go to the maximum on the sentence. And the maximum for these charges is ugly. You want to buy the bullet now? I'll bet you can get it at a discount from one of your friends."

There was a slight pause. "So I went to the jeweler's, so what? I needed some jewelry."

"Sure you did. That's why you were upstairs with a bunch of people. They were helping you pick it out."

"Yeah, I like a second opinion."

"How much did you pay that Russian piece of shit to bomb my offices?"

Silence.

"OK, next question. How much did you pay Mike to arrange those murders?"

Silence.

"No good, Qin. I have everything I need."

"I didn't pay Mike."

"You're working as a source for the Tianjin MSS office, but not a good one, and definitely not a smart one. It was an especially bad idea to put that bomb in the Yanji office of State Security, my office. A very bad idea. That makes you not only a traitor and a terrorist but also an embarrassment. They especially don't like being embarrassed. It looks bad. So you know what they do? They get rid of embarrassments without a trace. Here today, gone tomorrow."

"Just a minute, Major."

"Don't try to bribe me, Qin. I'll cram it down your throat just before they shoot you."

"I'm not bribing you. I'm only thinking out loud. We can think out loud, can't we?"

"Go ahead. But I want to bring you in before dawn, so don't drag this out."

"OK, here is what I'm thinking. It was a mistake, but you've got to admit, it was only a little bomb. No one got hurt. I made sure Dmitri made it small, more noise than anything else."

"A bomb is a bomb."

"Sure, I know that."

"Who let Dmitri into the building?" I already knew the answer, but I wanted to see if Qin would give it away.

"Who do you think? Look, Major, let's be blunt. It doesn't matter whether you like me. This city is starting to grow. Things are getting better for everyone."

"No, not everyone. Not for Mei-lin."

Another pause. "I told you, that wasn't me. What's the matter? Lonely? We can find someone pretty, just take a few days is all."

"Qin, you disgust me. Time's up. Don't bother packing a bag."

"Wait a minute, will you? Things will get better for everyone, just watch. Sure, the wheels get greased. Come on, Major, you know that. How else are things going to get done? When has it been any different?"

I sensed a change in his tone. He had caught on.

"Look out your window, Qin. The sky is getting light in the east. What's your point?"

"The point is, if you get rid of me, you'll have to deal with a new mayor, and none of the new breed understands the world, much less anything about running a city. They will do whatever Beijing tells them to do, and we all know what that means these days. It's as bad as it was under Mao."

"You don't want that on tape."

"Come on, Bing, there's no tape. You want a deal; otherwise you wouldn't have called me first. You would just have busted in the door and grabbed me. OK, I like it here. You want me to dial back? I can do that. As long as I'm here, I can hold off the political types from the capital. We should coexist. Am I right?"

"You are only right about one thing, Qin. I'll be watching. And I'll squash you like a bug if that's what I think needs to be done. Keep away from Mike."

"I don't like him. Nobody likes him. And I didn't have those diners murdered. That would have been stupid." He laughed. "Bad for business."

"And don't bother phoning your old contact from Tianjin. He's on his way out of here as soon as I sign the papers." I hung up. It wasn't much, but Qin knew I had a rope around his neck. Sleazy and revolting as he was, it was better for everyone if he stayed put.

If one of the new breed of hatchets for Beijing showed up as his replacement, it would be worse.

I sat thinking for a few minutes, then walked back into Uncle O's workshop. For a change, it was neatly organized, everything in its place. On his workbench, under an antique wood plane he brought from Korea, something he'd once told me his grandfather had given him, was a piece of paper. It was a poem in neat Chinese characters.

> *The perfumed words return each night.*
> *Too soon they disappear,*
> *Like small waves weary of*
> *A long familiar shore.*

Lisbon
2015